Praise for bestselling author
Raye Morgan

"A wonderfully romantic story that proves love is truly worth fighting for.... Readers will remember this novel long after turning the final page."
—*RT Book Reviews* on *Trading Places with the Boss.*

"Give *A Little Moonlighting* a try.... You will be able to smile, sigh and close the book feeling very content."
—*TheRomanceReader.com*

"In *Jack and the Princess*, Raye Morgan does an excellent job of reminding readers that Prince Charming doesn't always come in the form you expect."
—*RT Book Reviews*

"Morgan's latest is a delightful reworking of a classic plot, with well-drawn characters... and just the right amount of humor."
—*RT Book Reviews* on *Beauty and the Reclusive Prince*

RAYE MORGAN

has been a nursery-school teacher, a travel agent, a clerk and a business editor, but her best job ever has been writing romances—and fostering romance in her own family at the same time. Current score: two boys married, two more to go. Raye has published more than seventy romances and claims to have many more waiting in the wings. She lives in Southern California with her husband and whichever son happens to be staying at home at that moment.

Raye Morgan
Jack and the Princess

Betrothed to the Prince

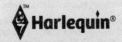
Harlequin®

TORONTO NEW YORK LONDON
AMSTERDAM PARIS SYDNEY HAMBURG
STOCKHOLM ATHENS TOKYO MILAN MADRID
PRAGUE WARSAW BUDAPEST AUCKLAND

Recycling programs for this product may not exist in your area.

ISBN-13: 978-0-373-68832-6

JACK AND THE PRINCESS & BETROTHED TO THE PRINCE

Copyright © 2011 by Harlequin Books S.A.

The publisher acknowledges the copyright holder of the individual works as follows:

JACK AND THE PRINCESS
Copyright © 2003 by Helen Conrad

BETROTHED TO THE PRINCE
Copyright © 2003 by Helen Conrad

CONTENTS

To royalty everywhere:
May they live on in our dreams
and stay out of our politics!

JACK AND THE PRINCESS

Raye Morgan

Chapter 1

Scaling the wall of a mansion and slipping from a balcony into an upper-floor room was probably a unique way of interviewing for a job. But Jack Santini was a pretty unique guy, and he decided it was the reasonable way to go. And all went well until he got to his destination. He hadn't expected to find a young woman in the room, much less in the bed, in midafternoon. As he came in through the open French doors, he was as surprised as she was.

He couldn't afford to have her scream and bring the household down on top of him, so he followed his instincts and grabbed her quickly, covering her mouth with his hand while he whispered in her ear.

"Take it easy, honey. I'm not going to hurt you."

She didn't struggle. Her first start of alarm faded quickly, and though he could feel hear heart beating wildly, she was looking at him sideways, more with wide-eyed interest than with fear. She was a pretty one, with shiny golden hair that curled around her face and huge blue eyes framed by thick black lashes. For just a moment he was intensely aware of how soft and rounded she felt, and his head was filled with her fresh, sunshine scent. But he shook it off. Years of training held him in good stead and he quickly regained his professionalism.

"You think you can stay quiet for me?" he asked her, his mouth against her ear.

She nodded and he loosened his grip, waiting just a few seconds to make sure she wasn't bluffing before completely releasing her. Springing up off the bed, he went to the door and listened, ready to leave as quickly as he'd arrived. There were people in the hallway, chatting back and forth. Probably maids cleaning rooms. He combed a hand through his thick black hair, frustrated. He was going to have to get past them if he was going to end up downstairs in the business office without triggering any sort of alarm.

That was his goal. He'd come to interview for the job as head of security for this estate. He liked to take a direct approach and test out what was going on, which is why he'd come into the property the way he had. His experiment was showing him that security here needed a lot of work.

But his test wasn't over. He still had to arrive at estate manager Tim Blodnick's desk without being let in the front door. He was anticipating the look he would see on Tim's face when he appeared out of nowhere. The next few minutes after that look would determine whether he took the job or not. Even though he was desperate as hell for something to pull him out of the swamp he was stuck in, he wasn't about to sell his soul. Time would tell.

The best thing would be to show up in front of Tim's astonished face in about two minutes. But the voices still echoed up and down the hallway, sounding casual, in no hurry. He couldn't leave the room until they'd gone. Stymied, he glanced back at the girl on the bed.

She was sitting back against the headboard, watching him, her eyes very bright. She looked wary but not really scared, and he supposed that was a good thing, although rather unusual. One yell from her and he would seem foolish instead of exceptionally expert, which was what he was going for. He was lucky she was staying calm.

"Where are you taking me?" she asked him, acting more like someone on the brink of an adventure than anything else.

He turned fully and looked at her, noticing again that she was one of the prettiest girls he'd seen in a long time. An employee, probably. The room was sparse, with nothing more than a simple bed, a straight-backed chair and a small dresser. There were no decorations, no fancy drapes. The house itself had the look of a fairy-tale castle from the outside. If she was part of the family who lived here, he would think she would have fancier digs. At the most, he expected she might be a visiting granddaughter of the old couple Tim had mentioned lived in the place.

"I'm not taking you anywhere," he reassured her, starting back toward the door. "I'm getting out of here as soon as the coast is clear."

Her pretty face took on a puzzled frown. "Wait a minute. Didn't you come to kidnap me?"

He spun and stared at her, both hands raised. "Whoa, hold on. I'm not kidnapping anyone." He frowned, put off balance by her odd reactions. "Why would I want to kidnap you?"

Her chin lifted as though she was gathering pride around herself. "Because I'm the princess, of course."

A princess. Oh, sure. He relaxed. She certainly looked like one, though, sitting there in her lacy nightgown with her hair tumbling around her face. She could have been right out of a picture in a Victorian novel. Too bad she also seemed to be a little nuts. Either that, or she was just pulling his leg.

"A princess," he said wryly. "Right. And I'm Robin Hood."

Robin Hood. Karina Alexandera Roseanova, Princess of the Royal House of Nabotavia, mulled that over and it made her smile. This very imposing man would fit perfectly into the role of the bandit with a heart of gold. He moved with a strength and agility that made her marvel, and he had the right audacious attitude for it, as well.

She knew he was mocking her, but that didn't bother her at all. In fact, it made this encounter all the more interesting. She hardly ever got this close to such an attractive man—especially one who didn't know who she was. He was scoffing at the idea of her being a princess.

He didn't know!

This gave rise to all sorts of intriguing possibilities. She didn't get the chance to come across as a regular person very often. In fact, her life was often monotonous, although seldom ordinary. For her to sit here and contemplate being kidnapped and not be frightened by the prospect should have been bizarre, but somehow it wasn't. She knew very well that one of the main reasons they had to have such extensive security here at the estate was exactly because there *were* Nabotavian rebels who might think grabbing the princess would give them leverage of one sort or another.

There had been a coup in Nabotavia shortly after she was born. Her parents had been killed in the fighting, and she and her three brothers had been whisked out of the country for safekeeping. Ever since, fears that one of them might be grabbed and taken hostage in order to manipulate events back in the old country had been a constant backdrop to their lives. She knew she ought to take the risk more seriously, but she was tired of spending her life jumping at every strange sound and distrusting everyone who looked at her too long.

She'd lived that way for years; had endured being moved from one boarding school to another just when she'd finally made friends, because there might be a threat. She'd spent her summers in places so unpopular, no one under fifty could be seen on the streets; and had sat through long dinners where her aunt and uncle and other relatives moaned and groaned about living in exile, while she dreamed of just being close enough to real life to see men who didn't wear dentures.

And now a gorgeous specimen of the most virile masculinity had been dropped right into her lap.

She watched as he went back to the door and pressed his ear to it, listening, it seemed, to see if the coast was clear. Remembering how it had felt when he'd held her in his arms, she shivered, even though she knew very well it had only been for emergency purposes. She hadn't had much male attention in her young life. That feeling was one she was going to cherish for a long time.

And she was going to need it, knowing the future she had in store for her. A shadow passed over her face as she thought of it, but she pushed it away quickly. She had the rest of the spring and most of the summer before her fate would be sealed. She meant to enjoy that small window of freedom to the hilt.

"You know…" she began, but he motioned for silence and she obeyed.

"Just a minute," he murmured, listening at the door and getting impatient. The maids were passing very close, laughing over some shared joke. If only they would get out of the hallway. At this rate he was going to be late, and the effect of his entrance wouldn't have nearly the same impact.

"Well," she began again, from right behind him this time.

He spun around, shocked that she had gotten up out of the bed and come so close without his noticing. He must be losing his edge. And guys in his business who lost their edge usually lost a lot more in the process. He was going to have to watch it.

"Shh," he warned her sternly.

She blinked and complied with his warning, going on in a stage whisper. "If you're not here to kidnap me, what are you here for?"

"Get back on the bed," he told her gruffly, feeling slightly dizzy from the sense of her warmth so close. He was tall and muscular, and suddenly he felt every bit of his manhood as he looked down at her delicate features. The white lace of her nightgown was edged by a threaded blue satin ribbon, emphasizing her femininity. She came to his shoulder, but her figure was slender. She looked light as a feather. Still, the outline of her breasts was clear through the lace, full and rounded and…

The bottom threatened to fall out of his stomach, like going fast over a dip in the road, and he had to look away quickly to keep control of his reactions. He'd just told her to do something, but he'd forgotten what it was, and she wasn't doing it, anyway. He frowned, trying to recapture his sense of reserve.

"You're not trying to burglarize us in broad daylight, are you?" she demanded as she thought of it. "Or maybe you're casing the joint?"

He had to look at her again at that one. She'd said it oddly, and he suddenly realized she had a very slight accent. "'Casing the joint?'" he repeated, his tone shaded with just a little ridicule. "You've been watching too many old movies."

"And you're avoiding the question."

He supposed she deserved to know the truth. "Listen, you've got this all wrong. I'm not burglarizing anything. I'm just testing the security system on this estate, evaluating how tight it is."

She rolled her eyes. "'Just testing.' Right." She said it in a direct copy of the way he'd responded when she'd mentioned being a princess. "And I'm the chimney sweep."

He couldn't hold back the slow grin she evoked. She was darn cute, if annoying, with her tousled locks and her pert attitude. "Okay, chimney sweep," he said. "Because that really is what I'm doing. Just give me a minute and I'll be out of your hair."

The word triggered something between them. Her hand went involuntarily to smooth back her curls, and his gaze followed, caressing the golden cascade of hair for a moment, then sliding down to take in the way her breasts filled the bodice of her nightgown before he met her gaze and realized she'd noticed the way he was looking at her. Her huge blue eyes widened, and without saying another word, she reached out and took up a light robe that was slung across the back of a chair, slipping into it and pulling it together in front.

He felt his ears burn and wondered why. Suddenly, incredulously, he knew. Dammit, he was blushing.

That was what getting mixed up with women did for you. It was Eve with the apple every time—sweet temptation that you had to pay for, big-time, later on. With a soft, internal groan, he turned back to the door. There was still noise in the hallway. Without bad luck, he would have no luck at all.

"They'll be gone in a few minutes," she told him calmly. "They're a pair of chatterboxes."

"Maids?" he asked.

She nodded. "They would be in here right now, only they think I'm asleep. I'm just getting over the flu."

He glanced at her again, realizing that his attention was being drawn back to her repeatedly because she was just so good to look at. "I was wondering what you were doing in here at this time of the day."

She gazed at him levelly, her head to the side as she scanned him. "Since you figured out that I'm not the princess, what do you think I am?" Raising her arms, she turned before him, her eyes crinkling with amusement. "What do I look like to you?"

He would hate to say. She would probably slap his face if he were honest about it. "I don't know." He shrugged, put on a forced frown and went to the window, looking out at the rolling green lawn that was her view. You couldn't see the street from here, but he could see the tall wrought-iron fence that guarded the property. Everything else was trees. You would have thought this was out in the country somewhere. You couldn't really tell they were in the middle of Beverly

Hills. "Maybe a nanny for the little kids or something," he said back over his shoulder.

"You think I look like a nanny?" She seemed pleased as punch, turning to look in her mirror as if to confirm his opinion. And that just confused him all the more.

"You *do* work here, don't you?" he asked, just to make sure.

"Oh, yes." Turning back, she nodded wisely. "I work very hard, in fact."

"Do you? What do you do, exactly?"

"I…well…" She avoided his gaze, her attention skimming over the room. "You might say I'm a sort of companion to…to the princess." She gave him an impish grin. "There really is one, you know. And to the duchess."

"The duchess? What duchess?"

She turned to stare at him rather majestically. "Do you mean to tell me you broke into this house and you haven't any idea who lives here?"

"I haven't a clue."

"You see, that's your problem. If you did better research before you set up your breaking-and-entering projects, things might go more smoothly."

He knew she was trying to tease him, but he shrugged again. "It doesn't matter. My old friend Tim told me he had a job for me as head of security. I'm in real need of a job right now. He gave me the address and I came on over."

She drew in a quick breath. "So you're going to work here?"

"Maybe." He frowned at her, realizing she was going to be one of his charges if he did get the job. It was evident she needed a few lessons in how to protect herself. "You know what?" He jabbed a finger in her direction.

"If I do, you're going to be one of my first cases. I'm worried about you."

"Me?" she squeaked, wide-eyed. "Why?"

He leaned toward her and she took a step back. "You don't really know who I am or what I'm doing here," he said accusingly. "You should be hysterical about now. Why aren't you?"

"Oh, please." She waved his question away. "I'm afraid hysteria is not my style."

His eyes narrowed thoughtfully. "You're taking this all too casually. Just for future reference, if a man ever comes bursting into your room again, I want you to scream this house down."

"Shall I do it now?" she asked obligingly.

"No!" Taking a quick step in her direction, he almost grabbed her, until he realized what he was doing and stopped himself. "No, not now."

She gazed at him with ill-concealed amusement. "So you're the only man allowed to come in off my balcony. Is that it?"

He resisted the urge to grin at her, knowing very well it would be disaster to let her think he could treat her as a friend. "You got it. If I become head of security here, there are going to be some changes made."

"Well, I guess so." She was teasing him in earnest now. "After all, old Mr. Sabrova never came into my room without knocking first."

"Who is old Mr. Sabrova?"

"The previous head of security. But then again, I don't think he could have made it up here even if he'd put a ladder up to the wall. He was pretty old. But a very nice man," she hastened to add, remembering her manners.

A very nice man, but like all the men around here,

over-the-hill and not very interesting. After all, old Mr. Sabrova didn't have jet-black hair, thick as an animal pelt, and sexy muscles that bulged right through the fabric of his crisp white shirt and snug dark slacks, nor did he have stormy gray eyes that hinted at mysteries unlike anything she'd ever encountered.

"You're going to have to wear a uniform, you know," she told him, suppressing a grin as she thought of how he'd look in the ridiculous getup Mr. Sabrova had favored.

"I'm used to uniforms. I've been a Navy SEAL and a beat cop in my time." But then he remembered. This was a strange house with strange practices. He turned slowly and looked at her. "What sort of uniform?" he asked suspiciously.

"Oh, white with gold braid and epaulets on the shoulders and a red hat and—"

"No way." He laughed shortly. "That's not *my* style."

She gave him a skeptical look. "That's the way we do things here. That's the way it's always been."

"Tell you what. It may just be time to modernize this whole operation."

She laughed softly. "I can hardly wait to hear you tell that to the duchess."

He gazed at her quizzically. "Is there a 'mister duchess'?"

"Oh, yes. The duke. He's a darling. I adore him. But he doesn't matter. It's all her, believe me."

He held his hand up to stop her from saying anything while he listened intently.

"They're gone," he said decisively. He opened the door a crack and looked into the hallway. Glancing back, he winked at her. "Thanks for the memories," he said. "See you around." And he slipped out into the hallway, closing the door silently behind him.

Kari stared at the closed door for a moment, then moved resolutely toward the telephone on the corner of the dresser. Picking up the receiver, she pressed a few numbers and put it to her ear.

"Blodnick here," said the gruff male voice at the other end.

She smiled. "Mr. Blodnick, it's Kari. I believe you have an appointment today with a man—an old friend of yours—about taking on the job as head of security."

"You're right. He's late."

"No, on the contrary, he was here quite on time. I'm afraid I detained him."

"You what?"

The shock in his voice was palpable, but she ignored it.

"If at all possible, I'd like to have him hired, please."

There was a pause, and the man cleared his throat. Then he said the only thing he could say. "Whatever you say, Princess."

"Oh, and, Mr. Blodnick. About the uniform. I think you should discuss designing something new for the security guards. Your friend may have some ideas on that score. It is a new millennium, you know. We need to get with the times, don't you think?"

"Sounds doable, Princess."

"Thank you, Mr. Blodnick."

She hung up the telephone and smiled happily. Suddenly she didn't feel sick at all. Maybe this summer wasn't going to be quite the boring disaster she'd expected it to be. It was, after all, going to be her last period of relative freedom. And when it was over, she would be marrying someone her aunt chose for her.

Something told her he wasn't going to be at all like the new head of security.

Her smile faded as she remembered that, and the familiar sensation of a fist closing down inside came over her. By winter she would be married and on her way back to Nabotavia, a place she didn't even remember.

"But that is weeks away," she told herself, closing her eyes and taking a deep, cleansing breath. "Weeks away."

Chapter 2

Jack tested the condition of the wrought-iron fence near where the hill rose behind the property and noted the results in his minirecorder. It was really too dark now to get a full picture, but he could see some of the more obvious features. He'd been head of security on this estate for all of six hours, and he'd already found a number of improvements that had to be made to bring the place up to standard, which was what he'd been told his goal would be. Upgrading conditions and managing a staff of five rotating guards were the main duties he'd signed on for. The pay was above average and included living quarters right here in the compound. It was a good job and he was glad he had it, if temporarily.

The estate was large, consisting of the main house, a few utility buildings, a five-car garage with chauffeur's quarters overhead, a garden house with the security office and the apartment where he would be staying.

The grounds were extensive, including a small stand of redwoods that gave the sense of being in a forest, a formal rose garden that seemed to be a special show-place for the estate, emblematic to the royal family themselves, a kitchen garden and three small pools connected by waterfalls, ducks and koi. Another waterfall recycled water into the swimming pool. Everywhere there was the sound of water.

He still hadn't figured out exactly who this was he was working for. Tim had been in a hurry to make a meeting in L.A. and had promised to fill him in later. He gathered these people were some sort of exiled royalty from some little country in Europe—situated somewhere between Austria and Hungary—he'd never heard of before. They certainly employed a lot of people, most of them from the same little country. So far he'd seen three maids, a cook, a butler, two gardeners and a chauffeur, plus, of course, the "companion" whose room he'd invaded.

Thinking of her, he glanced up at the house, his gaze focusing immediately on the brightly lit window of the room where he'd been, and the memory of how soft and rounded she'd felt in his arms flashed in his mind. Resolutely he pushed the image away. She was dangerously attractive and deeply appealing, but he wasn't in the market for that sort of thing. Getting involved with a woman had messed him up one too many times. If he hadn't learned his lesson by now, there was no hope for him. He was going to have to keep his distance from that one. And that shouldn't be too hard to do. The security of the place needed a lot of work. He was going to be very busy.

And, turning to go back up toward the house, he

nearly ran smack into the very woman he'd been trying to avoid thinking about.

"Whoa!" He jerked back, just missing her, and annoyed that he hadn't heard her approach. The ubiquitous waterfall sounds masked everything else. He was going to have to see about making some adjustments there.

"Hello," she said, glancing toward the house and stepping back farther into the shadows the long rose arbor made along the edge of the property. "I thought I might find you out here."

He frowned, not pleased to see her. She was too damn pretty for her own good. "I'm just going in," he said gruffly, and turned to go.

"Wait. I've brought you something."

He turned back and looked at what she was carrying, but he couldn't quite make out what it was in the darkness.

"I brought you a lemon tart from dinner. I know you didn't get one."

He hesitated, knowing he was being a fool. But a lemon tart—it was only his favorite food, and his stomach growled just to remind him that he was hungry as a bear. One little lemon tart. What could that hurt? Besides, it would be rude to cut her off when she was being so friendly. Reluctantly he turned back.

"Thanks," he said simply, and followed her back into the arbor to a bench where the light from the lanterns around the nearby swimming pool brightened the area. They both sat down, and she handed him the plate and a fork.

He took a bite, savored it, then gave her a lopsided grin. "Thanks a lot," he said sincerely. "This is really good."

She smiled back. She was glad she'd come out now. At first she hadn't been sure. All through dinner she'd watched for him out of the tall dining room windows, but she hadn't caught sight of him. So she'd decided to take a chance once her aunt was safely off to visit her friend who lived a few blocks away. She'd gone to the kitchen, snatched a lemon tart and come out searching. Luckily she'd found him right away.

"So, Mr. Jack Santini," she said, showing off that she'd found out what his name was. "You decided to take the job."

"A man's got to eat," he said, taking another bite of the tart as though to illustrate that very concept. "And from what I've seen so far, you people eat pretty well."

She supposed that was true. They employed a wonderful cook. The food here at her aunt's was certainly better than anything she'd ever been given at any of the many boarding schools she had attended. One of her goals for the summer was to learn to cook. What if it was true that good food was the way to a man's heart? Hmm...

She looked at him and felt a ripple of excitement flow through her. He was so attractive, so...well, so male. What could she do to get him to stay with her a little longer after he'd finished the dessert? Maybe she could get him to talk.

"Tell me about yourself," she said brightly. "Are you married?"

He took a last bite of the tart and gazed at her levelly. She was dressed in a sweater and slacks and had her hair tied back in a ponytail that looked completely appropriate. She seemed impossibly young. And young was something he had never seemed to be.

He wasn't sure if he'd always been such a pessimist,

but lately it felt as though his life always had a sense of waiting for the ax to fall, wondering when things would get worse. And they usually did. Right now he was on suspension from the police department, cut off from the career as a police detective that he loved, taking this job to fill in the gap and hold him over until a hearing on his future was held.

It wasn't as if he was complaining. The suspension was his own fault. He knew very well what he'd done. Given the same circumstances, he very likely would do the same thing over again. His instincts always seemed to put him in position to go overboard protecting someone else—particularly if she was a woman—and end up hurting himself. He had to be careful not let that happen anymore.

And he had to be careful not to let anything he did here make things worse as far as his suspension went. And how could that happen? Well, he could let himself get involved in a flirtation with this pretty young thing. That ought to just about seal the deal on his doom. But he wasn't quite that stupid. Or that weak.

And she wanted to know if he was married. He gave her a sideways look and said, "Why would you care about a thing like that?"

"No reason. I'm just making small talk."

"Small talk." He couldn't help it. She made him want to laugh. "Okay, here's some fodder for your small talk. I'm thirty years old. I was born in San Diego, grew up all over the place. Was a Navy SEAL for a few years, then joined the Rancho Diego Police Department. I was engaged once, for about five minutes. But I've never been married. And I have no kids."

He left out a few things, such as the fact that his parents had died in a car accident when he was young and he'd been shuttled from one place to another, living with various relatives, until finally he'd ended up in a group home for problem teenagers. He understood that his early rootless existence was behind his strong need to find his identity in organizations such as the police force. But that understanding didn't make the need any less powerful.

"Whew." She whipped her head around as though she'd just been hit with a strong wind. "I guess that takes care of that. Now I feel like I've known you all my life."

He handed her his empty plate, knowing it was time to get up and walk away. But that would be a little abrupt. He supposed he could spare a few minutes to be courteous. "You may know me, but I don't know you," he told her. "Your turn."

She blanched and looked away, using the moment to set the plate down on the bench beside her. She'd almost forgotten that he didn't know yet who she was. He would know soon enough—perhaps in minutes. But she wanted to prolong him not knowing as long as she could. She hated the way people changed once they were told she was royal.

Sometimes she wished she could shed that royalty like a used and useless second skin, cast it off like a worn-out dress. She'd been quite rebellious about it a few years ago as a teenager.

After all, to her, royalty meant such loneliness. Since the loss of her parents, when she was a baby, she'd always had her aunt and uncle. But her brothers had been raised elsewhere. The two oldest, Crown Prince Marco and Prince Garth, had been raised by another uncle at his family home in Arizona. Prince Damian, the closest to her in age, spent most of his early years living with their mother's twin sister and her family. She had only seen them all on special occasions. For most of her youngest years, she'd lived under the rule of a governess. Children were occasionally carted in to play with her, but the situation was hit-and-miss. She was excited when she went away to school at fourteen. Finally she would meet people of her own age.

But developing relationships was still hard as she moved to each school with a whole retinue, taking over entire sections of the dormitory like an occupying force. That, combined with the fact that she changed schools so often, meant that friendships were still tough.

She hoped things would be different once she was married. Though she hardly expected to find true love in an arranged marriage, she did expect her mate would be a friend, someone to talk to, someone to share life with. She'd settled down now. Her small flash of rebellion was in the past. She was sworn to do her duty and she was ready to fulfill her role. She only hoped she would marry a man she could like.

That was the current state of her affairs, of who she was, but Jack Santini didn't want to hear all of that.

"I'm not very interesting," she said quickly. "I'll tell you something about the family, though. What would you like to know?"

"Your name, for starters."

Her name. Well, that was easy. "Kari."

"Kari." He said it slowly, as though he wanted to remember it, and that made her smile. "Just Kari?" he added.

"Isn't that enough?"

"Most people have a last name, too."

She shook her head. "I've got too many of them. They would only confuse you." She turned to look at the swimming pool through the leaves of the rose vines. The light from the lanterns made ghostly reflections on the inky water. "But we were talking about the family. Aren't you curious about them?"

"The family." He considered for a moment. "Okay. Tell me what I should know."

"The Roseanovas are a very old family. They ruled Nabotavia for almost a thousand years. Then, twenty years ago they were overthrown by rebels. The December Radicals, they were called." She rolled her eyes to show what she thought of them. "The king and queen were killed…."

She stopped, surprised that her voice was quavering over that last statement. It was her own parents she was talking about. It had been so long ago, when she was just a baby, and she didn't remember them, except for what she knew from old pictures and stories. She'd thought she was used to that, but for some reason, her voice was betraying emotions she thought she'd tamed. Taking a deep breath, she went on. "And many others were forced to flee from the country."

"Including you."

"Oh, yes. Also the duke and the duchess, and—"

"And the princess? I've been told there really is a princess."

She nodded, eyes sparkling. "And you doubted me," she charged. "The princess was smuggled out of the country, along with her three older brothers." Then she looked at him curiously. "What did they tell you about her?"

He shrugged and stretched back, leaning against the railing with his legs extended out before him. "Nothing. Tim was more concerned that I not get on the wrong side of the duchess than anything else." He cocked an eyebrow. "Is that the duchess you were talking about?"

She nodded. "Yes."

"So she's pretty hard to please, is she?"

Kari hesitated. She didn't want to say anything against her aunt. After all, the woman had raised her—in a way. How could she put this delicately? "You know the wicked stepmother in the Cinderella story?" she ventured.

He grinned, his white teeth flashing in the gloom. "Sure."

She gave a soft laugh. "She's sort of like an updated version of her."

He chuckled. "And what are you? Cinderella? Do they make you do all the dirty chores?"

"Not quite. But there are certain expectations and standards that must be met." She waved the topic away. "But you'll see for yourself tomorrow. She's planning to have Mr. Blodnick perform an introduction. Something of a royal audience," she added with a gleam in her eye that was close to teasing.

He noticed. She was getting more and more familiar with him. He knew he ought to get up off the bench and head for somewhere as far as possible away from this beguiling female. But for some reason he just couldn't do it. Instead he turned away again and sat staring off toward the swimming pool, telling himself not looking at her would be almost as good as leaving. And knowing he was lying.

"So I'm going to meet the people I'm working for," he noted with a shrug. "That's pretty routine, don't you think?"

"Oh, not at all. It's very important that the duchess and the princess approve of you."

"I've got no reason to think they won't," he said with complete confidence. "I know what I'm doing. And I'm a likable guy, after all."

She studied him critically, her head to the side. Likable was one thing. Absolutely gorgeous was another. What would her aunt think of having her guarded by a man like this? Wouldn't she have second thoughts? Wouldn't she notice that an electricity seemed to spark between them at times? And once she did notice, wouldn't she get rid of this man as quickly as possible?

The answer to most of those questions of course was yes. It was going to be up to Kari to find a way to make sure she didn't think them.

"Well, the duchess won't like you, no matter how nice you are, because the duchess doesn't like anyone," she told him pertly, overstating the case, but only a little. "But the princess...now that's another matter." She pretended to think hard, her brow furled. "What will the princess think of you?"

He had to turn and look at her. There was something odd about her tone of voice, and he couldn't quite put his finger on what it was. He knew she was teasing again, but he wasn't sure why.

"What's she like?" he asked, watching her face.

"The princess?" She shuddered. "Oh, she's ugly as a bulldog. She's slow and dull and she has no real wit about her."

He stared at her for a moment, then a reluctant smile quirked the corners of his wide mouth. "You're a real good friend of hers, are you?"

"Oh, very," she said in all sincerity. "We're close as...as...as sisters."

"Sisters." He nodded, and his smile took on a more

cynical twist. "Funny, I heard she was pretty." He watched for her reaction.

And she gave him one, rolling her eyes. "You know how people are sometimes. They endow celebrities with beauty and talent they don't really have, just because they *are* celebrities. Well, people do the same thing with royalty."

"Do they?"

"Oh, yes. I've seen men look at the princess and not even notice that she squints and walks into walls and that her feet stick out at funny angles." She nodded emphatically, her eyes shimmering with laughter. "I've even heard people say she's beautiful." She shrugged, hands out in a "go figure" gesture.

"Poor, demented souls." He was laughing at her now.

"Exactly!" She laughed back. "That's how blind people can be."

Their gazes connected and suddenly she was aware of how soft the air felt, how different from anything she'd ever noticed before. She sobered, still looking into his eyes and feeling very strange, almost like floating.

"Are you saying I'm blind, too?" he asked, though his voice seemed to have dropped an octave.

"Oh, no," she assured him. "I just wanted to warn you, so you could be prepared." She caught the hint of a clean, masculine scent and wondered if it were a flower blooming nearby or his aftershave. She wanted to get closer, just to see. "I wouldn't want you to fall into that trap," she added somewhat breathlessly.

"Why?" he asked her lazily, his eyes half-closed. "Are you afraid I'm going to fall for the princess?"

Her shrug had a sensual languor to it that made him think—for some reason—of naked bodies on satin sheets.

"You might," she murmured, her gaze locked with his. "Stranger things have happened."

The magnetic pull between them seemed to have a life of its own, generating heat and electricity that made Jack feel it was inevitable that they would kiss. The soft darkness, the sound of water, the scent of roses, all combined to draw them closer and closer. But Jack had the sense and experience to know what was happening, and he knew it was wrong—and that he was the one who had to stop it. He started to straighten, to pull away, but Kari stopped him.

"Hold still," she said. "You've got a smudge on your face."

It was only a crumb from the pie crust on the lemon tart, caught by the barely visible beginnings of a growth of dark beard alongside his mouth. Her heart began to pound as she leaned forward to get it. What was she doing? She had no idea, but she wanted to touch him so badly. Reaching out, she brushed the crumb away, then let her fingers linger there as she looked up into his eyes, just inches away from hers. A change came over them as she watched. She saw a darkening, as though a cloud had covered the sun, and then she caught her breath. For the first time in her life, she saw raw desire in a man's eyes and knew it was aimed at her.

The strange thing was, it didn't frighten her at all. Instead, a thrill shivered through her, making her feel alive as she'd never felt before. Her hand turned, cupping his cheek with her palm and fingers, and she looked at his lips, suddenly needing his kiss as though it would keep her from dying. Her own lips parted and she drew closer…closer…her heart beating wildly, her blood singing in her veins.

Jack's groan came from deep within his soul and

it came with an effort he was almost too overcome to
make. Reaching up, he circled her wrist with his fingers and pushed her hand away.

"You'd better go in," he said roughly, hoping she
didn't notice that his breath was coming too quickly,
that his own heart was beating right along with hers.
He didn't think he'd ever felt this aroused before without doing something about it. Why it had happened so
quickly and so effortlessly with this woman he barely
knew, he wasn't sure. He only knew he had to avoid the
temptation she represented if he wanted to keep from
ruining his own future—and that he had to protect her
from himself.

That she was an innocent was obvious. That her naiveté seemed to excite him in a way he hadn't been excited in a long, long time was not something he was
particularly proud of. His first instincts had been right
on the money. He was going to have to avoid her at all
costs.

Suddenly they were both aware of voices. They
turned and looked toward the house. A figure filled
the lit window of Kari's room.

"Oh-oh!" Kari jumped up from the bench, picking up
the plate as she went. "I'm going to have to go in. The
duchess is looking for me." She flashed him a quick,
wavering smile. "Good night."

He watched her go and groaned again, leaning his
head back against the railing. Five minutes with the
woman and he was thinking about how she would fit
into his bed. And she was the kind of woman that had
"trouble" written all over her. If he was going to give
in to the urge to mess around, it would have to be with
a woman who had been there and done that and knew
the score, not some sweet little innocent looking for

someone to love. How had he let that happen? Whatever it had been—it couldn't happen again. If he had to get tough, that was exactly what he would have to do. But he had to stay away from Kari. That much was a given.

He was a little out of his depth here. What was he— an ordinary police detective, a guy who'd grown up in foster homes with no family of his own, who'd had to struggle to get an education and build a life for himself, with no background to depend on—doing here, working for royalty? Oh, well, it was just for the summer, just until he could get reinstated for his job. He supposed he ought to appreciate the experience. He would never have another one quite like it.

Chapter 3

"Karina, will you stop looking at yourself in the mirror?"

The duchess glared adamantly across her impressively decorated dressing room at her charge. They were prepared to go out to an engagement, but were waiting for Tim Blodnick to announce that he was downstairs and ready to introduce them to Jack Santini.

"You're developing an unhealthy interest in your own reflection."

Kari took one last look at the impeccably dressed woman in the mirror and sighed. For the first time in her life she actually cared how she looked in more than a passing way. She would have thought her aunt would be glad she was finally taking something of an interest.

The image was of a slim young woman wearing a royal-blue silk sheath with princess seams and a scooped neckline. She had on white gloves and spectator pumps.

A small pillbox hat with a skimpy veil for decoration sat perched atop hair that was carefully arranged in a comely twist. And, of course, she sported tasteful pearls. No princess of her age would go out without them. At least, that was what her aunt always told her.

She looked like a picture from a history book. What would happen if she ripped off these relics and put on a nice tight sweater and a leather skirt? Her aunt would have her committed, no doubt about it.

"First you tell me to take a look at myself more often and try to make my image conform to what a princess should look like," she commented. "Then you criticize me for doing exactly that."

The duchess turned and gave her an assessing look. The woman herself looked well groomed and elegant in an obviously expensive lime-green silk suit that suited her coloring. Her hair was cut short and chic and dyed an attractive shade of silver. She looked altogether imposing, which was precisely what she was.

"It is very important to get the look exactly right," she counseled her niece. "But it is just as important not to let anyone know it was any effort. Your royal style should flow naturally, like the waters of the Tannabee River that runs through the heart of Nabotavia." She made an elegant gesture with her hand. "Perfection is fundamental and imperative. But never allow anyone to see you attempting to achieve it."

Kari smiled to cover the annoyance she felt. She wanted to let it out, to rip the hat off and toss it out the window, to trade in her dress for jeans and a tummy-tickler T-shirt. She wanted to be a normal and very casual young woman, just like the young women she saw from the limousine window as she was whisked from one official engagement to another.

Well, she couldn't do that. But sometimes her sharp tongue was just too quick to be stopped. "I see," she said brightly. "In other words, all's fair in the quest for royal superiority. Lie, cheat and steal—just don't get caught."

The duchess turned away, looking in need of smelling salts. "Much too vulgar for a princess," she murmured faintly, but, glancing at her diamond-studded watch, she quickly regained her sharply efficient attitude.

"I hope Mr. Blodnick hurries along and brings this new fellow he's hired as head of security. I'm not sure I approve of this move he's made. I usually expect to meet the management-level employees before they are offered a contract."

Kari turned away and hummed a little tune trying to look innocent. If she told her aunt that she'd been behind the quick approval of the man, she knew very well her aunt would fire him on the spot. The duchess would be great at marshaling armies and taking over small countries, but she didn't have a lot of understanding in her soul.

She would certainly never understand what had happened in the arbor last night. But then, Kari didn't really understand it either. All she knew was that all she had to do was think about almost kissing Jack Santini and her breath stopped in her throat. She had been so forward! She knew very well that it had been her doing the seducing, not him. In fact, she didn't like to think about how he had reacted, because it made her worry that he'd been laughing at her the whole time. Had he thought she was silly?

No. Whenever she remembered the way he had groaned, as though he'd had to rip the sound out of somewhere deep and tortured, she got chills. She didn't think he'd been laughing. But still, she didn't know what he thought and that was making her nervous.

"Karina, please, don't slouch like a teenager."

She straightened without really hearing what the woman was saying. That was actually her usual reaction to the constant stream of advice and reproach. She usually got along well enough with her aunt, but it was her uncle she loved. The duke was her father's half brother, and to her, an orphan left alone in a very scary world, he represented parental love in a way her aunt never could. Her aunt was the taskmaster, the instructor, the maker of hated rules and regulations. Her uncle was the man who had taught her how to whistle, how to find the Big Dipper on a clear night, how to tell robins from blue jays. He was the one who read bedtime stories to a sleepy little girl, who always had her favorite candy hidden in his coat pocket, who carried her up to bed when she fell asleep over her toys. And though he had retreated more and more from any sphere where his wife took charge, he was always available for Kari when she needed someone to talk to.

The telephone rang and the duchess took it. "He's ready," she told Kari. "Let's go down."

Kari hesitated, her pulse speeding up just a bit. She had to admit she was just a little nervous. She was looking forward to seeing Jack again, and yet she wasn't looking forward to his reaction once he realized she was the princess. She didn't think he'd guessed—although someone might have told him by now. Maybe when she walked into the room he would already know and she wouldn't have to see the look of shock in his eyes as he realized what she'd kept from him.

As she followed her aunt down the stairs, she realized

she was dreading that. At first she'd thought it would be fun—that he would look surprised and she would laugh. But having gotten to know him a little better last night, she knew that wasn't what was going to happen. He wasn't going to like the fact that she'd tricked him.

"Duchess Irinia Roseanova, allow me to introduce Jack Santini, our new manager of estate security."

She came into the room just in time to see Tim present Jack to the duchess, but not in time to be addressed along with her. Jack's attention was all on her aunt and that was just as well. She hung back, waiting for him to look around and notice her.

"We've lived very quietly recently, Mr. Santini," the duchess was saying. "But all that is going to change as spring opens into summer. We have a number of entertainments planned, and we will need extra security during them."

"What sort of entertainments do you have in mind?" he asked.

"We will be giving dinners, card parties, a tea or two and, of course, the ball."

"A ball?"

"Yes. The ball will be held at the country club, not here on our premises. However, I'll expect you to be in charge of security for the ball, and that will entail quite a bit of work. We're expecting almost two hundred people to attend."

They went on talking about plans, and Kari watched on tenterhooks. Jack was dressed in black slacks, a black long-sleeved shirt and a silver tie. She wondered if this would be the new uniform, and that made her smile. He was so very handsome. Still waiting, she tugged off her gloves and held them in one hand. When he was presented and he bent to kiss her fingers, she wanted his lips to touch flesh, not fabric.

And suddenly he was coming her way and looking right at her, and Tim was saying, "And I believe you've met the princess casually, but I'd now like to make a formal introduction. Princess Karina Alexandera Roseanova, may I present Jack Santini?"

Tim turned back to speak to the duchess, leaving Kari and Jack to deal with the rest of the introduction alone. She raised her gaze to meet Jack's and found it unreadable. That only made her more uneasy, so she held her head high and extended her left hand in a formal, if rather haughty, manner.

He took it gingerly, looked down at it, then back into her eyes. "What am I supposed to do with this limp fish?" he asked in a low voice just loud enough for her to hear.

She caught her breath. He was angry. Well, she supposed she couldn't blame him. But neither could she let on to her aunt that there was any sort of relationship between them.

"It is customary that you kiss my hand," she told him imperiously, keeping her gaze cool and distant.

Grabbing her hand more firmly, he used it to pull her closer and murmured, "I'd rather spank your bottom," before he let her go.

"Oh!"

Her cheeks colored and her blue eyes glittered and he immediately regretted what he'd done. But not very much. He was quite serious. The girl needed a little discipline. He felt like a fool and he was furious with her for leading him on and letting him say stupid things. Still, there was a facade here that had to be maintained.

He brushed her fingers with his lips and then dropped her hand like a hot potato.

"So happy to meet you, Princess," he said, sarcasm spicing his tone.

But then his gaze met hers again and he saw her remorse. His anger began to fade. After all, what had it really hurt for him to think she was just an employee for a time? Thank God he hadn't taken advantage of the kiss she'd offered him the night before. At least there was that.

"I'm glad to see that your squint has healed, Princess," he added, just to show her he was still annoyed, but wasn't going to hold it against her. "And that you are no longer walking into walls."

She bit back a smile, obviously relieved but still looking a bit contrite. "Yes, I'm doing very well," she said coolly, her nose in the air. "With therapy, I may even get my feet to go straight again."

The duchess turned from her talk with Tim and frowned in their direction. "Karina. Is something wrong?"

Kari sent a brilliant smile in her direction. "Oh, no, madam. Nothing at all."

They waited for the duchess to resume her talk with Tim, and then Jack leaned closer and said, "You could have told me the truth."

Her eyes flashed as she looked at him. "I did. You were the one who refused to believe it."

He knew she was right but he hated to admit it. Of course, if he'd only thought about it, he would have known. The clues were everywhere for him to see. As he thought back over their conversation the night before, he could see that she'd practically spelled it out for him. He was the one who'd been too dense to put two and two together. Well, what did it matter, anyway? Her being the princess only made it more imperative that he stay away from her. Maybe it was all to the good.

She turned to walk toward the windows, pulling her gloves on as she went, and he followed her, no longer annoyed with her and rather captivated by the quaint picture she made, all decked out in her old-fashioned attire.

"You look like something out of the fifties," he told her softly as they stopped to gaze out over the lawn. "What's the deal with the little hat?"

She touched it and smiled. "That's the way we royalty are supposed to be, you know," she told him. "Timeless. Classic. Straight out of the past and walking boldly into the future."

She looked up at him, laughter in her eyes, and he found himself smiling down at her.

A princess. What the hell had he gotten himself into here?

But their moment was already over. Tim and the duchess were coming toward where they stood at the window, and the duchess was addressing him. He turned to face her.

"I'm glad to have met you, Mr. Santini," she was saying, looking very regal. "I'm sure you will do a splendid job, as long as you stick to the basics. Right now we're going to need someone to accompany us for the afternoon. We are going to a Ladies' League meeting. Princess Karina will be the guest of honor at their tea, where she will present a short speech on the history of Nabotavia and the latest developments from that part of the world. Even in such a benign setting, she must be guarded, you know."

"Very well, madam," Jack said mildly. He'd already

known about this and was prepared. His gaze skimmed over Kari's and away again. "I've assigned Will Strator to accompany you. He should be waiting in the driveway at this very moment."

He didn't have to look at Kari to sense her disappointment. She'd thought he might be coming along. Well, he wasn't going to get caught in that game. He had other guards who could watch Kari when she went out in public. He wasn't going to do it.

"Goodbye," she murmured as she slipped past him. "You're missing a great speech."

She left her scent behind, and he inhaled it for a moment before turning away to get back to work. And then he wished he hadn't. Memorizing the perfume she wore would only make it worse when he thought of her at night. Because that was all he was going to do. No doubt about it. This was more of a hands-off situation than ever. The woman was a princess for God's sake. As if things weren't bad enough.

Three Days Later

"Oh, Mr. Santini."

Jack turned back. The duchess had just finished filling him in on some changes she wanted made to the alarm system and was calling him back as an afterthought.

"The princess has an appointment to make some dress selections at Goldmar's at two o'clock. She'll be going alone, as I have some visitors coming. But she'll need protection."

Jack gritted his teeth. Every man he had available was already assigned. "I'm afraid we don't have anyone free at this time," he started to tell the duchess.

"Then you'll have to go with her," she said impatiently. "Protecting the princess is your first priority. Never forget that."

Of course it was, and he felt it as strongly as anyone. He knew she couldn't go out alone. He'd been briefed about the Nabotavian rebels and the threats that were periodically made against the family, and against Kari in particular. It was a turbulent time for the country, with the rebels losing favor with the population and a constitutional monarchy being restored. From what he gathered, there were numerous factions from the old country who would like nothing better than to get their hands on the popular princess in order to push their own agenda. Of course keeping her safe was the most important part of his job. He'd hoped the appointment might be canceled, but it didn't seem to be an option.

"Of course I'll handle it," he told her crisply. "I'll be ready at one-thirty."

In the three days since the introduction in the parlor, he'd managed to find ways to stay out of Kari's path for all that time. He was getting pretty good at knowing instinctively when she was liable to show up in any given area, and in making himself scarce at just the right moment. He'd even managed to stop thinking about her forty times an hour as he had at first. He was on the right track. As long as he kept his distance, the temptation she represented would fade more and more.

The worst had been the day it had been warmer than usual and a group of Nabotavians who lived in another part of the state had arrived for a visit. The party had included two young women about Kari's age, and the three of them had gone for a swim. Though he'd heard the laughter and the splashing, he hadn't thought much about it. But when he walked out of the guard office, there Kari had been, poised on the diving board, about to take a plunge into the water, wearing an alluring one-piece suit. She'd been calling to one of the others and hadn't noticed him, and that was lucky, because he'd turned to stone for a moment, unable to move, as he'd stared at her, every masculine response in his body coming alive and aching.

She'd been so beautiful in an innocent, untouched way. Her skin had gleamed golden in the sunlight, her hair a golden-blond halo around her pretty face. Her slim body was perfect, with her breasts swelling inside the swimsuit top; her long, graceful legs and those intoxicating curves. Desire had risen in him like smoke from a fire, and he'd choked on it.

He'd finally gotten himself under control and turned away, muttering every obscenity he could think of under his breath as he got out of there as quickly as he could. But the picture of her poised in the air like a bird would stay with him for the rest of his life, no matter how hard he tried to erase it.

So he approached their impending outing with some reluctance, but when he met Kari at the car, she gave him a brief smile and entered the large Cadillac, inviting him to sit in the back with her. He sank into the luxurious seating, trying to forget what he knew about the body beside him so modestly clothed in a chic linen pants suit. After only a quick glance her way, he sat looking straight ahead as the chauffeur began to guide the car out onto the city streets. They rode along in silence for some time, and he'd just about decided that she'd taken the hint to heart and realized that they shouldn't attempt to have any sort of relationship when she spoke.

"Why do you hate me?" she asked softly.

He looked at her, startled. She was staring straight ahead. He glanced at Mr. Barbera, the chauffeur. There was a Plexiglas barrier between the front and back seats, but he knew that didn't always mean that sound wasn't traveling from one side to the other.

"Don't worry, he can't hear us," she said, still staring ahead and letting her lips move only slightly as she spoke. "He's half-deaf. But he can see. And he will tell everything he sees to my aunt, you can count on it."

How reassuring. Jack sighed, wishing he were anywhere but here.

"I don't hate you," he said, following her example of moving his lips only as much as he absolutely had to and staring out the window while he spoke.

"You've been avoiding me like the plague."

"I'm not avoiding you," he lied. "I'm just trying to do my job."

"I thought we could be friends."

There was no particular overt emotion in her voice, but he thought he heard something—some tiny tremor, some vague vibration—that made him look at her again.

"Kari...Princess." He turned his head away again. "Look. You're royalty. I'm the serf, or whatever. I work for you. We are on completely different levels. It's hard to be friends that way."

Her outrage at that statement made her careless, and she completely forgot to hide what she had to say, turning to him and demanding, "What! Did you grow up in Europe or something? You sound more like a Nabotavian than I do. We're in the U.S.A. Everyone is supposed to be equal."

He frowned, talking directly to her. "There are always levels, even if people pretend to ignore them. Be realistic."

They had arrived at the large exclusive department store and Mr. Barbera was pulling up before the entrance. A doorman rushed to get the car door. Without saying anything more, Jack got out and helped Kari to her feet. Giving the chauffeur a wave, she turned toward the store and he went with her.

"Anyway," she said in a conversational voice as they walked along through the fine jewelry department. "I'm not asking you to marry me. I just want you to be my friend."

They came to an elevator and stood side by side, waiting for the doors to open.

"You know you want more than a friend," he told her softly, watching to make sure they were not being overheard by any of the customers. After all, he shouldn't be talking this way to her. But he didn't have much choice.

"How do you know what I want?" she demanded, turning to look up at him, her blue eyes huge.

He hesitated. This really wasn't the time or the place. But once begun, this topic was pretty difficult to abandon until it had been dealt with. He looked down into her eyes and felt something twist in his chest. If only she weren't so damn appealing.

"The vibes between us tell it all," he told her shortly, willing her to understand without too much explanation.

"Vibes!" She said the word as though she scorned it.

The elevator doors opened and they went aboard. Jack pushed the button to close the door quickly so that they wouldn't have to share the elevator with anyone else. He had a feeling she would continue this conversation no matter who was listening.

Once they were underway, he turned to her. "Yes,

vibes. You feel it, I feel it. If we hang around together too much, something is bound to happen."

Her eyes were even larger now, and they seemed to melt as he looked into them.

"Will it?" she said softly.

"Yes." Every part of him wanted to take her in his arms. Something about her looked so vulnerable right now. He wanted to reassure her, tell her not to worry. But he hardened his heart. "I've got more experience at this type of thing than you do. I know it will."

The doors opened on their floor. They stepped out. The showroom was before them, and a beautifully groomed woman was smiling in their direction. Kari looked around, then turned and grabbed his hand.

"Let's not argue anymore," she said, giving him a wobbly smile. "Let's just enjoy the afternoon."

He blinked. Didn't she get it? He was working here. He pulled away from her.

"I'll stay in the background and stand against the wall while you…"

"Oh, no you don't. You'll come on in with me." Her smile brightened as she took his arm. "They don't know I'm a princess. To these people, I'm just another spoiled girl from Beverly Hills. It would be perfectly natural for me to have my boyfriend along." Perfectly natural and perfectly normal. Things she would love to be. Things she really couldn't have. But just this once…

He was shaking his head, though he knew it wasn't going to make any difference. "Princess, I don't think this is a good idea."

"Please. I want you to."

He stared down into her beautiful eyes and swallowed hard. He should say no. He tried. But he couldn't do it.

"All right," he heard himself say.

She beamed up at him. "Good!" And she led him into the showroom.

Chapter 4

The showroom attendants were prepared for Kari and quickly accommodated her guest. A table had been set up in front of the stage. She and Jack sat down next to each other.

"We have a nice viewing ready for you, Miss Rose-anova," the coolly efficient looking young woman told her. "Your aunt asked that you be shown a selection from a number of lines. If you would prefer to limit the number—"

"Oh, no. I want to see it all. Oh, and we'd like tea, please. And scones would be nice, don't you think?" Kari smiled at Jack, then at the helpful attendant. "Thank you very much."

Jack leaned close and muttered, "What are you doing?"

"I already know what dress I'm ordering," she told

him softly. "But the more I look at, the more time we'll have to talk."

"Talking isn't part of my job," he reminded her grimly, his gray gaze flickering in her direction and then away again.

"Maybe not, but keeping me happy is."

His face darkened, and she knew right away she'd said exactly the wrong thing. Catching her lower lip with her teeth, she winced, staring straight ahead. That had sounded bratty and immature and she deeply regretted it. Right then and there she vowed she would never let herself sound like that again. She tried to think of a way to take her words back, but it was too late as the first of the models began to mince across the stage.

The model paused, posing, but her gaze flickered over Jack before she got it under control. Kari stifled a chuckle. She nodded to the model and then to the attendant, who wrote down her wishes on the order slip. Kari took the opportunity to lean close to Jack and whisper to him.

"Do women always look at you like that?"

He raised an eyebrow innocently. "Like what?"

Her eyes sparkled. "You know very well what she was doing."

But another model had taken the stage, and it was time to examine the heavy silk gown she was displaying. One after another they came, while a background tape playing gentle standards filled in the atmosphere, but Kari hardly noticed. A few she ordered set aside, most she didn't, but her mind was much more on her companion than it was on the dresses.

He was sitting very still, and yet she thought she could feel that he was very alert, his senses on guard, his mind weighing everything. She had the urge to distract him, to make him pay more attention to Kari, the woman, rather than the princess who needed to be guarded. But she curbed her impulse. She wanted his respect as much as she wanted anything, and if that meant she would have to apply a little dignity to her bearing, that was what she would do.

Finally the attendant announced an intermission and the scones and tea were served on lovely porcelain china with sterling silver utensils. Kari took a sip of the hot liquid and smiled at the man by her side.

"You're bored to tears," she said calmly. "But you're very good at hiding it."

"I could never be bored around you, Princess," he said softly.

And it was true enough on a human level. Though he had some reservations about spending all this time merely sitting in a department store showroom, gazing at models and indulging a pretty princess, it did seem to be part of the job. This was a far cry from his usual routine, where periods of investigation and analysis were interspersed with violent episodes—short and dangerous but ultimately rewarding when criminals got the prosecution they deserved.

The rewards here were very different, he admitted to himself as he gazed at Kari's pretty face. Different... but just as dangerous.

"I'll tell you what *is* boring," he said as he bit into a scone. "The clothes you're looking at. I didn't know there were still stores that sold things my grandmother used to wear."

She sighed. "I know. That's why we shop here. No one else carries these relics." She rolled her eyes. "My aunt likes to keep me firmly in the past. I'm just lucky she can't find hoop skirts for sale anywhere close."

He looked at her speculatively. "There were some younger styles on mannequins on the floor we came in on. Why can't you look at some of those?"

"Oh, because my aunt…" Her voice trailed off and her blue eyes widened as she realized what she was about to say. He was right. Why couldn't she look at some more fashionable things? She'd fallen into the habit of letting her aunt dictate these matters to her. She sat up straighter. "What a good idea," she said, looking around for the attendant.

"You'd like to see something from our young adult collection?" the woman said when Kari rose and went across the room to ask. "Of course. Your aunt requested these more mature styles, and frankly we were quite surprised to see how young you were when you came in." She smiled and gave Kari a wink. "Don't you worry about a thing, my dear. We've got consultants who know what's hot. It will only take a few minutes to set it up. But we'll need some further measurements." She eyed the very conservative sweater set Kari was wearing. "And perhaps you'd like to go ahead and try on a few representative items, just to get a feel for the sort of thing that suits you."

Suddenly a tedious task was becoming interesting. Kari felt as if she was going on an adventure. She looked over at the table and gave Jack a smile, then turned as two teenage girls came out from a side door with measuring tapes in hand.

"Would you like me to ask your young man to wait outside?" the older woman said.

"Oh, let her boyfriend stay," one of the girls who had a name tag that read Sheena said, laughing.

"We won't be doing anything too risqué," Mae,

the other girl teased, giving Jack the eye in an open, friendly manner.

Kari looked across the room at Jack, and he met her gaze with resignation, just barely shaking his head to let her know he wasn't taking all this too seriously. She laughed softly and lifted her arms so that the others could begin to measure her.

She assumed they would just get her height, her waist, and maybe her shoulders, but soon she began to realize they were pulling the tape around every part of her, one saying the measurement while the other wrote down the number, and she began to feel a little more self-conscious.

"Get the breasts," Sheena called out to Mae in what Kari thought was an unnecessarily loud voice. "Take a deep breath, honey, and push your chest out. If you got 'em, flaunt 'em, I always say."

Mae pulled the tape tightly around the relevant items. "And you got 'em, honey." She called out a number that made Kari blush, followed by, "Woo-hoo!"

Her cheeks were hot. She glanced quickly over to see how Jack was taking this and found him staring relentlessly at the wall. At first she was hoping he hadn't been paying attention, but then she noticed the twitch at the corner of his mouth and realized he was working hard trying not to laugh. And that made *her* laugh.

Moments later she was behind a folding screen that had been set up for her, trying on clothes the likes of which she'd never seen before, with a lot of help from Mae and Sheena, both clucking over her like a pair of bantam hens.

Jack waited restlessly, wondering what he had put in motion here. From where he sat he couldn't see much, but he could hear a lot of disjointed comments, and he had to admit they were making him curious to see the finished product.

"No, honey, you don't wear a bra with that. The point is to look sexy. Let it all hang out."

"Ooh, add three inch heels with ankle straps…"

"I know it seems tight. Here, Mae and I will help pull it on. If we all three shove at once…"

"Oh, those cranberry hot-pants are fabulous on you! Come on, try this black metallic net top with them."

The outfits sounded intriguing. The only problem was, Kari wasn't coming out from behind the screen to show them off. Every now and then he could hear her soft voice in a demurral of one kind or another. It was pretty obvious the clothes were a little far out for her at this juncture.

"Ohmigod!" Sheena cried at one point in a piercing voice that could have cracked open glaciers. "Look how cool she looks in the green velour spandex capri leggings with the see-through crop top!"

"Oh, yes! Eat your heart out Britney Spears!"

Jack reached out and poured himself more tea. As visions of Kari braless and in metallic spandex filled his head, his mouth seemed to be getting drier and drier, and at the same time sweat was popping out on his forehead. He pulled out a handkerchief to mop his face before he realized what was going on, and he had to shake his head, embarrassed for himself. His imagination was running wild. If she didn't come out from behind that screen soon, he was going to have to get up and go take a walk around the building.

"Ready?" she said at last, and he looked up to see her look out shyly, then emerge in a long, slinky dress that glittered like Las Vegas and clung like a second skin. "What do you think?" she asked, looking at him hopefully.

Oh, Baby! was what he thought. But he didn't say it. "Very nice," he said. "It's…ah…very nice." And he started doing some shallow breathing in order to hold off a meltdown as she walked slowly before him, turned and started back.

"You hate it," she said accusingly.

"No." He gave her a strained smile. "No, I definitely do not hate it. But I don't think you'd better buy it."

"Why not? Doesn't it look good?"

"It looks too good." He gave her a wistful look. "I'm supposed to be protecting you. I don't need the extra risk factor."

She paused, looking worried, then noticed that his eyes were dancing, and immediately she laughed. "You're bad," she said, waving a finger at him. "You are very, very bad."

He grinned at her and she went back behind the screen, changing into her own clothes and joining him again, despite the urgings of the two girls to try a few more. Rock music was blaring from the speakers now, and young women came dancing out in one fashionable outfit after another.

Kari leaned close and whispered, "My aunt won't like this," to Jack.

"Maybe it's about time she let you pick your own clothes," he murmured back.

She nodded. "Of course it is. I know it. The whole world knows it. Now how do we tell her?"

She went ahead and ordered a few items to be sent to the house for her to try on later. Jack watched her and liked what he saw—liked it too much. Her look, her scent, the sound of her voice—everything about her was turning him on in a way that reminded him of his teenage years. Uncontrollable lust wasn't a pretty thing and he wasn't crazy about it in any case. He liked control, liked to think he could manage himself and events around him. But for some reason the attraction he was experiencing with this young woman was like nothing he'd ever known before.

Forbidden fruit, he told himself. That had to be it. He knew he couldn't touch her so the need to touch her was building like a summer storm inside him. If he didn't watch out, he might become the most dangerous thing she faced in her daily life. And he was the one who was supposed to keep her safe.

To keep her safe. The words went straight into his soul. That was his job now. Suddenly he wondered if he was taking it seriously enough. She was quick and bright and self-assured, but there was a vulnerability that surfaced when he least expected it. And whenever he saw that, something in him responded and he wanted to pull her close and make sure no harm could touch her. But that was mostly a man-woman thing. Was he ignoring the most dangerous aspects of this project? Was she in real jeopardy?

"So what is next on the royal agenda?" he asked as they waited for the attendant to finish the tally and present the list of outfits that would be delivered the following day.

"The parties, of course."

"Why so many parties?"

She gave him the impish smile that always made the corners of his mouth curl into a responding smile despite all his best intentions. "To get me married. I'm supposed to try out all these men. They'll be bringing them over in herds."

His smile faded as the horror of the situation finally became clear to him. Summer at the Roseanovas was going to be a regular marriage market. She was going to be auctioned off to the equivalent of the highest bidder. This might be what royalty routinely did, but it sounded barbaric to him.

"And at some point you'll choose which one will be your husband?" he asked, frowning at her.

"Well, the duchess will choose. She will decide who is the most suitable."

He was speechless. How could she be so casual about it? He was outraged himself, and ready to threaten bodily injury to any man who got too close to her.

"But it doesn't really matter," she told him reassuringly, putting a hand on his arm as though she sensed his agitation. "I'm not marrying for love. It's my duty."

Her duty.

He pictured a gray-haired geezer with a lecherous grin taking this lovely young woman in his arms, kissing her, taking her to bed…and his stomach churned as adrenaline raced through his system. He wanted to hit something—preferably the jaw of the disgusting mythical bridegroom.

He cleared his throat, forcing back his natural reactions and attempting to maintain his cool in any way that might be possible.

"When do they start bringing them in?" he asked, hoping she didn't notice how strained his voice sounded.

"Who?"

"All these eligible bachelors they are going to be parading in front of you in order for your aunt to make her choice."

"Ahh." She nodded wisely. "Actually, the first dinner is tomorrow night."

He squared his shoulders as though preparing for an onslaught. "Okay," he muttered to himself. "No problem."

She made a face at him, but then continued on. "We'll start small. There will be three or four of them at the first dinner. But don't worry. My aunt has assured me these men aren't very important. We have invited them as a courtesy, so they will feel they've had their chance. But they won't be considered in the end."

"'Had their chance'?" He looked at her quizzically.

She laughed and preened. "Of course. I'm quite a prize, you know." Grinning, she made sure he understood she didn't take it all so very seriously. "I don't mean personally, of course. I mean what I represent."

But *he* meant personally. She was very much a prize. She was beautiful and lively and carried herself with a natural nobility that couldn't help but shine through. Any man would be lucky to get her hand in marriage.

So why was there a knot forming painfully in his gut? It made no sense. He tried to tell himself that things might get easier once the men started hanging around. At least her mind would be occupied. Yes, that was it. Get her busy. Then things would get back to normal.

But what was normal? The way the allure of her perfume got caught in his head? The way her face haunted his dreams? The way he felt her presence beside him even when he didn't turn to look at her?

Maybe normal wasn't so safe, after all.

Jack was sometimes disconcerted by Princess Karina and her candid reactions, but when it came to his job as head of security of the estate, he was confident of being on solid ground. Here, he knew what he was doing. With the approval of the duchess, he ordered new security fencing, a new alarm system for the house proper to be turned on between midnight and six in the morning, and a cell phone for Kari.

The cell phone arrived the morning after their department store expedition. On his way to deliver it to the house, he found Kari sitting with a book in the very elaborate rose garden. The Roseanovas, he'd learned, used the rose as the symbol of their royal house. The rose garden was laid out as a map of Nabotavia, with paths standing in for rivers, making a maze. Kari was sitting where the capital, Kalavia, would be. The huge rose bush covered with deep red roses was supposed to stand for the castle where her family had lived since the Middle Ages.

She was a vision in the early light, with sunshine streaming through her hair and her face still a little sleepy as she looked up to greet him. He held out the cell phone.

"What am I supposed to do with this?" she asked, holding it between her thumb and forefinger as though it weren't clean enough to touch.

He maintained his composure, though she looked pretty comical. He'd promised himself he wasn't going to fall for her charms any longer—or at any rate, he wasn't going to let it show when he did feel that warm curl of attraction unfold in his chest. That always looked so doable when he was in his own apartment, preparing his plans. After all, he'd fulfilled tougher assignments in his time. But when he came face-to-face with her, plans tended to crumble.

He had accompanied her back from the showroom display the previous afternoon, only to find the duchess waiting as they walked in, a suspicious look on her face as she watched their interaction sharply. They were a bit later than expected, and he could understand her concern. But he'd quickly assessed the situation and engaged the duchess in conversation, keeping a cool head despite the fact that they were smuggling in popcorn for the duke.

The princess had told him about the popcorn as they were leaving the department store showroom, making their way back downstairs in the elevator.

"My uncle loves it," she'd explained. "And my aunt forbids him having any. She's very strict about his diet, you know. And she has some sort of idea in her head that popcorn is bad for his digestion."

"I'm sure she's only looking out for his best interests," he murmured, though he wasn't sure of it at all.

"Possibly," she responded breezily. "But I think he deserves a treat now and then, so I get him popcorn whenever I can sneak it in."

The elevator doors opened and she began to lead him toward the counter that stocked such things.

"It's got to be the candied kind," she said instructively. "And it's got to be in a vacuum pack, because of the smell, you know. That always gives it away. And if the duchess catches me..." She made a face that revealed dire consequences in a comical fashion.

He had to hold back a grin, but he allowed himself one comment as they came to a stop at the counter and began to wait for service. Looking at her sideways he murmured, "You're awfully sneaky, for a princess."

She laughed. "You don't understand royalty at all if you don't understand how sneaky the whole system is. To be royal is to put on an act. It's all a false front." She sobered, getting philosophical. "We have to try to be larger than life, because that is what people expect of us. If you just come across like an average, everyday person, people start to pout." She demonstrated, putting on a silly voice. "'What's the point? Who needs royalty like this?' I've even heard it said that the Russian revolution became possible when the people saw Czar Nicholas and realized he was just a scrawny little man. People began to say, 'Well, who's scared of a czar like that?'"

He had to laugh at her antics. She was absolutely adorable. He stood beside her and watched as she purchased her popcorn, feeling a wave of affection for her that made him groan inside.

But once they were home and faced with the suspicions of the duchess, he worked quickly, distracting her attention with a list of security concerns for her to deal with while Kari gave him a wink and slipped away, suitably disguised popcorn in hand, to visit her uncle.

There was no longer any doubt in his mind—the princess was a very special person. And she deserved every bit of creative protection he could manage to provide. Equipping her with a cell phone was only the beginning as far as he was concerned, and here she was, resisting his efforts.

"Hold it like this," he said firmly, taking her hand in his and showing her how to hold and flip it open, then immediately pulling away when he realized he was back to treating her like a pretty girl rather than a royal presence. Somehow he had to get it through his thick head that there was a wall between them, a wall he would be a fool to try to breach.

"The best thing to do would be to wear it at your waist. See, it has a clip at the back. That way you'll always have it with you."

"Is that really necessary?" she asked, still looking

as though she would just as soon drop it in the nearest waste receptacle.

"It's just another element in our security system. It's meant to make you safer, to give you a means of communication in case anything should happen." He frowned at her. "What is your hesitation? Every girl your age in the civilized world carries one of these around with her at all times. Most wouldn't know how to function without one."

She shrugged, not at all convinced. "You still haven't told me what I am supposed to do with it."

"It will come in handy if you need to get a hold of help quickly. And you can use it to call your girl-friends."

She raised her head and met his gaze honestly. "I don't have any girlfriends."

She said it without irony, without bitterness, without guile. So much so that for just a moment he thought she must be joking.

"What are you talking about? I've never known a woman who didn't have friends. It's part of their nature."

She shook her head. "Not me," she said simply, a certain sadness shadowing her blue eyes.

He was still having trouble with this concept. "What about those two girls who were over swimming with you the other day?"

One perfectly sculpted eyebrow rose. "Were you watching us?"

"No, of course not." Suddenly his ears were burning again. What was it about her that made him do that? It had never happened with anyone else. "But I did happen to see them with you," he went on doggedly, hoping she didn't notice the color of his ears.

She shrugged. "I'd never met them before and I doubt I will see them again. I believe they were just passing through, though I didn't really get a chance for a good talk with either one of them. Besides, it would be too risky to make friends with anyone in the Nabotavian community. Too much chance for treachery." She shook her head. "I'm quite serious, Jack. I have no real friends." A slight smile played at the corners of her mouth. "I did have an imaginary friend when I was little. I called her Bambi." She looked at him quickly, wishing she could take that admission back. She'd never told anyone before. Was he laughing at her?

No. His eyes were stormy, and he was filled with a certain anger as he contemplated what her life must have been like growing up this way. What sort of archaic and sadistic system kept this lovely young woman from living a normal happy existence like that of others her age? What had all this protection and elitism done to her? And was it really worth it? No girlfriends, no life... And he thought *he'd* been deprived growing up with no family. Suddenly he realized that they had more of a common bond than he'd ever thought possible.

"Well, you should have a friend," he said tersely. "In fact, I'm going to look into getting you one."

She stared at him for a moment, and then a smile just barely crinkled the corners of her eyes. "I didn't know you could order them up," she said. "Darn! I would have bought one years ago if only I'd known."

He didn't smile. In fact, he felt more like he needed to hit something and he turned away from her.

But she followed, putting a hand on his arm to get his attention back. "You mustn't blame us for our old-fashioned ways," she told him earnestly, seemingly reading his mind and knowing how he felt about her upbringing.

"We've lost our country. We hang on to as much of our traditions as we can manage. They are all we have left."

Of course. He knew that. Swallowing hard, he forced himself to remain casual and even attempted a look of unconcern. She had her life and he had his. There was no reason their two existences should touch in any form whatsoever, except in the most professional way.

It wasn't easy to figure out why she had this ability to reach in and take hold of his emotions the way she did. Regardless, he couldn't let it show. In fact, it was probably time he put some actual distance between them, before the duchess walked out into the yard and saw them talking. Instinctively he knew she wouldn't like it at all.

He looked down at her hand on his arm, and she removed it, flattening it against her own chest. His gaze followed, and for some reason he couldn't pull away. Her fingers were slim and tapered and looked beautiful against the lightly tanned skin showing above the scooped neck of her lace-edged top. The vision she made touched him, made him yearn for her. He ached to take her in his arms.

Their gazes met and held for a long, quivering moment. But as each second ticked away, he was gathering the strength to do what had to be done. And finally he gritted his teeth and looked away.

"I've got to get going," he said gruffly. "You practice with that cell phone. Get used to it. It won't hurt you to join the modern world, at least this little bit."

When he looked back, he found her smiling at him in a way so wise, he immediately feared she could read his mind and knew exactly what he was thinking. But she didn't make any comment, turning from him, picking up her book from the bench and starting toward the house.

"I guess I'd better get going, as well. I have a lot to do to prepare for this evening." She turned back and gave him her impish grin. "Tonight is the night. Madam Batalli is due soon to do my hair. Let's hope she manages to make me beautiful."

He nodded, mixed feelings grinding through him. "So you're pretty excited," he noted dryly.

"Well...sort of." She shrugged. "This is the first step toward the beginning of the rest of my life. I'm about to launch, in a way. The way debutantes are presented. The way young ladies were introduced to society in the old days."

He nodded again, fighting the impulse to say something to her. It would be better to let her go, he knew. He had no business imposing his thoughts. But he just couldn't leave it alone.

"Princess..." He stopped, shoved his hand in his pocket and turned to go, then turned back. "Listen, be careful, okay?" he admonished awkwardly. "I mean, about the man you pick. You deserve the best. Don't settle for anything less. Okay?"

She nodded, her eyes filled with the bright light of the sun. Suddenly she took a quick step toward him as he turned to go again.

"Wait...look," she said, making an elaborate show of attaching the cell phone to the waist of her slacks. "Here, I'm putting it on. I'll be so much safer now, in case I get lost in the woods or fall down a rabbit hole or something like that."

She looked up expectantly at him, like a child hoping for approbation. Then she sighed, as though she realized she was going over the top.

"I appreciate the attempt to protect my interests. Really, I do. And I'll wear this faithfully as a token of my appreciation." She gave him a sharp salute, like a cute toy soldier at attention.

He bit back his own grin. "Thank you, Princess," he said formally. "Just remember to use it if you do find yourself in any sort of sticky situation."

"Oh, I will," she said. Her eyes lit up as she thought of something. "And once I memorize your number, I'll be able to call you anytime, day or night."

He hesitated warily. "Sure, if you're in trouble…"

"How about when I'm lonely?" she asked softly, her eyes luminous. "Or when I need some good advice?"

His face darkened. "Princess…"

"I know, I know," she said lightly, turning away and starting for the house again, book in hand. "I'm being frivolous." She looked back at him from the doorway. "But I'm going to memorize your number, anyway." She put her hand over the cell phone at her waist and added, in a voice just above a whisper, "I think you would make a wonderful friend."

And then she was gone.

His heart twisted inside him, and he stood where he was, muttering every obscene swear word he could think of—anything to keep from feeling the emotions she triggered in him.

Chapter 5

Looking the current crop of suitors over later that evening, Jack tried to remain objective. If he was going to provide Princess Kari with the proper level of security, he had to understand what was going on around her. Emotions couldn't be allowed to cloud the issue.

He stayed in the background during dinner, blending in with the help and watching as the duchess and her guests were served an elaborate meal at the long, dark dining table. Huge candelabras lit the high-ceilinged room, casting shadows on the richly flocked walls. The duchess sat at the head of the table. Seven adults as stiff and mannered as she was were scattered up and down each side, and four young men sat between them, attention all on Kari, who sat at the other end. The conversation was polite. It seemed almost formulaic to Jack, as though each was reading from a script she'd learned for the occasion.

But that all changed as the party finished dessert and retired to the game room for liqueur in tiny crystal goblets and more animated conversation. The adults sank into plush chairs around a large felt-covered gaming table while the younger ones gathered at the far side of the room, encouraging Kari as she played a few light tunes on the piano.

All four of the young men were very handsome, though one had a dissolute look and another seemed bit vacant. They were all much younger than Jack had expected. There were no old lechers looking for a young bride here tonight. That should have been a relief, but somehow it didn't help. He still hated seeing them crowd around her, vying for her attention.

"She looks like Scarlett O'Hara at the barbecue," he muttered to himself as he stood, feeling restless, in the dim light of the patio off the gaming room.

A chuckle nearby told him he'd been overheard and he turned to find the duke coming up to stand at his elbow. "You hit the nail right on the head," the duke told him softly, nodding. "Look at her. Isn't she the most fetching thing you've ever seen?"

Jack turned back to take in the scene reluctantly. The older man's admiration was well-founded. Kari was wearing a violet dress that fitted her bodice like a glove, then flared out at the hips into a filmy cloud of transparent fabric that played teasingly about her long, lovely legs. It was one of the dresses they had looked at the day before, so he assumed her choices hadn't been completely vetoed by her aunt. Kari's hair was swept up into a cascade of curls that was old-fashioned but appealing, and her face was shining with joy. Jack had never seen a woman look lovelier. He was afraid to leave his gaze on her for too long, afraid a part of him would begin to burn inside. She was just as her uncle said, completely fetching.

The young men circling her were another matter, and the duke filled him in on their identities himself.

"Now Leonard Bachman's lineage goes back to the Holy Roman Empire," he noted, pointing out one with a decidedly superior look to him. "Eugene is one of the British royal cousins," he added, nodding toward the blonde. "Not very bright, I'm afraid, but awfully good at cricket. And Nigel is a very nice lad. I once thought I was in love with his mother."

That got Jack's attention. He smiled at the duke, really looking at him for the first time and realizing how sweet he looked for a man his age. His hair was either very blond or had turned a stunning shade of white, and was combed back in a debonair style that belonged to swells of another age.

"The one to watch out for is that redhead," the duke continued, unabashed. "He has a very wild reputation among the younger crowd. I don't like the look of him. He brings to mind a young Oscar Wilde."

Jack nodded. "I'd been thinking something along those lines myself," he murmured.

"Good. I'm glad you have an instinct for these things." The duke nodded his handsome head approvingly and patted Jack's shoulder. "I trust you'll be keeping a close watch on our young lady. And making sure none of these young swains get too fresh with her?"

Is that what I'm supposed to do?

He only thought the words, but the question was a good one. He knew he'd been hired to keep Kari safe, but no one had been very clear on the extent of that safety. Was he expected to make sure she didn't risk breaking her heart? Was that a part of it all?

I hadn't understood that morals patrol was part of the job.

Again he didn't say the words aloud but thought them as he muttered something agreeable instead.

The duke went on telling him anecdotes about each of the guests. The stories made Jack grin, and even laugh once, and he wondered why the man was being so friendly. He'd met him on occasion for only a few moments at a time, but he was acting as though they'd known each other for years. Something told him Kari was the reason. She must have mentioned him to her uncle. But what could she possibly have said that would make the man feel as though they were practically comrades?

He threw a casual glance in her direction. She was laughing, and the redheaded gallant was leaning toward her, touching her cheek, saying something that was obviously impertinent. Every muscle in Jack's body clenched. The young man drew back his hand, and Jack slowly, purposefully, made himself relax. Whether the family wanted morals patrol or not, his instinct was doing the job on its own.

"Well, I suppose it is time to honor the scene with my royal presence. Frankly, I'd rather stay here chatting with you, but duty calls." The duke gave him a sad half smile. "As for my young lady, I'm sure you'll take good care of her," he said with a wink, then straightened his tie and set off to join the party.

Jack frowned, not sure what the duke had meant by that. Suddenly Kari's head lifted and her gaze met his across the room. She caught him off guard, and her smile shot straight into his heart. He saw a connection in it, a recognition that he should be in on her private joke. Suddenly he knew exactly what she was thinking just as though she'd whispered the words in his ear. She was having the time of her life but it wasn't serious—he wasn't to take it as such, and she wanted him to laugh at it with her. She wanted to share her joy with him.

He couldn't let that happen. The emotion knotting his stomach had nothing to do with humor. Telling himself to ignore this wasn't working. He was caught in a maze with no way out. Unless he took the initiative and made an escape route for himself. He took a deep breath. Time to do just that. Moving farther back into the shadows, he pulled out his walkie-talkie and called Greg Pinion, his right-hand man. It was time to hand the rest of the evening over to someone better equipped to handle the torture. He was getting out of here. A man could only take so much.

Kari bit her lip. Jack was leaving. She could tell. As he briefed Greg, she could read the signs. He was transferring the assignment and heading off to do something else.

Suddenly the delight drained out of the evening. Much of what she'd been doing had been an act meant to impress him. It had been fun, even thrilling for a time. There was certainly nothing boring about being admired. But more than that, she'd wanted Jack to see her as the center of a lot of male attention. She was sure that was a wicked thing to want, and now she was pretty sure it had backfired on her.

Of course, she was being foolish and she knew it. Much as she liked Jack, much as her pulse rate quickened whenever he was near, she knew there was no future for the two of them. She had gone through periods of feeling rebellious in the past, but that was all over now. She knew her destiny. She was going to marry and do her duty. She owed that to her parents and to her culture. In another few weeks she would be engaged to be married to an eligible nobleman of her country.

She caught her breath. That thought always made her feel as though she'd just fallen off a very high ledge. Married. How could she be married when she knew nothing—nothing at all—about men? She couldn't help being terrified of the whole situation.

"This isn't about love and kisses and romance," her aunt had told her often enough. "You don't need to know anything at all about men. That's irrelevant. This is about duty to your family and your country. It is about securing the future of the nation, helping your brothers to make it stronger. That is what you were born for."

Of course she would do her duty. But other girls got to date and flirt and have fun with boys they didn't intend to marry…didn't they? She was never going to be allowed to live like a normal person, but this one little thing…this friendship with a man who made her feel light-headed…couldn't she at least have this? Was that so horribly selfish?

She looked around at the faces of her admiring new acquaintances. Every one was well connected, handsome, charming. The man who would be picked as her spouse would be a lot like one of them, only probably a bit older—someone stable, ready to settle down, but of the right family and with the right connections. Someone eminently eligible for her hand, just as these were. Perfect for her.

This was what she'd been waiting for all this time. The days of being stuck with the old folks were gone. She was now allowed, even encouraged, to have fun with young men. She ought to be like a kid let loose in a candy store.

And yet compared to Jack these handsome suitors seemed colorless and uninteresting. It was lovely to be the center of their attention, but she'd had enough for tonight. She was ready to give up this pretense for the time being. She wanted to see Jack again. Ached to see him.

The handsome redhead was leaning close, murmuring sweet nothings meant to make her swoon, but she wasn't really listening to him. Her heart beat faster as she made her decision. Yes, she was going to see Jack again. Tonight.

Jack leaned back into the pillows he'd piled against the arm of the couch and yawned, turning off the television. Dressed only in slacks, he'd been flipping channels and finding nothing that could hold his interest. It was late. He'd been putting off going to bed but he'd waited long enough. Maybe now he would finally be able to fall asleep without thinking about…

He swore softly. No, he wasn't even going to let himself *think* about thinking about her.

This fascination with the girl was completely unlike him. He'd spent most of his life as a man's man, more at home with a group of buddies than with a girlfriend. He figured that was because of the way he'd grown up, in foster families and group homes, usually with a boy or two for a pal and very little contact with the opposite sex.

That had all changed in high school, of course, but though he'd dated a lot of pretty girls, he'd been more at home with his football teammates. Girls made him nervous. He just didn't understand what they expected. It seemed to him they said one thing when they really meant something else, and his head would swim as he tried to figure out what was going on.

The mystery girls posed faded as he hit his twenties. He even had a few fairly long-term relationships. But somehow his heart had never been truly touched. And when each relationship ended, he didn't look back with any sort of remorse. Women were easy to get when you wanted one.

The single thing he did regret, however, was letting a woman mess with his life in a way that might turn out to be downright disastrous. It had already played havoc with his career. Now he was waiting to see if his partnership with Lucy Dunlap—and the mistake of trusting her—had turned his future to dust. By the end of the summer he would know.

There was a sound at his door, a knock so soft, at first he wasn't sure if he'd imagined it. He frowned. Someone at his door at this time of night could only mean trouble. Assuming it was one of the guards, he rose from the couch and sauntered to the door, ready to point out that a call on his cell phone would have been a quicker way to get his attention.

But he never made that little speech, because he pulled the door open and found Kari on his doorstep.

"Hi," she said in a voice meant to be muted to the outside world. "Let me in, quick."

Stunned, he did as she asked and immediately regretted it.

"You can't be here," he noted sternly, lurching back. "Don't close that door."

But she did, snapping it shut before he could reach it and then turning to grin at him. "Shh!" she said with a finger to her lips. "No one knows I'm here."

She'd dressed herself all in black, from her slinky

turtleneck sweater to her soft jersey leggings. Her face was scrubbed clean of the makeup she'd worn earlier, and her hair was combed out and floating softly around her shoulders. Every time he saw her she looked more lovely than before. It was like a disease, and he was suffering from a rare and possibly fatal case of it.

"Why didn't Greg stop you?" he demanded, glowering at her. "He's supposed to be guarding the back of the house."

"I waited until he was distracted by something and I sneaked right past him," she said proudly.

"If he's that easy to fool, I'll have him fired in the morning."

Her eyes widened in horror. "Oh, no, don't do that. It wasn't his fault."

"If he can't do his job…"

"No, don't you see?" She gave him her most irresistible impish smile. "It isn't that he's so bad at what he does. It's all because I'm so good at what I do. You can't punish him for…for that…"

Her voice faded at the end because she'd finally taken in the condition she'd found him in. Her gaze trailed over his naked torso, lingering on the hard, chiseled muscles of his chest, his strong upper arms, the washboard panels tapering into his slacks.

"Oh, my," she said in a tiny voice.

He groaned and turned, rummaging in the couch, throwing pillows aside, looking for his shirt. "This is exactly why you shouldn't be here," he warned, finally spotting it and yanking it out to slip into. "You have no business coming to my apartment," he went on as he hastily worked with the buttons. "If the duchess knew you were here, she'd pack you off to a convent."

"I had to come," she said in a strangled voice. She

took a deep breath, then blinked hard a few times, regaining her equilibrium as he covered up his gorgeous flesh. "I need your help."

"What for?"

She looked at him expectantly, throwing out her hands. "Aren't you going to ask me to sit down?" she said. "Isn't that what people usually do when someone comes to visit?"

He hesitated. He wanted her out of there as quickly as possible, but he knew darn well she wasn't going to budge until she'd said her piece.

"Have a seat, Princess," he said at last, biting out the words crisply. "And tell me what you need help with."

She sat gingerly on the edge of the couch, while he dropped to drape himself casually on the opposite arm, as far from her as he could possibly get. She noted that, then looked around at the simple living room, the small kitchen just off it, the hallway toward the bathroom and bedroom. Bookcases lined the walls, though there wasn't much filling them. The old security man had lived here for years, but when he'd left, he'd taken a lot of the furnishings and Jack hadn't replaced them with many personal items. She knew he was only here for the summer, but she was disappointed he hadn't set out more clues to himself and his life. She wanted to see what he liked to read, maybe some pictures of friends, a favorite item from his past. But there was nothing she could put her finger on. Jack seemed to enjoy being an enigma.

"It would be so much fun to have a place of my own," she said wistfully. "A place I could decorate my own way and have people over to visit." She sighed. "Don't you just love being on your own?"

He shook his head, his mouth twisted cynically. "The

female urge to nest," he said. "It seems to be universal." His mouth hardened. "But this isn't getting us any closer to your problem."

"My problem?"

His brows drew together. "You said you needed help."

"Oh. Of course." She smiled at him. "This is going to sound a little strange. But it's actually quite serious. You see, I need to learn how to kiss."

He choked, which set off a short coughing fit.

She leaned toward him. "Do you need a good thump on the back?" she asked hopefully.

"No!" he said, leaning away from her. "I'm fine. It's just…" He coughed one last time and shook his head, looking at her in wonder, squinting as though that would help him see her better. He manufactured a glare, just to show her he was serious. "What did you really come here for?"

She thought for a second or two, then shrugged. "The kissing thing was it."

He groaned and she added defensively, "I thought it was a good idea. I think you ought to teach me how to kiss. Because I really need to know."

He looked at her uneasily. She was so pretty, so impossibly desirable, and so completely unaware of the danger she could have been in. She shouldn't be saying things like this to a man like him. Still, he wasn't totally convinced that she wasn't pulling his leg.

"Why?" he asked suspiciously.

"Don't you think it's something I ought to know?" She didn't give him time to answer, talking fast. "I've been taught how to dance, how to make small talk, how to drive a car. Don't you think it would be best if I were taught the intricacies of kissing? After all, I might be doing quite a lot of it this summer."

He stared at her for a moment, then turned away, muttering something she couldn't quite make out. So she went on making her case.

"You know that song, 'Sweet Sixteen and Never Been Kissed'? You could change the lyrics for me." She let out a tragic sigh. "Bitter twenty-two and never even been touched by any man." Her face changed and she almost smiled. "Except you, of course," she added, dimpling playfully.

"Me?" His head whipped back and he stared at her. "What are you talking about?"

"When you came into my room that day. Remember? You grabbed me." She sighed dreamily. "It was great. I think about it every night before I fall asleep."

"Well, don't." Rising, he began to pace the room, running his hand through his thick hair as he did so. This was no good and could get a lot worse. He had to play it carefully. "Just forget about it."

She just smiled and he stopped before her, arms folded across his chest.

"Are you seriously trying to tell me you have made it twenty-two years without once being kissed?" he demanded.

"Of course."

He shook his head. "How could that be?"

"I've never been left alone with a man. I always have someone with me." She shrugged. "That makes it rather difficult to fool around."

He shook his head again, hardly knowing whether to believe her or not. The experience she was portraying was so far removed from that of the average young woman her age, it seemed like a fairy tale. But then, she *was* a princess, wasn't she? So fairy tales would seem to apply.

"There was no point in letting me date," she went on helpfully. "I always understood that perfectly well. Why should I go out with boys who have no chance of ever marrying me? What if I fell in love? It could be disastrous."

"It still could be," he noted softly, staring down into her beautiful eyes.

She held his gaze, head high, but there was an excitement quivering deep inside her. "I think I can handle it," she told him quietly.

He shook his head slowly. "You don't know what you're talking about," he told her. It took effort, but he forced himself to turn away and begin pacing again. What was he going to do with this girl?

She watched him, a slight smile tilting the corners of her wide mouth. "You're probably right," she said. "But don't you see? That's just the problem." She waited a moment, but he kept pacing, hands shoved deep into his pockets, so she went on. "It occurred to me tonight that I really haven't had enough experience in handling men. I need help. My older brothers aren't here, so I can't turn to them. My uncle is hopeless and the duchess would just snap at me." She turned her palms up appealingly. "So I have no one else to turn to but you."

He stopped, turning to look at her. It was still an improbable scenario. Beautiful young princess appeals to lonely cop to teach her to kiss. No one else would believe it. Why should he?

"What happened tonight?" he asked her softly, his eyes searching hers, looking for evidence that there was more to this request than she was admitting to. "Did one of them try to...?"

"No, nothing like that," she said quickly. "But I want to be prepared, in case anyone ever does 'try' anything. I need to know what's possible, what to look out for. How can I defend myself if I don't understand what's going on?"

She was getting through to him. She could see the tiny seeds of doubt beginning to germinate. She was starting to persuade him to see it her way. Time to get back to the heart of the matter.

"But what I really need to know," she said softly as she looked up into his eyes, her own wide with innocence. "What I really need is lessons in how to kiss."

"Oh, no," he said, backing away from her. "There's no reason in the world you need to know how to kiss."

She rose, following him. "You wouldn't want me kissing some count or earl and having him think I'm just a callow schoolgirl who doesn't know what she's doing, would you?"

He stared at her, once again wary of being fooled by her innocent act. "Oh, come on, Princess. I imagine that's exactly what they want. Someone who's completely...untouched." He choked on the phrase and his mind was flashing words like *pure* and *virginal*. He had to turn away so she wouldn't see what that did to him.

"If you won't teach me how to kiss, I'm going to have to look for someone who will." Her eyes narrowed speculatively. "I suppose I could ask Count Boris," she mused.

He turned back, frowning fiercely. "Who the hell is Count Boris?" he growled.

She smiled at him. "The duchess's younger brother. He's coming for a visit soon. I haven't seen him since I was about ten years old, but I remember that he seemed very handsome to me at that time."

She waited, watching the conflicting emotions play in his dark gaze. It was all so blatant she was almost embarrassed. But she knew instinctively that she was never going to get anywhere if she left it up to him. So here she was, doing the best she could manage.

"What exactly is it you want to know about kissing?" he asked her, though she could see it cost him something to give in, even to this extent.

"I thought maybe…you could show me how?"

"Oh, no." He shook his head firmly. That was obviously out. Completely out. Wasn't going to happen.

"Well, at least you could give me some advice," she said sweetly.

"Advice?" He looked relieved. "Advice. Sure. Why not? I'll give you some advice." He pointed at the couch. "You go sit down. You make me nervous standing so close. And I'll think up some advice to give you."

She went back to the couch obediently, slipping out of her shoes and curling her legs up under her, looking very comfortable. He stood on the other side of the room, arms across his chest, gazing at her.

So now he was supposed to be some sort of expert. What the hell did he know about man-woman relationships? Poor thing, she didn't realize he was the last man she should be asking. You didn't get great helpful hints from someone who had failed at what you were aiming at. He could tell her what to avoid. He could tell her relationships weren't worth the effort. He could tell her not to trust anyone. That was pretty much the way he handled his own life. But somehow he didn't want to steer her in the same direction. Maybe she would be lucky. Maybe she would find something good in this rotten world. He didn't want to ruin that for her.

"Okay, the first thing you have to realize is that as a woman, you have all the power."

"The power?" She blinked in surprise. "How can that be? Men are bigger and stronger and…"

"Sure, men who are thugs can overpower you physically anytime they want to. But that's not the sort of power I'm talking about. With any normal man, it's going to be up to you to control things."

He stepped closer to where she sat, the subject suddenly as engrossing to him as it was to her. And that was odd because he'd never thought this through before. But now that he was considering it, there seemed to be a lot of theory floating around in his head, and he had to wonder how long that had been going on.

"You're beautiful, appealing and very sexy," he told her earnestly. "Men are hard-wired to react to that sort of thing. They can't even help themselves. Around a female like you, they're helpless."

She bit her lip to keep from snickering at him. Men helpless—what a concept. If men were so helpless and easy to control, why wasn't Jack kissing her right now? She took a deep breath and waited, listening intently.

"Which makes them very dangerous. Because a helpless man is going to feel cornered and is likely to do something stupid. So you have to learn to treat every man with a firm hand, but with some compassion at the same time." He frowned, shaking his head. "Is any of this making any sense?" he asked her. "What I mean is, you have to learn to play your cards very close to the vest, and to be aware of what kind of reaction you are getting at all times."

She laughed softly. "Oh, Jack, you're the quintessential law enforcement officer, aren't you? So suspicious of everyone."

He didn't welcome her comment. "Look, you asked my advice."

"I did, indeed," she said quickly, looking suitably abashed. "Sorry. Please continue."

He made her wait a beat or two, then went back to pacing as he warmed to his subject. "Okay, talking specifically about the prospective husbands—well, put it this way. Any guy worth his salt is going to want to kiss you. It's up to you to hold your kisses safe. They're worth a lot. It's up to you to decide who you value enough to squander them on."

She dangled a foot over the edge of the couch. "What if I decide I want to kiss them all?" she asked breezily.

"No!" He stopped short, frowning at her. "No, because a kiss isn't just a kiss."

She gazed at him quizzically. "Then what is it?"

He thought for a moment, wanting to get this right. "It's an invitation. It's a promise. It's a way a woman opens the door, even if just a tiny crack, into her soul."

She gasped softly. She hadn't realized Jack could be so poetic. "Just a little kiss can do all that?"

She watched him wide-eyed. She was beginning to understand what he'd meant. She thought she felt a little of the power he'd been talking about in the way she could feel that he was drawn to her. It was intoxicating. It made her think things possible she might not have dreamed of before coming here. What if...?

She rose and planted herself in his pacing path. He turned and almost ran into her, reaching out to steady her with his hands on her shoulders.

"I think you should show me that kiss now," she said softly.

The look that flashed in his eyes might have been

alarm, or it might have been something more dangerous. She wasn't sure. At any rate he turned her down.

"I don't want to kiss you," he said flatly.

Her lips tilted at the corners. "Yes, you do," she said
daringly. "I vote we be honest about this. Okay? You
want to kiss me. And I very much want you to. So
what's the holdup?"

He thought about turning away, but it had become
impossible now. She was too close. Her scent was filling his head. And he couldn't seem to pry his fingers
off her shoulders. But he had to try to keep this thing
from steering off the cliff.

"Princess…"

"Scaredy-cat," she taunted softly, smiling up at him.

She felt so fragile in his hands, so deliciously pliable.
Light as a breeze, sweet as a rose.

"No," he said, as much to himself as to her. Hell, he
was strong enough to resist this. This was nothing. "No,
we can't do this."

"Jack," she said, cocking her head to one side and
looking deep into his eyes, "if you won't kiss me, someone else will be my first. Please be the one."

Resistance crumbled abruptly, and something close
to pain was squeezing his heart. "Well, maybe just a
small kiss," he heard himself saying. "A quick one. Just
so you see…"

Oh, who was he kidding?

"No hands," he warned, releasing her shoulders. "No
touching."

She clasped her hands behind her back and he held
his hands in fists at his sides. She leaned toward him,
and he leaned toward her. She closed her eyes.

The first thing that surprised her was that his lips
were so soft. He was a hard man with a hard body and

she'd expected hardness. But no. His lips were as soft as kitten fur and smooth as whipped cream. And yet it wasn't comfort she was feeling. Heat curled through her like smoke, fire began to lick in her veins, and every nerve ending seemed alive and aware as they had never been before.

She kept her hands clasped behind her but she arched toward him, instinctively wanting to feel her breasts against his chest. At the same time, her lips parted slightly and the tip of his tongue touched them, and then he jerked back, breathing quickly and scowling at her as though he was very sorry for what he had just done.

"I didn't mean to do that," he began, then swore softly, turning away.

She was standing there, all dewy and luminous, her lips still parted, and he knew she wanted more from him. And there was no denying every part of him wanted the same thing—and more. He grimaced, feeling like a man drowning in golden nectar, a man who had to claw his way back to the surface. But he was a man who usually did what he had to do, and he managed. And when he could breathe normally again, he turned on her sternly.

"Look, I think it's time for some plain talking. You want truth? Let's both face some facts." He pointed at her almost accusingly. "You are a princess. You're royal. You were born to be one of the elite." He ran his hand distractedly through his hair, setting it on edge. "I come from the opposite end of the spectrum. I'm nobody. I come from nowhere. I've got nothing."

She winced, hating that he was talking like this. "Jack…"

"In fact, the only reason I was available to take this

job was because I'm on suspension from the police department. I'm being investigated. I might get fired."

That was news to her, and she didn't know what to say. Still, she made an attempt. "Jack, that doesn't matter. I can tell what kind of man you are."

"Can you?" He shook his head. "Sometimes I'm not too sure about that myself. You know where you come from. There are books full of your genealogy. I don't know anything about my background except that there's got to be an Italian in there somewhere. I was raised without roots, without history, without money." *Without love,* he could have added, but he would rather have died than say it. "We can't…I mean, you know there is no chance for there to be anything…"

Kari rolled her eyes toward the heavens and turned with a sigh, slipping back into her shoes. She'd tried. But now she was getting angry.

"Save your breath," she told him evenly, tossing her hair over her shoulder as she stepped past him. "I'm not a foolish child. And I'm not falling in love with you. You take all this much too seriously." She stopped at the door, looking back. "I just wanted to learn how to kiss. That's all."

Pulling the door open with her head held high, she disappeared into the night.

Jack stared into the dark for a moment, then strode after her. He didn't say a word as he passed her, but went straight to where he knew Greg was standing sentry duty and engaged him in conversation, giving Kari cover to get into the house without being seen. And when he finally got back to his apartment and closed the door and leaned against it, closing his eyes and laughing softly, he realized one thing—she'd taken his lesson about power to heart, and she was a quick study. Maybe he wasn't going to have to worry about her social relations after all.

But there was something else, something that made his laughter fade quickly. He knew it was going to be a long and sleepless night as he fought his body every minute.

Chapter 6

"Stay away from Jack Santini. He's no good for you."

Kari looked down at her perfectly polished pink fingernails and chewed on her lower lip while she waited for Mr. Blodnick to finish his tirade.

"If I'd known something like this would happen, I'd never have hired him. But I darn well should have known, shouldn't I? After all, I knew all about his suspension from the department. That was over a woman, too. His partner, of all things. I should have kept that in mind…"

"Mr. Blodnick," she said quietly, having had her fill of his overreaction. "If you please."

"Oh." The man calmed himself quickly. "I'm sorry, Your Highness. But when you ask me a question like that—"

"Mr. Blodnick, nothing has happened. No transgressions are being contemplated. All is well." She pulled her robe more tightly around her shoulders. She was dressed for a swim, but had stopped by to ask him questions because she knew her aunt was out of the house at the moment and wouldn't notice. "I merely asked you to tell me what you know of Mr. Santini's background. Idle curiosity, nothing more. There is no need for you to let it upset you so."

"Your Highness…Princess…are you sure? Because if I were to be the cause of ruining your life, I would really feel bad about it."

Kari laughed and reached out to squeeze the man's hand with a great deal of affection. "I'm sure. Now tell me. What did Jack Santini do to deserve a suspension?"

He looked like a man being tortured on the rack. "Have you talked to the duchess about this?"

"Be serious. I'm the one who told you to hire him, aren't I? Do you think I would give her a chance to tell me how wrong I supposedly was?"

He shivered at the thought. "I wouldn't think so."

"Exactly. So come on, mister, spill the beans."

He shifted in his seat and looked very uncomfortable at being in the position of having beans to spill. "I don't really know the details. And I've only heard of it in the most general terms, so…" He coughed. "Well, from what I've heard, he let his feelings for his female partner get the better of him and ended up getting blamed for something she did."

His words cut into her hopes, but she wouldn't allow him to detect that. "I see," she said, all calm and casual.

"There is an ongoing investigation. And a hearing in late August. If he's cleared, he'll be back on the force in no time. But if the board rules against him…"

She nodded. "Was there a romance involved?" she

asked, hoping her voice didn't betray how much this was costing her.

He hesitated. "You got me. All I know is, women are always falling for Jack. So I imagine it was something like that."

She smiled, rising from her chair. "Thank you, Mr. Blodnick. You've been very helpful."

He grimaced. "And you won't tell the duchess?"

Her short laugh held a trace of irony. "I'll never lie to her. But I certainly won't volunteer anything unless I'm forced to by circumstances."

"Good." He shook his head with a worried frown. "I'd hate to see him lose this job. I think his being employed here will look good to the board. Just in case he needs that extra boost. And him getting fired would look very bad."

There was no doubt about that.

But Kari left the man's office with a heavy heart. She had absolutely no right to be jealous, but human emotions were difficult to control, and she was feeling rather glum at the moment.

It had been almost a week since that night in Jack's apartment. He'd been avoiding her ever since. She knew he was right to do that. She knew that it was best for them both. They should just stay away from each other.

She'd been wrong to go to him that night. She'd been even more wrong to insist he teach her how to kiss. And yet, whenever she thought about it, she couldn't really regret it. It made her smile when she remembered how he'd tried to avoid kissing her. It made her gasp to remember what his kiss had felt like.

Still, he was right. They couldn't be together. There was no place for them as a twosome in this world. She needed to set her sights on her future, on the man who would be her partner as she returned to her country and began to serve her people the way she had been born and bred to do.

And there was a new angle. The more she was finding out about his situation, the more she realized that his position was quite precarious and could be threatened if anything happened to cause him to lose this job. Just from things she'd heard and things he'd said, she was putting two and two together and getting a rather scary scenario. It would be cruel to him to pursue him in any way. So she just had to stop it. Now, if only she could stop thinking about him as well.

Stepping out onto the veranda, heading for the pool enclosure, she stopped for a moment. She could see Jack in the distance, standing in front of the five-car garage, talking to one of his agents. At the other end of the property, she caught sight of her aunt, giving orders to one of the gardeners. Chin high, she ignored them both and went straight toward the swimming pool, dropping her robe on the deck and diving in without hesitation. She swam ten laps before she paused.

There, she thought. That's better. But she knew she was fooling herself.

She didn't know enough about men. That was the crux of the issue. Her brothers were always so far away, and her uncle was so often remote. After dressing, she quietly slipped down to the rooms the duke kept for himself and knocked on the door. Once he bade her enter, she opened the door and looked in.

"Hello, my favorite uncle," she said with forced cheer. "I've come to ask a favor. I need you to tell me something." She smiled at him tremulously. "Will you tell me about my father?"

* * *

Jack was carrying a ladder into the library the next day when he realized Kari was already in the room, sitting at a desk, books and papers spread out all around her.

"Hi," she said, looking up cheerfully.

"Oh." He stopped. He wanted to work on some wiring that had come loose in the alarm system, but he could do that some other time. "Sorry, I didn't know you were in here. I'll just go and let you have some privacy."

"No need to do that. I just came in here to transcribe some of my notes. You won't be bothering me." When he still hesitated, she flashed him a look of pure exasperation. "Don't worry. I'm not going to try and corner you to get another lesson in kissing or anything like that." Her mouth tilted in a slight smile. "That was childish. Immature. Manipulative. And I'm sorry I did it."

He turned to look at her questioningly, and her smile got rueful. "Oh, rats," she said. "That's a lie. I'm not sorry at all. But I know I should be, and I'm trying hard to be. It's just that, so far, it's not working."

He couldn't help it—she made him laugh. And she made him want her with a yearning that was quick and deep and stronger than it should be. For just a moment he let himself dream, looking at her as she sat at the desk, her blond hair in disarray, her lacy blouse twisted, her short skirt revealing long, lean and gorgeous tanned legs that seemed to draw his gaze straight up to where it didn't belong.

What if she were just an ordinary woman? What would he be doing right now? Flirting, no doubt about it. Giving off signals. Looking for response. Wondering

how long it was going to take to get her into his bed.
Anticipating how sweet it was going to be to taste her
nipples, how his hands were going to explore until he'd
found all her most responsive secrets, how he would
awaken her to things she'd never known before. At the
same time, the need for her would build and build in
him until it was almost unbearable, until he would slide
into her body and take her all the way, and finally find a
relief for himself so intense it would almost bring him to
tears as her soft cries of pure wonder and delight filled
his ears.

Whew. He blinked hard, forcing himself back to earth
and looked at her quickly, hoping his thoughts hadn't
been too obvious. But she didn't look alarmed. She was
saying something about the notes she was compiling.
He cleared his throat, still standing before her with the
ladder in his hand.

"Notes?" he asked, scanning the books and papers
she had spread out before her. "Are you giving another
speech?"

"No. Thank goodness." She sat back in her chair,
crossing her long legs and looking completely comfortable with herself and her circumstances. "Didn't I tell
you about my three main goals for my summer?"

"No," he said, forcing his gaze to avoid looking at
those lovely legs. "I don't remember anything like that."
But then, he could barely remember his name at this
point. He looked at the ladder he was holding. It took a
moment to recall why he had it with him, but once he
did, he went into action, setting it up along the far wall,
greatly relieved to have found something to do besides
standing there drooling all over the sexy princess who
was supposedly in his care.

"Okay. I'll tell you now." She put down her pencil and

rose, walking over to where he was beginning to climb up the ladder. "I have three big goals for my summer. Number one is to write a book about my mother's life. A biography. I'm actually using that as a device to explore a history of my country."

He was up high now. She looked very petite and young from his upper perch. Still, he had to admit, the way she carried herself gave her a presence you just couldn't deny. No one would have to be told that she was royal. And from up here, her breasts looked so damn appealing...

"You remember that she was killed by the rebels when we escaped from Nabotavia. She and my father both."

He nodded as he reached into the vent with pliers. Maybe he could cut into a wire and get electrocuted, thus putting himself out of this misery. But misery wasn't really the right word for what he was feeling. Sweet torture was more like it. And if he were honest, he would have to admit it felt dangerously delicious, despite everything.

"That's why I want to find out all that I can about her and write it down. Before it's too late and everyone forgets."

He finally realized what she was talking about, and that caught him up short. Here she was discussing her murdered parents and he was off in fantasyland instead of giving the subject the respect it deserved. He quickly vowed to mend his ways.

"What about your father?" he asked by way of catching up as he threaded the wire into place.

"He's had a ton of books written about him," she said, wandering down the wall of floor-to-ceiling stacks and pulling out a book about the king, waving it at him, then shoving it back in. "But my mother hasn't. I want to use her story to fill in the lives of women of her time." She looked into space. "I want to write a memoir about Nabotavia, about how it used to be before the revolution. My uncle is helping me with it, but I'm also interviewing some of the older servants to get anecdotes from their lives, as well as some of my aunt's friends when they come to visit. I really want to get a lot of different perspectives." She turned back to see if he was still paying attention.

"How are you doing it?" he asked, snapping closed the opening he'd been working on.

"I have a little recorder I use. I just turn it on while talking to people. Then I transcribe the tapes later, go through and edit, pick out the parts I want to use. My uncle looks my work over and makes suggestions."

"Really." He was impressed, now that he was paying enough attention to understand what she was doing. His image of a pampered little princess whiling away her time eating bonbons and accepting flattery from the huddled masses was fading fast.

"Once I get it into a form I can live with, I'll have a few other Nabotavians of the old school look at it and tell me what they think. Eventually I hope to have it printed up and put into the national library."

"I think that's great." And he really meant it. She was quite ambitious in her way, and he admired that.

"Do you?" She glowed under his praise. "I hope it turns out to be something Nabotavia can be proud of. I live for my people, you know."

He winced. She'd finally hit a note that sounded sour to him.

"What are your other two goals?" he asked her, changing the subject as he started back down the ladder.

She threw out her hands and dazzled him with a bright smile. "Number two is this—I want to learn to cook."

He stopped at the bottom to look hard at her. "Why would you want to learn that? You'll always have others to do that for you."

"That's exactly why I need to know. I don't want to be a silly princess who couldn't feed herself if anything went wrong." She slipped back onto the library table, sitting on the end, swinging her legs. "Things happen, you know. And I want to be prepared. And I don't want to be someone who gives orders and has no idea what others have to do to perform chores for her." She chuckled softly. "Besides, I don't think you've ever been at the mercy of a royal chef. It can be quite an experience. If he goes on a kick, say he reads that anchovy paste on everything brings good luck or something like that, you might just be faced with a week's worth of inedible food. I've seen it happen. Not a pretty sight. It's smart to be prepared for the worst."

He nodded, bending down to pack his gear into a toolbox. "And number three?" he asked.

"And number three, of course—I have to get married."

Straightening, he looked at her and nodded again. "Of course." His fingers curled around a pair of pliers. "How are things coming on that front?"

"Well, our next dinner is Friday night. The more serious candidates are due to arrive. I'll be wearing one of the dresses I chose the other day and having my hair done in a special new style in the afternoon."

"You're having your hair done again?" It seemed to him that the hair dresser was a daily visitor lately.

She laughed at his naiveté. "I have to look my best,

you know. Madam Batalli will be coming to help me before every party, and especially before the ball in August."

"Really." He frowned thoughtfully, still holding the pliers. Madam Batalli was an older lady, almost elderly. One would think a princess would want to try some younger style ideas. "And all to catch yourself a royal husband."

She went perfectly still, staring at him. "You don't approve."

He lost it. If he'd only stopped for a moment and thought. After all, he was no one but an employee. He had no call to react the way he did. But by the time that realization had taken place in his mind, it was too late. The words were out.

"Damn right I don't approve. This is like some ritual out of the Dark Ages. This is like selling your oldest daughter to the highest bidder. I wish you'd reject it. I would think that a woman like you, with all you've got going, could tell them all to go to hell and walk out of here."

Her head jerked back as though he'd slapped her. "Gee," she murmured. "Don't hold back. I wouldn't want you to feel as though your opinion had been overlooked."

He grimaced, rubbing his neck. "Sorry," he said gruffly. "But you asked."

"Indeed I did." She gazed at him seriously. "So I take it you don't think much of royalty."

"I didn't say that," he replied. "It was useful once. I think royalty was nice while it lasted, but it's had its day and should get off the stage."

"But what if the people of a country want their royalty?" She shook her head. "It's a double-edged sword, you know. The people are locked into their traditions, and we're locked into providing something they want to have. I was born into a certain situation and I owe it to my people to fulfill my role."

He was beginning to wonder how he'd ended up in this position. It certainly wasn't a comfortable one. "Your people kicked you out," he noted dryly.

She whirled to face him. "No they didn't. That was only one small segment that took over. And now they are gone and the people seem to want us back."

"So you think you're really going back?" He'd heard something along these lines, that Nabotavia had held a plebiscite and the royalty was being begged to return. Funny how once he had the name of the little country in his mind he seemed to be hearing about it everywhere.

"Oh, yes. That's what this is all about. That's why I have to marry right away. By the end of the year, we'll all be going back. And it looks as though my oldest brother will be crowned as the new king."

Jack frowned, wondering what that would be like. "Does he want that?"

"Well, of course. It's his destiny. His destiny and his duty." She saw his skeptical look and went on a bit defensively. "We were all raised with a sense of what our duty is, and I think that is a good thing. It helps to raise us above selfish concerns. Don't you find you become a better person once you commit yourself to a larger cause? Especially when it involves doing good for others."

"I suppose so," he murmured doubtfully, but memories were floating into his mind, reminders of when he'd been a Navy SEAL and how he'd felt when he'd been active in the police force. She was right. He'd always been happiest when working for a bigger issue.

"You know about that," she said, as though she'd read his mind again. "You're a cop."

He glanced her way. "Yes, I am."

"Do you still feel a sense of duty to the police force, even though you're under suspension?"

His gaze hardened. He wished he hadn't told her about that. Still, it was hardly a national secret. "Sure I do," he said speaking curtly. "The situation I'm in was my fault, not theirs. I could have avoided it if I'd been smarter."

"From what I've heard, you were protecting your partner."

He groaned, looking away.

"I also heard your partner was a woman." She stopped right in front of him. "Did you love her very much?"

He looked down into her eyes, wondering why she was pushing this. "Princess, look. I know you live in a fairy-tale world, but most of us have to deal with a more mundane existence. Things don't follow the usual story lines."

She cocked her head to the side, regarding him with a piercing look. "There's nothing fairy-tale about my world. Just the names. Otherwise, it's very boring."

"So is being a cop. The cop shows on TV—they hype that up to make a good story. Real life is not like that."

"So you're saying you weren't madly in love with her?"

He almost had to smile at her dogged determination to get the straight scoop. "No, I was not madly in love with her."

He was in pretty heavy duty "like" there for a while, but he didn't have to tell her about that. Liking Lucy, feeling a lot of sympathy for her, all that had clouded his thinking at the time. And that was what ought to remind him of how important it was to keep a distance. He'd just about ruined his situation on the force by letting personal relationships get in the way of his duty. He'd be damned if he would let that happen again.

He started away, hesitated for a moment, then turned back. "I probably should warn you. I've ordered that the dogs be let loose to roam the estate during the night."

Her head came up and she stared at him. "The dogs?"

"Yes. The Great Danes that are kept in the kennel behind the garage. I found out they were originally purchased to be guards, but no one ever followed through and actually trained them. So I've hired a trainer who says they can start right away."

She nodded thoughtfully, her eyes cool as she gazed at him. "I see. So…is this because you want to guarantee I won't come visiting you at night?" She cocked an eyebrow in that royal way she sometimes had. "Are these vicious beasts supposed to take the place of poor old Greg who 'couldn't do his job right'?"

He made sure that his expression didn't change. "It has nothing to do with that, Princess," he said.

"Really." She didn't believe him for a moment. "I see. Well, thank you for warning me. I'll be on my guard."

He turned, ladder in hand, and almost ran into the duchess as she made her regal way into the library. She nodded to him curtly, then frowned as she looked at her niece.

Kari sighed. She would have liked a bit longer with Jack, but now he was out the door and there was no hope of clearing the air between them. And she was left with the duchess looking as though she'd walked in on a romantic tryst.

"Oh, Aunt, don't look so cross. We were only talking."

The duchess looked skeptical as she dropped into a chair at the library table. "I'm not sure it was such a good idea to hire that man," she fretted. "I now hear that he has had problems in the past and is currently under suspicion of using his status as a police officer to cover criminal activity."

"He's completely innocent," Kari blurted out, then regretted it as her aunt looked at her sharply.

"How on earth would you know that?"

"I just...Mr. Blodnick told me," she improvised quickly. "And he has known him for years."

The duchess drew her head back and narrowed her gaze. "I think I'd better have a talk with our Mr. Blodnick."

Kari's heart was in her throat. "You're not going to have him fired!"

Her aunt turned and stared at her. "Why is that so important to you? What's going on here?"

Kari knew she'd made a big mistake reacting as she had. Now she was going to have to summon all her acting powers if she was going to turn this around. Very carefully she composed herself and managed to look casual and unconcerned, if slightly offended. "Oh, Aunt, there's nothing going on. Heavens, I've got enough on my mind right now. But I wouldn't want anyone fired just because rumors circulate about him." She smiled at her older relative. "And I wouldn't want anyone fired because of me."

"It wouldn't be because of you."

Kari threw out her hands. "Why not? He was hired because of me."

"True." Her aunt seemed at least partially mollified.

"Anyway, I don't have time to deal with that this week. I'm going to be traveling to San Francisco overnight. I'll be back in time for our Friday night dinner, however." She sighed, looking at Kari. "But you mustn't worry your head about these things. You just concentrate on readying yourself for matrimony, my dear. And the return to Nabotavia. Those are the only things you need to think about." She rose from her seat at the library table.

"By the way, my younger brother, Count Boris, will be arriving next week. He'll be staying with us for the rest of the summer." Her smile seemed to hold much pleasure at the thought of her brother arriving. "He was quite fond of you when you were a child. I hope the two of you will still get along."

Kari was breathing a sigh of relief and hardly paid any attention to this talk of Count Boris. "I'm sure we'll do fine," she said airily, not giving it a second thought.

"Oh, yes," her aunt agreed, smiling as though she was quite pleased at the prospect. "I'm sure you will."

Chapter 7

Princess Kari was in the kitchen the next morning when she got a surprise. Something was making a funny electronic sound, and she looked around the room for the source, then put her hand over the small bulge at her waist, realizing it was her cell phone. She'd been faithfully wearing it around for days without having any action at all.

"It's ringing!" she cried to no one in particular, since the room was empty except for her. She'd never had a real cell call before. Grabbing it, she flipped it open and said, "Hello?"

"Hi, Princess. It's Jack Santini."

"Jack!" Her heart leaped. "This is so exciting."

"What's wrong?"

His voice was filled with concern and she laughed. "No, it's just that you're my first call. Ever."

"Oh." He seemed to find that puzzling, but not interesting enough to pursue. "Are you alone?"

"Yes."

"Good. I've got some news. You know your hair appointment for this afternoon?"

Now it was her turn for puzzlement. "Yes."

"I'm afraid Madam Batalli can't make it today. I've found you someone new."

Kari frowned. "But I've had Madam Batalli since I was sixteen."

"All the more reason to try someone else. Don't worry. She's fine as far as security goes. Her name's Donna Blake. She's actually a good friend of mine."

"Who you just happened to have handy." Kari wasn't sure she liked this. "You haven't fired Madam Batalli have you?"

"No. Of course not. I can't do that. I just…sent her on a little vacation."

"What?"

"Never mind that now," he said quickly. "I just wanted to warn you. I think you'll like Donna. Here's her number." He rattled it off rapidly. "You can call her to confirm. She's waiting to hear from you."

"Jack…"

"Trust me. You'll like her. I've gotta go."

She clicked off, slightly confused but at the same time strangely happy. She'd had her first cell phone call and she liked it. Jack had actually called her.

"May it be the first of many," she declared out loud.

But the more she thought it over, the more her spirits drooped. Maybe this wasn't such a good thing after all. As she analyzed it, she began to think she might just know what Jack was doing. He figured if he contacted her by phone, he wouldn't have to risk any more face-to-face encounters. He was already calling out the dogs at night to keep her away and now he was using the phone to fend her off in the daytime. She had a sudden epiphany. Women used the phone to draw people closer. Men used phones to keep people at a distance.

So that's your angle, she thought, pursing her lips. Well, we'll just see about that Mr. Jack Santini. We may just have another card up our royal sleeve.

Pulling the cell phone off her waist, she pressed in his number, tapping her fingers against the counter while she waited for him to answer.

Jack hung up, letting out a long breath. She charmed him every time. She was so open, so innocent, so lacking in guile of any kind. It gnawed at him that he was now manipulating her as baldly as any woman had ever tried to manipulate him in the past. In some ways you might almost say he was sending in a spy. Well, not exactly a spy, but something almost as repugnant.

But that wasn't really fair. Donna was no spy. She was a darling and Kari needed a friend. As soon as he'd decided to try to provide her with one, Donna had leaped immediately to mind. He and she had both lived in the same group home the year before he'd joined the Navy. Though she'd been a few years younger, they'd struck up a friendship that had lasted ever since. They had even shared an apartment for a while, platonically, when he'd first been discharged from the Navy and she'd just finished cosmetology school. Donna had a basic decency and bright view of life that Kari might respond to. In his experience she had warmed the heart of everyone who had ever met her.

Kari had said she had no friends. Well, Donna would be a friend if Kari would let her be. He couldn't go so far as to manipulate the way the princess would feel about Donna, but he was pretty sure he knew how his old friend would feel about the princess. He couldn't imagine anyone not loving her at first sight.

Still, his conscience was nagging at him a little. The duchess wouldn't have approved, but she was out of town for the day—or Jack would never have tried to pull the switch this way. Maybe he was just being selfish, bringing in one of his own personal pals to be buddies with Kari. It was probably unethical as all get-out, but it wasn't necessarily illegal. He sighed. It was hell getting involved in a personal relationship, but here he was, stuck in one, whether he wanted to be or not.

His cell phone rang and he reached for it automatically.

"Hello?"

"Hi," Kari said. "It's me."

"No kidding." He couldn't help but smile at the sound of her voice.

"Since we're now in cell phone contact, I thought we ought to work on secret signals," she said pertly.

That opened his eyes. "What?"

"In case I get kidnapped or something. If I have my cell phone with me I could give you a call and tell you my location using code words if we have them set up ahead of time."

He had to smile at her enthusiasm, but at the same time he knew he had to squelch it. "The first thing that any competent kidnapper will do is strip you of your cell phone."

"Oh." She paused, but not for long. "Well, what if they're not competent? I'll bet the Sinigonians wouldn't have thought of doing that."

His brows drew together. "Who are the Sinigonians?"

"The people who kidnapped me before."

Shock catapulted him up off his chair. "You were kidnapped before? Why didn't anyone ever tell me?"

"Oh, it happened so long ago. It was no big deal."

No big deal. He swore softly, shaking his head, and when he spoke again, his voice was like struck steel. "Where are you?"

"I'm in the kitchen. But I'm very busy…"

"Don't move. I'll be there in less than a minute."

She sighed happily as she closed her phone and put it back at her waist. Sometimes things really did work out for the best. By the time he arrived in the doorway of the kitchen, she'd barely gotten back to work on the counter she was cleaning.

He stepped into the room and looked around suspiciously. The huge light-filled space gleamed with copper-bottomed pans and stainless steel appliances. Only the island butcher-block counter was a mess, covered with flour and the remnants of dough that Kari was cleaning. He looked at her as though he could hardly believe what he was seeing.

"Where is everybody? Do they leave you alone in here?"

"Very funny." She went back to scrubbing down the wooden counter. "Cook and I have been making the dough for dinner rolls. She's gone to take her midday nap, and I'm cleaning up."

"You're kidding."

"Why would I kid you about that? Here's the dough." She pulled out a large flat tray to show him the saffron-colored dough waiting to rise. She displayed it with all the pride of a creator. "Isn't it beautiful?"

"It's beautiful all right. I just can't believe…" But he looked at her flour-dredged hands, then her wide eyes, and cut his comment off without completing it. "So you're cleaning up."

"Yes," she said defiantly, going back to her scrubbing. "I'm cleaning up." She glanced up at him from under her tousled hair. "What do you think? That I'm making this up?"

"No. No, it's just that…well, you're a princess. You don't need to do this."

"Oh, yes I do," she said calmly. "Besides, I like doing it."

He watched her for a moment. Right now she could have been any young woman in any kitchen in the country, doing chores that needed to be done. But no, he took that back. She was much more beautiful than any other young woman of his acquaintance, and the way she was scrubbing that counter, putting her whole body into it, she was also more hardworking. She was a puzzle. And she was also the cutest thing he'd ever seen.

He shook his head over her desire to play scullery maid, but decided to let it go. "Okay," he said crisply, crossing his arms at his chest. "Tell me about this kidnapping."

She shrugged, pushing back a stray hair with the back of her hand. "I told you it was long ago. No one has ever said anything about it to you because for the most part, I'm sure, they've all forgotten about it. It wasn't very significant, even at the time." She went back to scrubbing. "I was about thirteen, I think." She rinsed out a rag and began to wipe the counter dry. "It was the Sinigonian family. They are kind of the Keystone Kops of our homeland. They are always trying to gain advantage over the other factions, but they are just so incompetent. It never works out for them." She rinsed the rag again, hung it to dry, and turned to face him.

"They only took me to their house in Santa Monica. My brothers came and rescued me before anything really happened."

Jack frowned. The entire operation sounded wacky, but he was considerably less alarmed than he had been when he'd first heard about it. He slumped onto a stool set at the counter, casually draping across it. "They didn't hurt you?" he asked her.

"Oh, no, not them." She plunked down on a bar stool next to the one he was sitting on, drying her hands on her apron. "They were very sweet to me, actually. Now the Davincas...that's a different story. You don't want to be kidnapped by them. They're a bunch of thugs. They took one princess and held her for ransom for weeks. They kept her in a vegetable cellar. It was horrible."

Jack shook his head. The Nabotavians seemed to be particularly enamored of nabbing royalty. "Were your kidnappers asking for a ransom?"

"Oh, no." She wrinkled her nose. "They only wanted me to marry their son, of course."

Jack gave her a look of outrage. "At thirteen?"

"The old-fashioned types think that's a great age. Catch her while she's young and too naive to complain, they say." She shrugged. "But they needn't have worried. My aunt has kept me young all these years." Her tone wasn't exactly bitter, but it was the closest thing to it. "I've been carefully nourished and coddled. I'm still like a thirteen-year-old girl. If you know what I mean." She held back her laughter. "Of course, I have recently been taught something about kissing, but not nearly enough to put me in the experienced category. Do you think?"

He avoided her gaze and steeled himself. He would be damned if he was going to let himself blush again.

She was taunting him and he knew it. She was also tempting him, and he wasn't going to take the bait.

"But that is neither here nor there," she admitted breezily. "The most important thing—of supreme importance—is to keep the blood line pure." She gave a casual wave in the air. "After all, succession and all that."

He risked a look at her and then he couldn't look away. She was wearing tight, patterned leggings he'd seen her eyeing at the showing the other day, along with a lacy white blouse and the red rose pin that symbolized her royal house, a pin she always wore. Her clear skin seemed to glow with a magic sheen that made him want to kiss her. But then, just about everything made him want to kiss her.

"I suppose that's pretty important for keeping the royal boat stable in troubled waters," he said gruffly, trying to keep his focus.

"Absolutely." She smiled, knowing he understood. "That's what happened to my darling duke. He's my father's half brother, you know." She dropped her gaze as she went on. "He was illegitimate. His mother was a lady-in-waiting to my grandmother. And that means he can never be king, you see." She looked up again. "My brother Marco will succeed. And whoever marries me will be very highly placed in the hierarchy of things." She sighed. "Unless, of course, they try to marry me off to a royal from another country. Then who knows what will happen to me?"

He wasn't going to say what he thought of this whole rotten system. She was wedded to it and obviously thought she could live with it. He got crazy thinking about how easily she could give her life up to others to guide for her. He had moments of a wild fantasy of carrying her off himself. Luckily he wasn't insane enough to think something like that might work. She was what she was and he was what he was.

"And never the twain shall meet," he muttered to himself.

"What's that?" she asked, but he shook his head.

"So tell me," he said instead. "What happened to these people? Did you have them prosecuted? Are they in jail?"

"Oh, heavens no. They're harmless little folks. We Nabotavians mostly take care of our own."

He had to look away and swallow hard at that one. Come on, come on, he told himself impatiently. Just because their system is nuts doesn't mean you have to fix it for them. Just let it be.

But he had to find out a few things. "So you're telling me they could still be out there, plotting to snatch you again."

She put her head to the side, considering. "Oh, I doubt that. From what I've heard they've given up on me long ago. They've already married their son off to some lower level princess."

"Uh-huh. Just how many princesses do you people have?"

"Oh, tons of them. At least, there will be when everyone returns. They're all cousins who married other cousins. You know how that goes. It's a mess, believe me."

His wide mouth quirked at one corner as he watched her. "So that's your problem," he said dryly. "Ever think you people might need to bring in some fresh blood?"

She looked up at him and smiled. "Sounds like a good idea to me," she said softly.

He grimaced and went on. "From the briefings I've

had, it's been my impression that the group called December Radicals is the one to look out for."

"Yes. They're the ones who killed my parents." She sat back, all smiles extinguished. "For a while they had all the power. But they've lost it over recent years, and they've been trying to get it back." She shook her head. "But there's no hope for them now. The country is becoming a democracy ruled by a constitutional monarchy. However, I suppose it's best to remember, as you were telling me the other night, that it is when people feel cornered and helpless that they are the most dangerous."

He nodded thoughtfully. It was a disturbing thought. From what she'd told him, he gathered that the Sinigonians merely wanted a bride for their boy. The December Radicals probably had something else in mind, like blackmail, ransom and revenge. The only thing he knew for certain was that he must never give them a chance to get their hands on her. Them, or anyone else who didn't have her best interests at heart.

Suddenly, inexplicably, he felt overwhelmingly protective toward her, and it was not on a professional level. It had everything to do with her huge blue eyes and the trusting way she looked at him and very little to do with a paycheck at the end of the month. He wanted her in his arms the way a starving man wanted bread, with a deep, primitive need that threatened to choke him.

And she seemed to sense that things were veering into forbidden territory, because she slid off her stool and made it clear that it was time for him to go. He got up more slowly, his inner turmoil not as easy to turn off once it had started simmering.

She looked about the kitchen, then set her jaw and faced him squarely. "I'm not going to fall in love with you, you know," she told him. "So you can quit worrying right now."

"All right," he said, because he couldn't think of anything else to say about a statement that so thoroughly took his breath away.

"I guess I'd better go give this friend of yours a call," she was saying, "if I'm going to get my hair done in time for the dinner tonight."

"Oh. Good." He stopped and faced her, reluctant to go anywhere she wasn't going to be. "Donna's a peach. You'll like her."

Kari took a deep breath and asked, "What is she to you?"

"What do you mean?" But he saw in her eyes what she meant. "Oh, she's a friend. We've been friends since we were kids." He wanted to reassure her, then realized doing that would only make things worse. "We both ended up in the same group home after bouncing around from one foster family to another. So we have similar backgrounds that tie us together."

"Unlike you and me," she said, her eyes dark.

"Unlike you and me," he agreed, his voice rough.

Suddenly she reached up and flattened the palm of her hand to his cheek. "There's no one else like you," she said softly.

He ached to taste her lips. Reaching up, he covered her hand with his own, then took it and pressed a kiss into the center of her palm, his gaze holding hers, burning into hers. Something passed between them, some connection was made on a nonverbal level that made them both breathless. He dropped her hand and turned quickly, leaving the way he'd come, and she stood where she was, savoring the lingering sense of the kiss she'd captured in her hand.

What did it mean? She didn't know. She didn't want to know at this point. She only wanted to feel, not to think. Closing her eyes, she held her hand to her own face and smiled.

Then she remembered the telephone call she still had to make and her smile faded as she remembered this Donna person. She hated this jealous feeling she had. She'd had it about his partner and now she had it about his hairdresser friend. Mr. Blodnick was probably right—he was the sort of man who women fell for in droves. There were always going to be women around him. And it really had nothing to do with her. So why did it make her heart twist in agony?

Kari started out the hair session determined to dislike Donna, but in very little time she realized that was going to be an untenable position. Donna's dark hair was cut in a bob that left her with bangs barely revealing bright green eyes that sparkled with interest and the joy of life. She started right out acting as though she'd known Kari all her life, without a hint that she might in any way be in awe of royalty.

"Here's what we'll do," she told her new client once they were alone in Kari's room. "While I'm setting up my equipment, you go through your snapshots and other pictures for the last year or so and pull out any you find where you think your hair looked its best. Also, if you have any pictures from magazines, or whatever, of hairstyles you'd be interested in trying, get those out, too. Then I'll sketch out some ideas using your facial shape and your bone structure as a foundation. And then we'll see what we can come up with."

They spent the next two hours together, giggling over pictures, trying out various outrageous styles, then settling on something less flamboyant but very different from the style Kari normally sported. All in all, it was the sort of fun that Kari wasn't used to, and she had to admit, she had a very good time. She ended the session liking Donna a lot, despite her original reservations.

Still, she wondered about the relationship Jack and this woman might have had in the past.

"So you've known Jack just about forever," she said, being carefully casual, as they began packing Donna's equipment and implements away.

"Oh, yeah, we go way back," Donna replied, giving her a quick smile that revealed her understanding of how things were. She stopped and looked at Kari earnestly. "Look, hon, don't be embarrassed if you've got a crush on the guy. Not many girls who meet him can resist a bit of one, you know. He's so cute and so very, very manly." She gave her a wise and knowing look. "I know you know what I mean."

Kari couldn't help but smile. "How about you?" she asked curiously.

"Me?" Donna laughed. "He's like a brother to me. Do you have a brother?"

"Oh, yes. I have three of them."

"Then you know what it's like. In some ways we're almost too close. There's not enough mystery left between us. You know what I mean? I adore him, but not that way."

For some reason—maybe because she just wanted to so badly—Kari believed her. Just before Donna left, they had a last look in the mirror together, both nodding with approval. The "do" was sophisticated, yet young and lively, with curls cascading down one side of her head and small tendrils teasing her ear on the other side. Kari was excited. She felt like a different person.

"Oh, I hope you can come again sometime," she told Donna impulsively. "I mean, I love old Madam Batalli, but…"

"Don't you worry about the madam. She's on her way to the Caribbean."

Kari frowned. "Whatever do you mean?"

"Didn't you know? Jack got her a position on a cruise ship. Seems she's always wanted to travel and this is her chance. She won't be back until fall."

Kari stared at Donna. "Why would Jack…?"

"He didn't tell you?" Donna shrugged and smiled at her, then launched into a long explanation, talking so fast Kari could hardly keep up with her thoughts. "Well, here's the deal. Jack told me about your situation, how you have to marry some dude you hardly even know, because of your duty to your native country. And I really admire you for that. I know I couldn't do it. But he also told me that you have wealth and you are going to have power, but the one thing you don't have, because of your position, is friends. He said to me, 'Donna, every woman needs a friend.' And you know, he's right. It's genetic. It's born in us. But he said, 'You go be her friend, if she'll have you.' And I told him I'd give it a try. I'd have to see if we got along. And if I liked you." She grinned. "And I guess you could say I like you just fine." She shrugged. "So that's where we are. And if you decide you want me to come back, I'll sure do that. But it's up to you."

Kari didn't know what to think. She'd seldom met anyone quite this straightforward. "Is this sort of like hiring you to be my friend?" she asked warily.

Donna gave an explosive laugh. "No! You're hiring me to be your hairdresser. The friend thing comes free." Impulsively she reached out and gave Kari a hug. "Darling, I'd love to be your friend. And I'd love to be your hairdresser. But if this just doesn't work for you, I'll understand." She turned to go. "Just remember, anything you say to me will be strictly confidential. Even from Jack. It's part of the hairdresser's code." She laughed, and as Donna left, her heels clicking down the hallway, Kari smiled. That laugh was infectious.

"I may just have a friend," she whispered to herself in wonder. And that was fun. But the fact that Jack had done this for her was harder to think about. A part of her wanted to find the angle, wanted to puzzle out the reason he might have done such a thing. What did he have to gain? Was Donna here to watch her for Jack?

"Or is he just a wonderful, wonderful man?" In her heart she thought she knew.

Chapter 8

The duchess hated Kari's new hairstyle. And she was furious to find that Madam Batalli was now working on a cruise ship. She'd come back from her overnight trip in a hurry to make it to the evening festivities, and she'd been presented with a fait accompli that she didn't agree with at all. She knew whom to blame.

"That Jack Santini man has got to go," she fumed. "I've been suspicious of him for quite some time and now he's overstepped his authority. We never should have hired him. I want him fired right away."

The atmosphere was electric with her criticism, but Kari's response stopped all that. She stood listening as her aunt went on and on, detailing how Jack was to be fired, and at last, when her aunt paused for breath, she made her statement.

"No."

The word echoed through the drawing room. The

duchess stopped and stared at her. Tim Blodnick, who'd been jotting down notes on just how the firing was supposed to go, gaped at her, as well.

"I don't want him fired," she said calmly, facing them both with quiet dignity. "I think he's done a wonderful job and I want him to stay."

The duchess regained her composure quickly. "My dear young lady," she said icily. "I don't think you know what you're talking about. Older and wiser heads will make these decisions for you. We're only thinking of your own good, you know."

Kari shook her head stubbornly. "I'm sorry, Aunt, but I won't hear of it. I'm over twenty-one and can make my own decisions now. Jack Santini stays."

The duchess fussed for a few more moments, but her tone was unconvincing. She'd been shocked by what Kari had done, but it was obvious she'd known it would happen at some point and she was beginning to be resigned to it. After all, truth to tell, Kari *was* the princess, and for the first time in her life, she was pulling rank. She'd never even dreamed of doing such a thing before. But it felt very natural now that it was done.

And though she wouldn't stop and frame the thought in full, a part of her knew instinctively that Jack had become more important to her than just about anything else.

In some ways the evening was like a rerun of the week before. There was a new cast of characters, but the circumstances were similar. Even the conversation seemed like something heard before. But the dinner was up to the usual high standards. Kari made sure Jack got slipped a roll, one of the ones she had helped Cook prepare that morning, then waited for his verdict.

When he gave her a surreptitious thumbs-up, she put her nose in the air with a "See? I told you so," display of hauteur. But when she peeked at him again, she caught him laughing, and that made her smile, as well.

Unfortunately, that incident provided the most interesting moment of the evening. This group of aspirants was older, more world-weary and not as prone to the sort of giddy courtship practiced by the younger set. Still, from the look in each eye she could tell they mostly thought she would make a pretty fine plum to be baked in their particular pie.

But that wasn't likely to happen. She found them all pretty boring. One was a future minister of health for the upcoming administration. Another was destined to manage the educational system for the newly reorganized country. A third was a sort of a rich playboy who had been married to a film star but was recently divorced. He drank too much wine and fell asleep during dessert and had to be carried to the couch.

The remaining gentlemen talked about politics and business—things she knew were important—things she knew she was going to have to begin paying attention to herself. But she didn't relish the idea. She was still too young for this, darn it! She needed a little more time. She needed some other sort of man. Someone like...

No, she wouldn't say it, not even to herself. But her gaze sought him out. He was standing in the shadows at the far end of the room, talking to her uncle, as he often did. But his gaze met hers immediately and he acknowledged her with a very slight, almost imperceptible wink. He looked as strong and handsome as any statue by Michelangelo, and it was quite clear his main object in life, at the moment, was to make sure she was safe. Watching him, she felt a surge of something hot and sweet that filled her soul, and her heart fluttered in her chest.

I'm in love, she thought. And the shock of it shivered through her.

No, she couldn't be. She couldn't let herself be.

Yes, I'm in love. I'm in love with a man who stirs my blood and is living his life to make mine better. A man who takes time out of his day to think about finding me a friend. How could I not love a man like that?

She'd told him only that afternoon that she wouldn't fall in love with him. But what else could she have said? If she'd told him the truth, he would have been worried about things he didn't need to worry about. Because it was clear as glass to her that she would do her duty, no matter what. Falling in love wasn't going to change anything.

The evening seemed to drag interminably. She was polite and she was cordial, but she was hardly engaged with her guests, and her aunt knew it. Still, she found to her surprise that she didn't care. She had a new sense of herself, and she was exploring that. She had little time and less interest in stepping back into her good-little-girl role. In some ways she'd entered a whole new world, and she wasn't sure how she was going to do there. But it was going to be interesting finding out.

Jack caught her look in his direction during the after-dinner session, when she stared across the room at him. It was odd the way he felt he could read her mind at times. He could tell that she thought she was in love with him. It had been coming for a long time, and he'd been dreading it. Nevertheless, he wasn't so sure the feeling wasn't mutual. He'd never felt about another women the way he felt about Kari. He'd never wanted one with this intensity, never cared about one with this much passion, never worried about one the way he worried about her. Her happiness was more important to him than his own. He didn't know whether that scared him or gave him some sense of pride—he only knew it was completely different for him and he wasn't really sure what he should be doing about it.

Kari surprised him again that night with another late visit after the suitors had gone, appearing at his door with both dogs at her side.

"Meet Marcus and Octavio," she told him blandly as he opened the door and registered shock at seeing her with the two of them, one nuzzling her hand, the other leaning his head against her hip and gazing up at her with pure doggy love. "They're great pals of mine—have been ever since they came here as puppies."

He wasn't unwilling to show his chagrin with a baleful smile. "I didn't know."

"Well, you know now." She returned his smile, her eyes shining. "But so what? I'm not the one they are supposed to be guarding this place against."

"No, but the fact that you have them licking your ankles and whining for smooches is not encouraging to me." He glared at them. "Come on, guys. Show some spirit. You're supposed to be warriors."

She laughed. "Oh, you leave alone. They're just fine. They'll wait outside while I come in and talk to you."

His look turned playfully sardonic. "No, they won't have to—because you're not coming in."

"Oh, yes, I am." She placed a hand in the middle of his chest and gave him a shove. He didn't move much, but she got in, anyway, because his standing in her way was only for show, not for real. "Excuse me," she said, stepping around him. And he let her, turning to keep an eye on her as she entered his apartment.

"How did you get past Greg this time?" he asked, looking her over in approval. She was back in black, but she'd left her hair in the new style, and he liked it.

She gave him a direct look. "I walked right up to him and told him where I was going," she said. "And he said, 'Watch out for the dogs.' And I gave a whistle and they came right away." She grinned at him. "You know what? I think I'm going to like this behaving like a grown-up thing. That little princess act of mine had just about played itself out."

"I don't know," he said a little sadly. "I thought it was pretty cute myself."

She smiled up at him and he winced, knowing he was going to have to pull back from this interchange if he didn't want it to start down a road he knew led to a blind cliff.

"Grown-up or not, you don't belong here," he reminded her.

She nodded with regret. "I know. But I had to come. I just wanted to thank you for bringing Donna to me. I think we are going to be friends. And—" her voice went lower and her gaze grew misty "—I want to thank you for caring about me."

Her words conjured up an array of emotions in him, some conflicting, all of them new and unexplored in his life. Shoot, he might as well admit it. She scared the hell out of him.

But he couldn't deny that she was right. He cared about her. "How could I not?" he said softly.

They stood so close that her perfume was making him dizzy, and yet he didn't dare touch her.

"Oh, Jack," she said with exquisite longing. "If only…"

"Yes," he said quietly, holding the passion in check. "If only."

The moment quivered between them and tears filled her eyes.

Jack cursed softly, turning away. "Go to bed, Princess," he said with a voice that sounded like ground glass. "Get some sleep."

She nodded, blinking back the moisture. "See you in the morning," she said softly, and in a moment she was gone.

Jack closed his eyes, let his head fall back and slumped against the wall. It was going to be another long, long night.

Count Boris arrived a few days later, amid much hubbub. It was plain that the duchess doted on her little brother, and he seemed to enjoy being made a fuss of. Despite all that, Kari's first impression of Boris was good. He was tall and blond and handsome—the very picture of a Nabotavian noble. He met her willingly, kissed her on both cheeks, then stood back to admire her. He was friendly, attentive and made her smile. All in all, he wasn't so bad.

"What do *you* think of Count Boris?" she asked Jack later that evening when she ran into him as she was coming in from her daily swim. The afternoon was lovely and sultry and water clung to her eyelashes in sparkling beads.

He looked at her steadily for a moment, then shrugged. "I'd say he's definitely a major part of the plan," he said at last.

She blinked at him, caught off guard by his cynical tone. "What do you mean?"

"It's pretty obvious your aunt had this rigged from the start."

"You mean, for me to marry Boris? Oh, no. I don't think so." Kari frowned, thinking it over. "Why would she set up the parties with all these other men?"

"Window dressing."

She shook her head. "You're just being suspicious, as usual," she noted. "It seems to be a well-ingrained character flaw."

He shrugged again. "Maybe so. How old is this guy, anyway?"

"Oh, thirty-five or so. Not all that old." Her impish grin surfaced. "Why? Did you think they were going to hand me off to some old decrepit graybeard?"

His eyes narrowed. "The thought had crossed my mind."

She laughed, holding her robe together with one hand. "I would run away first," she said impulsively.

"Oh, yeah?" he responded, wishing she would loosen her grip on the robe. He would have loved to see her in that suit again. "Where would you run to?"

She sighed. "That's just it. I don't know anything about the world. You would have to help me."

The trouble was, such ideas were beginning to sound appealing to him. He'd seen the count and he'd seen the duchess looking at Kari and every instinct he possessed told him this was a setup. The guy seemed okay, but Jack didn't like the way he was being foisted on her. Hell, if push came to shove, he wouldn't mind giving her a hand at evading these people for a while.

Then he had to laugh at himself. Talk about euphemisms. He knew it was time to stop thinking along these lines, when he started referring to kidnapping as an evasive action. Kari's future was her own to shepherd. It was none of his business what she decided to do. But he knew that all the cards were in the hands of the people who wanted her to marry Boris. She'd been indoctrinated in this path from the time she was born. Who was *he* to get in the way of the grand scheme? Besides, doing anything crazy would guarantee his main objective—to get his job on the force back—would fail. And then where would he be?

Still, Kari's happiness was a factor. He couldn't deny that. He just couldn't figure out how to deal with it. But the thought of Boris walking off with her rankled deep inside him. On a certain level he would feel that way even if she suddenly decided she was madly in love with the count. He wouldn't like it.

Where had this dog-in-the-manger attitude come from? It wasn't like him. He wasn't usually the jealous type. If he were honest, he would admit that he hadn't often cared about anyone enough to give much of a damn about whether or not they stayed true to him. Why should this be any different? She wasn't his, she could never be his, and yet, something in his gut told him that she *was* his. And that just wasn't right. Somehow his job was getting confused with his personal emotions, and no good could come of it.

It was probably time he got out of here—quit this job and moved on. He wished the hearing would come sooner so he could get his life sorted out. In the meantime, he had to drill it into his own head that Kari was going to marry someone at the end of the summer, and it wouldn't be him.

The next few weeks were a constant round of dinners, afternoon teas and chamber music evenings for

Kari—any excuse to gather a group of Nabotavian men together and run them past the princess, for her consideration. It was fun at first, but as time went by and they kept coming, it became tiring, and the men tended to blur together in her memory. Only Count Boris stood out, and he was nice, but he didn't excite her the way a certain other male icon did.

She was learning a lot about cooking, which was good. And she was making headway on her biography of her mother, devoting at least two hours a day to research, filling out little cards that she kept in a metal box, inputting details into a data base on her computer. It was a big job that would take her years. But all in all, she felt her summer was a productive one on many levels.

Still, her only real joy was getting away now and then for afternoon drives with Jack. She'd found the perfect ploy to arrange this, as she had to go to research libraries in outlying cities in order to find material for the biography. She would have Cook fix her a large box lunch the night before, and then she would take off early, before the duchess was up to stop her with invented errands to run or visitors to entertain. And she managed to convince Jack that he was the one who ought to go with her. And once he'd gone a time or two, she didn't have to argue any longer. He seemed to look forward to their trips as much as she did.

They seldom talked much as Mr. Barbera drove them along the freeways, then into the countryside, heading for libraries that always seemed to be in distant towns. Kari would then often have the chauffeur drop them at their destination. She would tell him to go see a movie or find a shady place to park and return to pick her up in three hours. That gave her time for an hour's worth of research—and two hours to stroll around the grounds or the town or the local park, with Jack.

And to talk. In the beginning they talked about what they were seeing and movies and books they'd read. But it wasn't long before they were beyond that. Kari had never had anyone to talk to about her hopes and fears and feelings. Mostly she talked and Jack listened. But he seemed to hear her. He even had a response now and then. And that was so new.

One golden sunny day they drove all the way to Santa Inez and spent an hour wandering the mission grounds. This time they left Mr. Barbera to doze in the courtyard by a Spanish fountain while the two of them took their lunch out under the huge old oak trees. They spent another hour talking softly, laughing a lot, and pretending there was nothing outside of the little world they made for each other.

Jack enjoyed these trips, but they were often more agony than ecstasy for him. Their relationship seemed stuck in a place it normally would not be. The way they responded to each other begged for another step to be taken. As it was, he was working very hard at not kissing her. He held her soft, slender hand now and then, and he often played with her fingers while they talked. That was dangerous enough, but to kiss...to have his mouth on hers, tasting her, taking in her essence, exploring her warmth...no, he couldn't do that without being tempted to go so much further.

So they talked about everything under the sun—life and art and music and why women talked all the time and why men didn't and whether liking rainy days made one a gloomy person at heart. He was surprised that he felt closer to her with just talking than he'd ever felt with women he'd had more physical relationships with. But then, in his experience, sex was often mere recreation. Getting to know Kari was something infinitely deeper.

Not that he wouldn't have liked a little lovemaking mixed in. Not that his body didn't remind him of that fact all the time. Still, something wise and cunning in his soul told him that making love with Kari right now would mess up his life—and hers—worse than anything else ever had. And that was the advice he was listening to.

Today he was lying back on the grass and she was sitting cross-legged beside him, her fingers playing idly in his hair. He'd just told her about the time he'd come home from junior high and found the foster family he was living with had moved away without telling him they were going. He'd lived on the street for weeks after that, until Children's Services finally found him again and put him in a new home. Funny, but he hadn't thought about that for years, and had certainly never told anyone before. Her interest seemed to dredge up memories without him even trying.

But eventually, as it always did, conversation came back to the marriage decision.

"So have you and your aunt decided yet?" he asked, looking up so that he could judge her reaction. "Is it going to be Boris?"

She sat back and sighed, looking cross. "I don't know. I know everyone wants us to pick Boris. But I don't think I could ever love him."

"No?"

"No."

A quiet feeling of satisfaction flowed in his veins, but it didn't last long. Left unspoken between them was who she could love, but they both knew who it was. Her eyes said it all. He looked away as satisfaction gave way to a wave of melancholy. This magic summer was almost over. In just a few weeks he'd developed feelings for this woman he'd never had for any other, and probably never would have. She was so special to him—special in his mind, special in his heart. And yet, very soon it would be over.

The hearing was tentatively scheduled for the day before the ball. On that day his future would be sealed, and by the next, so would hers be. Over those two days he would find out whether or not he was still on the force, she would find out whom she would marry. Some man—some man other than he himself—would claim her for his own, would take her into his bed, into his life. And Jack would be left behind.

The melancholy turned into a surge of nausea, and he had to get up and walk away for a moment, settling his system down. He could hardly stand the thought of losing her like that. And yet he didn't really have her. You couldn't lose what was never yours in the first place, could you? She wasn't his. She could never be his. She belonged to Nabotavia. They had both known that from the start.

She would probably be marrying good old Boris and sailing for her homeland and a glorious homecoming. Meanwhile, if he was lucky and was reinstated in his old job, he would be back in his lonely apartment on Wilshire. There would be poker with his friends on Friday nights and a date with some interchangeable beauty on Saturday, but most of his time would be spent with his nose to the grindstone, just as it had before he'd met Kari.

And that was the good outcome. What if he didn't get reinstated? There had been a time when he'd thought his life might be over if that happened. There might be nothing worth living for. But now he knew that was nonsense. He'd found something infinitely more important than making it back on the force. In just a few weeks of knowing Kari, his life and his outlook had changed immeasurably.

How could that be? It didn't seem possible. Knowing Kari had opened up a window onto a world he'd never even known existed. Was that window just going to close again? Or would he go on and do something different, be something different, because of having known her? He didn't know. But he didn't want to think about going on without her.

Returning to where she sat, he dropped down to sit beside her. The sun was sparkling in her eyes, making them look as though they were shooting sparks all around her pretty face. He loved the look of her, the clean scent, the way she moved her hands when she talked. There were times when she looked so good to him, pain shot through his body. That wasn't normal, was it? He'd never felt that way with a woman before. But then, he'd never known a woman like Kari before.

"So you're not ready to commit to Boris just yet?" he asked, unable to stay away from the topic that hurt the most.

She shook her head. "He doesn't love me, you know."

"How do you know that?"

"I can tell. The way he looks at me." She gave him a lopsided smile, looking at him sideways. "Like I'm a car he's thinking about buying. And the only reason he's thinking about buying it is because he might look good riding around behind the wheel."

He laughed, but that only seemed to encourage her, and she went on with her analogy.

"Oh, he's thinking about making the purchase, but

he's got to look over the numbers first, got to see if it will really be a good deal." She giggled, enjoying her own joke. "He'll probably consider haggling over the price. Ask for more accessories. Kick the tires."

"Hey." Reaching out, he curled an arm around her shoulders. "No kicking of the tires. Not on my girl."

My girl. He heard himself say it and noticed her tiny shiver of pleasure. She smiled up at him, but then he sobered, realizing that the underlying problem was no joking matter.

Summer was fast wrapping up, and with the end would come so many changes. Jack broke one of his own rules and kept her there in the shelter of his arms until it was time to get up and find Mr. Barbera and head for home again. He just couldn't let her go, she felt so warm and soft. There was comfort in that. Comfort, and a whole new level of sensual gratification.

A little more than a week before the ball, two of Kari's brothers arrived. The excitement over their arrival made the interest in Count Boris's visit pale by comparison. Maids scrubbed everything shiny, Cook baked special treats, Mr. Barbera waxed and polished all the cars, and Kari paced the halls, waiting for the signal that they were coming up the driveway.

And then they were in the foyer, two strong, handsome men, impeccably dressed, bearing all the dignity and swagger that royalty deserved to display, yet with the hint of a sense of humor showing and a warmth that belied their troubled background. Marco was the more wiry of the two, handsome in a rugged way, his face rather gaunt, as though he'd had troubles to bear—which he certainly had. Garth was gorgeous in a devil-may-care, confident way that drew women to him like moths to a flame. Kari ran into their arms, both at the same time. Oh, how she loved her brothers!

They were both older than she and had been raised in a different part of the country, but there was a bond between them that overcame all that, and whenever they were together, their shared sense of family shone through. And that happened again now. They spent an hour chatting formally with the duke and duchess in the parlor. The duchess then took the brothers on a tour of the estate, pointing out any changes since their last visit, while Kari went down to the kitchen to check on the progress toward the dinner and to relay requests for some favorite foods. A little later the three siblings burst out of the house like children on school break and huddled in the garden where they could talk and laugh and tease each other without being admonished by their aunt.

Finally Garth went off to check on the dogs, and Marco looked at Kari, getting serious. "What's this I hear about this fellow, Jack Santini?"

Some of the joy ran out of her day. She stopped to sniff a red rose. "I don't know. It would probably depend on who you heard it from."

"The duchess was my source," he said, crossing his arms over his chest and looking at her from the heights of his imperial prestige. "She made it quite clear that she thinks he's a bad influence on you."

"A bad influence!" Kari laughed, but she was only covering up for the tremor in her fingers. Marco was her oldest brother, a sort of father figure and symbol of authority to her. She couldn't help but care what he thought of her. "Oh, you know our aunt," she said dismissively. "She tends toward extreme judgments at times. She takes things too seriously."

"Indeed she does. But she's not crazy. And if she thinks there's a problem, I'm going to have to look into it."

"Oh, Marco." She turned and looked at him in some distress.

His dark eyes took on a worried look. "What is it? Do you have some sort of relationship with this man?"

Her chin lifted. "Yes, I do. It's called a friendship." She sighed and patted his arm. "Don't worry, dearest brother. I know my duty."

Crown Prince Marco was the one who had done the most to instill in her a sense of what she owed her culture, from the time she was a little girl. And he led by example. His beloved wife had died two years before, leaving him with two darling children, and he had agreed to marry a princess of a competing faction of Nabotavian power in order to facilitate the return. Kari knew it was hard for him to even think of marrying again, but he would do what was best for them all. She'd always admired him so very much. She would never do anything to disappoint him.

"I'm calling a meeting on the afternoon before the ball," he said. "We'll get together and we'll discuss the major candidates for your hand. It's time we made a choice." He touched her cheek. "And you are prepared to abide by our decision?"

"Of course." She held her head high, but she couldn't meet his gaze and her cheeks colored. "This is what I was born and raised for. I will do what is expected of me. I'm ready to play my part in reestablishing our country. It's my destiny."

"Good. I'm so glad you've left that teenage rebellion stage behind."

Her eyes flashed. "Marco, I haven't been a teenager for a very long time. I'm a woman."

"Yes, I can see that. And a very beautiful one at that." He took her hands in his and smiled at her. "Princess Karina, our parents would be very proud of you."

"I'm glad to hear you say that." Her eyes suddenly shimmered with tears. "I miss them so much."

He pulled her into his arms, pressing her face to his chest and murmuring comfort to his little sister. "Kari, Kari, what a life you've had to lead. I'm sorry I haven't been here to help you through much of it. But it will all be worthwhile once we ride back into Nabotavia in triumph."

"If you say so," she said against his chest. "You know I trust you implicitly."

And she did.

Her brother Garth was a completely different matter. Garth had little of Marco's quiet reserve. Daring and impulsive, he had gained a reputation for his roving eye and cavalier wit. He was ready to return to Nabotavia as well, but Kari thought she detected a somewhat more reluctant state of mind. He didn't say anything specifically to her but she caught his look of irony at times, especially when Marco was waxing poetic about how wonderful it was going to be to go back.

And Garth quickly perceived, before they had been on the estate for twenty-four hours, how things stood between her and Jack. Despite that, Garth and Jack got along famously right from the start. While Marco treated Jack with suspicion and wariness, Garth took him on as a buddy he could hang out with, so much so that Kari had to admonish him to let Jack alone so that he could get some work done.

Garth was complimentary about the job Jack was doing.

"I must say I'm impressed with the security measures you've taken. The old estate is tight as a drum. It's like a different place." He'd gazed at Jack speculatively. "We could use this sort of creative thinking in Nabotavia. We'll be starting from scratch with the security forces. I've been researching the most modern techniques. If you have the time, I'd like to go over some of my ideas with you. See what you think."

Kari watched this exchange, proud of them both— her brother for the way he was open to new ideas and searching for answers wherever he might find them— and Jack for being so good at what he did that he inspired interest from her family members.

At a later encounter she heard Garth saying Jack ought to consider coming to Nabotavia to work. She was short of breath for a moment, then her excitement dimmed, realizing that might not be such a good idea after all. Later she asked Jack about it.

"Have you given any thought to what Garth said the other day? About coming with us to Nabotavia and taking charge of the security at the castle?"

He turned slowly to meet her gaze. His eyes were dark but every emotion was revealed in their murky depths. "No," he said shortly.

He didn't have to elaborate. She knew exactly what he meant. Being there, in sight but not being able to touch or to talk, would be a nightmare. She agreed with him. The answer had to be no.

Having her brothers around made the return to Nabotavia seem so much more real to her. All her life she'd heard about the beautiful little country with its snow-capped mountains and thick green meadows laced with clear running streams. Her uncle had once told her that the capital, Kalavia, had been as quaint and charming as a storybook town before the revolt. Would it still be as wonderful a place as she had always heard?

She hoped so. But never mind. If it wasn't, she and her brothers would soon make it so again. It was what they had been born to do.

Chapter 9

The day of the ball was getting closer and closer. It was only a few days away when Kari began to wonder if she were losing her mind. She woke up one morning with a brand-new thought, and once she'd had it, she couldn't understand why she'd never thought of it before.

"Why do I have to get married, anyway?"

It was true. This was a new age. Women didn't do the things they'd done a hundred years ago. Just because she was going back to a country that was behind the times didn't mean she had to be back there with them. Did it? Had the rest of her family even considered this? What if she brought it up and made them see...

But no. She knew that wouldn't fly. Still, it gave her something to think about.

By that evening she'd admitted to herself that it wasn't that she didn't want to marry at all—that was just a smoke screen—it was that the only man she ever wanted to marry was Jack. It was a relief to admit it. She wanted to marry Jack and hold him in her arms and have his children and live with him forever.

But it seemed so impossible. His life was so different from hers. Did she think she could just move into a little house with a picket fence and walk her children to kindergarten and all those normal things that people did? No, of course not. She could never live such a sweet and simple life. She would always need protection, because there would always be people trying to grab her for political influence, even if she claimed to have no part of Nabotavia any longer. She would always need more security than that sort of life could afford.

On the other hand, could she take him with her to Nabotavia? No. That wouldn't work, either. The princess marries the security guard—the system just wouldn't allow for it. The gap between their stations would be insurmountable in Nabotavia and there was no use pretending otherwise.

So she was back to her original premise of the day— not to marry at all. What would her family say if she presented them with that option? She rolled her eyes. She could hear the screaming and see the renting of garments now. No, it wouldn't go over. Still, she had to think of something. She only had another day or two to find a solution. Time was flying.

Kari was just getting out of the pool the next afternoon when Jack came right out onto the pool deck, something he'd never done before. She was surprised and, for just a moment, a little shy, because she was still in her suit and hadn't reached her wrap yet. But as his gaze devoured every inch of flesh she was showing, her own pride grew. The look in his eyes told her he liked what he saw. He waited while she pulled her robe around her, then held out a piece of mail he had received.

"I just got confirmation. The hearing is tomorrow. I'll be gone most of the day."

"Tomorrow," she said, pulling her robe tightly around her and tying it with a sash. "But that's the day before the ball."

He nodded, enjoying the way she looked with her hair wet and slicked back, her skin browning lightly in the sunshine. "I can't help the timing."

She nodded. She knew that. "So you'll know by to-morrow evening if you've been cleared or not?"

"Yes."

Shading her eyes against the sun, she stared at him for a long moment, then smiled. "Well, that will be a relief." With a hand on his arm, she led him into the arbor where they had met that first night. She didn't think they could be seen from the house once under the vines and she needed to look at him and maybe even talk to him more intimately than the glaring stage of the pool deck allowed for. "Jack, tell me what you think your chances are," she said as they both sank down to sit on the bench.

He gazed at her levelly, his gray eyes honest. "I've got to think they're good. I'm innocent." Reaching out, he took her hand in his. "And you know what's going to happen. If I'm exonerated, I'll be going back on the force right after the ball is over."

Her heart froze in her chest. "Oh, Jack."

"You won't need me anymore after the ball, anyway," he said, his hand tightening on hers. "You'll be all set with your new fiancé to take care of you."

"Jack." She let him see her pain and he responded with remorse.

"I'm sorry," he said, dropping her hand and looking away. "That was uncalled for."

She scooted closer to him on the bench and slipped her hand into the crook of his arm. "You've never told me what your suspension is all about," she said quietly.

He nodded, covering her hand with his own. "I know. And you deserve to be filled in." He hesitated, wincing a bit. "It's just that I'm not exactly proud of my behavior. I didn't do anything illegal, but I was stupid."

She waited, not saying anything. He looked down at her, took a deep breath and went on.

"It was a simple matter of being too cowardly to confront my partner about illegal activities she was obviously engaged in. I think my natural affection for her—and we were very good friends—blinded me to what she was doing. I was in a sort of denial. I just couldn't believe… Anyway, by the time I finally fully realized it, I had held off doing anything about it for too long."

"What was she doing?"

"Stealing drugs. We'd make drug busts and all the confiscated material wouldn't end up in the evidence room where it belonged."

"She was selling it?"

"It was a little more complicated than that. She had a brother who was addicted. I think she was giving it to him to sell to support his habit." He stretched his legs out in front of him. "Anyway, by the time I'd decided I was going to have to turn her in, she'd already been spotted by internal affairs and they assumed I might be in on the thefts. There was no evidence against me, only the circumstantial elements." He shrugged. "They did what they had to do, but I'm hoping the truth will set me free in the end."

"Oh, I hope so, too!"

He smiled down at her, slightly awed by her blind faith in him. Why wasn't she suspicious? He could have made the whole thing—and especially his innocence—up. But she believed in him. "For a princess you've got a very cute nose. Did you know that?"

"Thank you." Her eyes shone with laughter. "For a cop you've got a very appealing mouth."

He groaned, half laughing. "So we're back on the kissing thing, are we?"

She nodded. "I feel sadly lacking in the proper instruction," she noted wistfully. "All I've had is one lesson. Hardly enough to become as adept as I'd like to be."

His large hand cupped her cheek as he smiled down at her. "Tell me this. Have you needed to put your lesson to use at all? Have any of the many applicants for your hand…?"

She laughed aloud. "I've had a few clumsy attempts made," she told him. "Remember the big industrialist with the walrus mustache? He kept whispering erotic suggestions in my ear during dinner and then he tried to kiss me as we walked out into the rose garden that night."

Jack held back the impulse to find the man and tear out his heart on the spot. Very carefully he kept his anger under wraps and maintained a calm exterior.

"But all I felt was this bushy hair all over my face and I made a rude noise as I pushed him away. That seemed to offend him." She shrugged. "Other than that, there was just the younger brother of the new minister of health and services. He caught me unawares and locked lips with me, but it felt so silly, I was laughing the whole time, and his feelings were hurt, too." She sighed. "I seem to be a failure at kissing. Maybe I need more lessons."

He grinned, pulling her close. "Maybe you do."

She lifted her face to his, and this time he didn't avoid the inevitable. He nibbled on her full lips for a moment, then used the tip of his tongue to go between them. She sighed softly, then gasped as he took possession of her mouth, opening to him and responding like a woman who badly needed to be loved.

"What the hell are we doing?" he muttered roughly as he pulled away, breathing hard after only a few seconds of the best kissing he'd ever had. "We're out in the open in broad daylight! Any gardener might have seen us, any delivery boy…"

She sighed, dropping her head against his shoulder. "That was even better than I thought it would be," she told him candidly. "The next time you kiss me—"

"There will be no next time." He frowned just to make sure she understood he meant it.

But she smiled. "Oh, yes there will be. Next time, *I* get to say when we stop. Okay?" Dropping a quick kiss on his neck, she rose to her feet and turned toward the house. "Bye, Jack," she said, giving him a quick wave. And she headed for her room with a song in her heart.

Her cell phone rang late in the afternoon of the next day. She answered it quickly.

"I'm clear," Jack told her. "I'm back on the force as of Monday morning."

"Oh, Jack, that's wonderful." Despite the fact that this meant he would be leaving, she was filled with joy for him.

"I'll see you when I get back," he said. "I'm going out to celebrate with a few friends I haven't seen for a while."

"Of course. I'll talk to you when you return."

She rang off, filled with conflicting emotions. Luckily there was a lot to do in preparation for the ball, so she was too busy to think about it too much. But by the time night fell, she was on the lookout for him.

She watched for him by the hour, but he didn't appear. If she walked to the end of the upper hallway, she could see his apartment from the window. She checked every hour, then every half hour, and finally every ten minutes or so, but it was after midnight before she finally saw a light come on in his rooms. She slipped out of the house and made her way quickly to his door.

"Jack?"

He opened the door and she flew into his arms.

"I'm so happy for you," she said, holding him close. "You're getting back everything you've wanted so badly."

His arms wrapped around her and his face was in her hair. "Not quite."

He said it softly, but she heard and she closed her eyes, loving him. She could stay there with him forever, holding on to his hard, warm body. If she just kept her eyes closed, maybe the rest of the world would fade away and...

She turned her face up and his mouth was on hers before she had time to will it to happen. And then she found out what a kiss could really be—all hot and wet and sliding, all hunger and need and excitement, a fuse that lit off a fire in her body, a sense of animal delight that she hadn't known about.

She wrapped her arms around his neck, arching

toward him. Suddenly she needed him to touch her breasts and she made that very plain. His hand slid inside her jersey top, slipping ever closer and she held her breath. When his fingers found their way inside her bra and curled around one swollen nipple, she gasped and an electric urgency crackled through her system, awakening parts she'd never known could feel like that. She moved her hips, yearning for him, wanting to feel her legs around him. Shuddering, she knew what her body needed with a knowledge as old as time itself.

"Maybe we should make love," she whispered breath-lessly, rubbing her cheek against his, reveling in the roughness of his evening stubble.

He jerked back and stared at her. "What?" he de-manded, as though he was sure he hadn't heard her right.

She searched his eyes, almost writhing with the way she wanted him. "Don't you want to?"

His head fell back and he groaned, still holding her by the shoulders as though he was afraid to let her go, afraid what she might do next.

"Of course I want to," he said gruffly. "But we can't."

She took air deep into her lungs, savoring her desire, not wanting to let it go. "I've never felt like this before. I don't know much about this sort of thing, but some-thing deep inside tells me I want to feel you sort of...I don't know...take possession of me."

He shook his head, half laughing, half despairing. "Don't talk like that, Kari. You don't know what you're saying."

"Don't I?" she said wisely, smiling at him.

He hesitated, searching for a way to make her realize she was asking him for something he would be a jerk to give her. "And don't forget," he reminded her dryly. "You've got to be pure for your noble husband."

She shook her head, her hair swishing around her pretty face. "I don't care about that. Of course I probably have to marry someone. But I don't think he will really care much, either." This was no time to give him a lesson in royal affairs, but in fact she knew a lot of things she wasn't supposed to know. And she had no illusions. Anyone who married her from the marriage mart her aunt had set up would not be marrying her for love. "I'll give him everything that will be important for him to have, but I won't be able to give him my heart. That's already taken."

Jack looked down into her beautiful smile and didn't know what to say to her. How could she be so open, so full of love for him? Didn't she know how little he deserved it? Lacing fingers with hers, he led her to the couch and sat down with her, curling her into the protection of his arm and leaning down to kiss her beautiful little ear.

"My future life is back on track," he said. "I know what I'm going to be doing. Now how about yours?"

She sighed. "You're wondering who I will end up with."

"Exactly."

"I don't know." She glanced up at him and shook her head. "The duchess has her favorite, but I'm not sure…"

"Boris," he said evenly, trying to maintain his natural logic and plain thinking. "They all want Boris. I suppose you'll do what's expected of you."

"Will I?" She shrugged. "What do you think I should do?"

"It's your life and your decision."

She nodded, considering, head to the side. "What if I chucked it all and ran away with you?"

His fingers tightened on hers. "You're not going to do that. You are a princess. You're going to do your duty. And I'm a cop, and I'm going back on the force. You're going back to Nabotavia. We've each got larger interests to serve. You told me yourself that is the best way."

She frowned, almost pouting. "I lied."

"No, you didn't. You told the exact truth. Much as it hurts now, there will come a time when we'll be glad we did the right thing."

She wasn't sure she believed that anymore. She'd believed it once. And it would be one thing if there was someone who would be hurt by their being together. But she didn't see that. People would be inconvenienced, maybe. Angered, surely. But no one would be really hurt if she didn't show up in Nabotavia with a consort by her side.

She knew she was being selfish. After all, look at what her brothers had been through. She'd had life so easy compared to them. Marco had the tragedy of losing his young wife, which would hang over him—and his two little children—for the rest of his life. And there was Garth who gave every sign that there was some sort of inner demon that drove him, something related to the flight from Nabotavia. And then there was Damian, who always held himself a bit apart from the others. He had some secret pain he wouldn't reveal to anyone. By contrast, she'd had a sunny life, punctuated occasionally by fights with her aunt, but nothing serious. Now all that was expected of her was to marry and go to Nabotavia to live a life of luxury as a princess. Wasn't this what every little girl dreamed of?

Yes, every little girl dreamed of it—but not every woman.

"If there was a way, would you want me?" She asked in all humility, her eyes huge.

He looked into those eyes and cringed. He knew he could string her along if he wanted to. He could keep her hanging on for weeks, months, even years. They could have clandestine meetings, sneak phone calls. And maybe even a real tryst or two. But it wouldn't be fair to her. It might actually ruin her life to let her get caught up in something like that. It would be far kinder to break with her now. And bottom line, he would do what was best for her. Because she was all that mattered.

"There's no doubt I want you," he said softly. "I can't hide it. Every part of me aches for you." He took a deep breath. Now here came the hard part. "But it's not really a big deal. I've felt that way before," he lied, "and I'll feel that way again. There are other women." He was really lying now, and she might be able to hear it in his voice, but he had to go on with it. "It's just the old man-woman thing," he said gruffly. "I'll get over it. And so will you."

She'd turned her face to him, and her eyes were filled with shocked pain, but she didn't flinch from the hard things he was saying. "It's not like that with me," she said calmly. "I know I'm in love with you. I'll never love anyone else the way I love you."

"That's just not true," he told her seriously, almost angrily. "Don't say it."

"It's true for me right now and that is all I know." Reaching out, she took his hands in hers. "Okay, here goes. I'm making a formal proposal. Jack Santini, will you marry me?"

Hadn't she heard a word he'd said? Yes, she'd probably heard all too well. He didn't seem to be as adept at lying as he thought he was. She'd heard, but she hadn't believed him. Still, he had to make her see...

"You know that's impossible."

She squeezed his hands very tightly and searched the depths of his eyes. "I want you to tell me some way it would be possible." She shook her head slowly. "You're the magic man. You have all the answers. You tell me. What can I do? Is there something? Is there someplace we could go...?"

He turned his gaze away. He couldn't stand to see her so sincerely handing him her heart. Not when he just had to hand it right back.

"No matter what you decide, I think you have to go back to Nabotavia," he told her quite seriously. "You've been living for that your whole life. Your whole family has. You can't just blow it off now at the last moment. You have to go back."

She closed her eyes and nodded. She knew he was right. "You could come, too," she tried.

But he was already shaking his head. "You know that's impossible."

"Why?"

"Kari, we've gone over this before. I can't be your groupie. I've got to have self-respect. I've got that on the force. I wouldn't have it in Nabotavia."

"So you're turning me down?"

He gathered all his nerve and looked her in the eye. "Yes, Kari. I'm turning you down."

She didn't say anything. Her face gave no hint of her emotional state. He could only guess. "When will you be leaving?" he asked her.

"Not until the end of the year." She bit her lower lip, then asked, "Will you come visit me before I go?"

His gaze met hers and he slowly shook his head. "Once you've made your choice, I don't think we'd better see each other again."

She nodded, rising suddenly, before he had a chance to realize her intention. "You're so sensible, Jack," she said as she started for the door. "Much more sensible than I am."

He rose and followed her. "Kari, are you all right?" he asked, touching her cheek.

She gave him a wobbly smile as she started out the door. "Oh, yes, I'm fine. But I do have to go." She smiled at him, her eyes already swimming in tears, despite her false bravado. "Goodbye, Jack," she said before she disappeared into the night.

The meeting was held in the library the next afternoon. All her family was there. Marco took charge, and he made the first speech, promoting Count Boris as the only logical choice.

"He's of a proper age," Marco noted. "He couldn't be from a better family. And he already has incentive to join with us. We won't have to worry about him trying to promote another faction. He's told me he has great affection for Kari and would be willing to do it."

Willing to do it! Kari bit her lip to keep from saying the words that came to mind.

"Of course I agree with you," the duchess said, beaming. "I think they will make a lovely couple."

"Whatever will make Kari happy," the duke said, though he looked rather resigned and not particularly enthusiastic.

"Why don't we see what Kari has to say about it?" Garth asked as his turn came.

"Thank you, Garth," she said slowly, looking from one face to another. "I just want to say that Boris is a very nice man and I like him very much." She nodded toward the duchess. "And I appreciate all of you being so concerned about my welfare. Really, I do. I love you all." She took a deep breath and forced herself to continue. "But I won't be marrying Boris," she said. "That won't be possible. You see, I'm in love with Jack Santini. And there is no way to change that."

All the faces staring at her exhibited shock of one form or another, but the duchess was the first to give it voice.

"I knew it! That gold digger. He's after her money, you can bet on it. I'll have him fired immediately. I'll…"

Marco put a hand on her arm, quieting her. "Tell me, Kari," he said in a voice too quiet, "what happened to your pledge to do your duty?"

His words were a dagger at her heart, but she didn't flinch. "I believe in duty, Marco. Duty should come before anything else, even personal happiness. I really believe that. But…I can't. I just can't take that next step." She took a deep breath and had to fight back tears. "I know I made you so many promises, Marco. And I was so sure I would keep them. But when the time came, things had changed. I'm so sorry."

The disappointment in his eyes cut like a knife, and she had to struggle to keep her breathing normal. The last thing in the world she wanted to do was make Marco feel that she wasn't keeping her end of their life-long bargain. But she didn't have a lot of choice. She loved Jack. She couldn't pretend otherwise.

"You little fool, you'll never marry him!" the duchess cried.

Kari tried to smile. "You're right," she said tightly. "I've asked him. He's turned me down."

This time the shocked silence only lasted a few seconds, and then everybody was talking at once.

Kari rose and looked at them all. "So the bottom line is, I won't be getting married. I realize it would be impossible to cancel the ball at this point, so I suggest we don't tell anyone about this just yet. We can send regrets later in the week, if you like. Otherwise, let's just enjoy the party."

Turning, she left the room, head held high, and as she went, she realized this was the first time she'd left such a family meeting without waiting to be excused by Marco or the duchess first. That thought gave her at least one small glow of consolation.

Despite everything Kari was feeling, the ball was wonderful, setting the night on fire with shimmering lights and beautiful music and a sense of excitement in the air. Donna had performed miracles on her hair, setting it off with a diamond tiara and giving her gleaming cascades of curls that seemed to go on forever. Her dress was a spectacular blue silk, threaded with spun silver, with a plunging neckline and a cinched-in waist that showed off her figure nicely. She shimmered like an angel every time she moved.

And she moved a lot. She danced with so many men she was lost in a blur. All attention was on her, and that was exhilarating, even though she felt a twinge of guilt that it was built on the faulty premise that she would choose one of these attentive men as her mate. Still, she couldn't help but revel in being the belle of the ball.

But one thing stayed with her the whole time—she was bound and determined she would get one dance with the man she loved.

Outside the building Jack was coordinating security. The ball was being held at a local country club, so he had the assistance of an extra set of agents but the headache of trying to mesh his forces with theirs. The building was beautiful, with high windows that flooded the greenery with light and verandahs as long and wide as the deck of a ship. From outside, he could easily see in, and he couldn't avoid seeing Kari. She was having a wonderful time. He kept telling himself that should make him happy. But it really didn't. Every time he saw her in the arms of another man, it seemed like another slashing wound in his heart.

Luckily, he didn't have to watch too often. His attention was distracted by his duties, and as often as not, by the duke, who came shuffling out every now and then for a chat.

The odd thing was, he really liked the old gentleman. Over the weeks they'd become quite friendly, and he'd heard all about the problems with the Nabotavian translation of Shakespeare the duke was working on, and how much he hated wearing the cravat the duchess insisted upon and how beautiful he thought his niece was tonight.

"I'll agree with you there," he'd told him.

The duke smiled rather sadly. "I know you do. It's a shame, really…"

His voice trailed off and then he looked at Jack. "Well, I've been to all the dinners, all summer long. Met all the suitors, each jockeying for position, hoping to catch the princess's eye. And I've got to agree with my niece. Not one of them can hold a candle to you, my lad." He patted his shoulder as he turned to start back to the party. "Sorry to see you go."

Jack stared after him, not sure what to make of his declaration. But then he saw Kari coming out of one of the long doors, and it slipped from his mind. It was just before midnight, and she'd managed to sneak away.

"Hi," she said, beaming at him.

He stood looking at her, his face displaying just how beautiful he found her. "You really do look like a princess," he told her.

"A princess in need of a handsome prince," she said, raising her arms to him. "Will you be my prince for one dance?"

He hesitated. "Out here?"

"Why not? We can hear the music."

He smiled at her, placing the walkie-talkie he'd been carrying on the nearest chair and erasing the distance between them in two quick steps. "Your wish is my command," he murmured.

It was a slow song, a simple song, about love and longing called, "I Love You in Moonlight," and the music was a perfect backdrop to their embrace. Once she was in his arms, she closed her eyes and let him sweep her up in the rhythm. She felt like Cinderella about to lose her slipper, like Belle dancing with the Beast. She was a princess and that meant she should be allowed a little time in a fairy-tale world. Shaking off reality, she sank into a dream and sailed away.

He held her close and buried his face in her hair, breathing as much of her as he could manage to capture, experiencing the curves of her body beneath the fabric, the sweetness of her skin. She seemed to melt against him, merging her body with his, soul to soul, heart to heart. For just this moment she was his, and he held her with tenderness and yet fiercely, ready to take on all comers, anyone who might come to claim her for their own, and for the first time he admitted to himself that he was in love.

She hadn't told him her choice and he hadn't heard it from anyone else. But maybe that was for the best. If he knew who it was and saw him here, face-to-face, there was no telling what emotional shape he might be in at the time and what he might do. Best not to know until he was away from here and from her. Then he was going to have to get used to it.

The song ended. Slowly they drew apart. She looked up at him, her smile gone. Raising her hand, she touched his cheek, and a look of pain passed through her eyes.

"Goodbye, Jack Santini," she said softly. "I hope you have a wonderful life. I hope you find someone wonderful to marry, and that you have many lovely children. I hope that you do well in your career and that your love for the police force is rewarded." Tears shone in her eyes. "You'll always be the only man I ever really loved."

He wanted to say something back, but he couldn't. There was a large and very painful lump in his throat. So he just watched as she turned and walked away. Every part of him cried out for him to stop her, to make her come back, to tell her it was the same with him— that he would never love anyone else the way he loved her. But he knew that if he did that, he would be tying her into a lingering relationship that would cripple her chances for happiness. So he had to keep his mouth shut and let her believe that he didn't really care. And wondered why his eyes were stinging.

Chapter 10

It was almost a month later before Jack heard Kari's name again. He'd been watching the papers, looking for an announcement of one sort or another, but there had been nothing. He'd assumed the Nabotavian community was just keeping a low profile on the matter.

He kept telling himself that was for the best, that the less he heard about her, the sooner he would stop thinking about her. But it didn't seem to be working. In fact, there were days when he thought about little else.

It was good to be back at work again. His new partner was a great guy. They got along well. Everyone had welcomed him back, and he'd been recommended as qualified to take the captain's exam when next it came up. Some of the senior officers had already assured him that he was slated for bigger things once he had the exam under his belt. Things were definitely looking good.

But he had to admit his experience working for Kari's family had broadened his outlook considerably. He wasn't sure how long he was going to be satisfied with his work on the force, now that he'd tried other things and found he had a certain knack for them. He was happy now, but he could foresee a bit of restlessness in his future.

He was feeling a little gloomy on the day he got the call that pulled him back into Kari's life. He was at his desk at the station house. His partner had gone out to get something to eat. The phone rang and he picked it up.

"Santini here."

"Jack." It was Garth's voice, and something in it hit his alarm button right away. "They've got Kari. They grabbed her today."

His hand tightened on the receiver. "Who?"

"I don't know. December Radicals, I suppose. She was on her way to a speaking engagement at the Pasadena Library but they were still in Beverly Hills when it happened. They shot Greg and Mr. Barbera and snatched Kari, drove off with her."

"Oh, my God." His stomach dropped and a coil of cold despair snaked through his gut. "When?"

"Just about ten minutes ago. The police have been called, but I thought maybe you could—"

"I'll get her back. Quick, give me all the details."

The details didn't help much. He was in his car only minutes later and moving without any real place to go, but he was in contact with the deputies who were on the case, and he could at least get closer to where the crime had occurred.

"Think!" he ordered himself. The last bunch who had taken her had put her in a house in Santa Monica.

If only he knew who had her this time. It would certainly help.

His cell phone rang. Assuming it was one of the other officers he'd contacted, he flipped it open. "Santini," he barked into it.

No one spoke. He waited another beat or two, then gave an exasperated sound and began to hang up. But just before he did, something caught his attention. There was background noise, and then a voice, coming from far away. Frowning, he listened more intently. Then he realized the voice was female. And lastly, that it was Kari.

He pulled over and shut off the engine, still listening, trying to make out the words. Suddenly things were much clearer.

"I see we're going south on the San Diego Freeway," Kari was saying, her voice projecting, her words enunciating carefully. "Are we heading for the border? No, I'll bet it's that airport in Orange County, isn't it?"

"Hey! Shut her up."

The dull thud of flesh smashing into flesh set his jaw on edge, and then he heard her soft cry. The evidence that someone had hit her would have driven him crazy if he'd let it. But he kept his composure. He knew he would have to remain calm if he were going to get her back unharmed. So he turned to stone. He had to.

The voices were muffled again, unintelligible. But he had his destination now. "Airport," he muttered as he started his car again. "Smart girl."

And he would bet they weren't heading for the public terminal. They'd chartered a plane, had it warmed up and ready to go. He knew just where that plane would probably be.

Using his police band radio, he called in what he

knew, then concentrated on the race to the airplane. If it was ready to go, there might not be time...

Reaching under the seat, he pulled out the magnetic flashing light, turned it on, opened his window and jammed it onto the roof of his car, then turned on his siren and began to cut through traffic like a knife through butter. Nothing was going to keep him away from that airplane.

He checked his shoulder holster to make sure his .38 was ready for action, but he wasn't going to use it if possible. Two people had already been shot, and he didn't want to risk something happening to Kari. Still, it had to be ready, just in case guile and strength weren't enough to do the job.

The airport was in his sight. He turned on a side street he knew of and headed for the cargo area. At first everything looked so peaceful and serene, he couldn't believe there was anything going on and thought he must have the wrong place. But then he saw them.

It was a small private jet and it was ready for takeoff. A black car had driven right up to the ramp and people were getting out. He would never make it unless...

Gritting his teeth, he gunned the engine right through a barrier. Splintered wood flew in all directions, but he was focused straight ahead. Adrenaline pumping, he raced across the tarmac and screeched to a stop at the airplane, jumped out of his car and raced for the ramp.

He didn't stop to think. There was no time for that. He reached the first man and tossed him over the side of the ramp onto the tarmac where he landed with a dull thump and remained motionless. The next man was pulling Kari toward the door of the plane, but she was struggling and he took the steps two at a time and reached the man before he could stuff her in the door. A good right hook got him to let go of her. A little pounding got him to crumple to the steps in a heap. Someone else appeared in the door of the plane, but Jack didn't wait to see who it was. He'd grabbed Kari by now, swung her up into his arms and was dashing back down the stairs to his car, ignoring the incredible percussion of a gun firing behind him, ignoring the bullet he felt barely miss his ear. He heard sirens as he placed her in the passenger's seat and raced around to the driver's side. They were ready to take off as the squad cars arrived, tires squealing, lights and sirens blaring. But just before they left the area, Jack signaled to an officer he knew, just arriving.

"I've got the kidnap victim with me," he said, showing his badge. "I'm getting her out of here."

The officer said something, but Jack didn't wait to see what it was. In another two minutes they were a mile away.

"Are you okay?" he asked her gruffly, not turning to look for himself.

"I'm fine," she said breathlessly. "I can't believe how you just crashed in and took me like that."

Something in her voice flicked a switch in him and he was finally able to begin to relax, to let the adrenaline subside. "You're here, aren't you?"

"Sort of."

He let himself look at her and, just as he'd feared, his heart broke in two and he had to pull over. "Ohmigod, you look…"

"Like something the cat dragged in," she conceded. "I know. I was flailing around a lot." She grinned crookedly. "I think I gave one of them a bloody nose."

He wanted to cry but instead he grinned. "My little

wildcat," he muttered. He couldn't stop looking at her, devouring her with his eyes.

"Yours?" She raised an eyebrow as she tucked some wayward hair behind her ear. "Why, whatever do you mean, kind sir?"

"I'll show you what I mean," he growled, reaching out to pull her into his arms with no hesitation, no second thoughts. She came willingly, laughing softly as he rained kisses on her face, turning her lips to his mouth, sighing as he began to devour her.

"Wait," he said suddenly, drawing back. "You aren't married, are you?"

"No." She shook her head. "I'm not even engaged."

"Good. But why not?"

"The night of the ball, I told them I wouldn't marry anyone but you."

He laughed softly. "You're crazy."

"I know." She reached up and caressed his cheek. "Crazy about you."

He kissed her gently, mindful of the bruises he knew she must have sustained. "I can't believe they didn't take that cell phone away from you."

"I know. They took my purse, they checked my pockets, but they didn't notice the phone attached to my waistband. It took me a while before I could worm my way around to where I could make the call. Luckily I had you on a preset."

"They didn't tie your hands?"

"No. They weren't nice," she said, putting a hand to where her jaw was starting to swell. "But they seemed to think I was a ninny princess who wouldn't have any resources of her own."

"Boy were they wrong."

She grinned, then shook her head as her eyes

darkened. "I kept thinking...as I was riding in the car...I kept thinking, what if they kill me? I'd never get to see Jack again."

Groaning, he pulled her to him again and held her close, rocking her against his heart. A fierce new resolve was building in him. He wasn't going to let her go. He was going to be in her life somehow, if only to keep her safe.

The whole family was waiting as he pulled up in front of the house. There was a sense of celebration in the air as they all talked at once and all tried to hug Kari at once and then to hug Jack, as well.

"Dr. Manova is here," the duchess told her. "He's in the upstairs sitting room, waiting to check you over."

"I don't need a doctor to look at me," Kari claimed unconvincingly. "I'm fine."

They all glanced at the bruise on her jawline, then looked away again.

"It's standard procedure," Jack told her reassuringly. "We have to make sure."

"Oh!" She shivered with frustration. She didn't want to be away from him. There was no telling how long he would be staying, and her eyes couldn't get enough of looking at him. "Don't leave while I'm upstairs," she ordered him, holding on to his hand as though she would never let it go.

"I won't," he promised, nudging her toward the stairs.

"You'll stay for dinner?" she asked, lingering.

He gave her a lopsided grin. "Sure."

Finally satisfied, she ran up the stairs, while Jack turned to face the rest of the family. They wanted details, and he gave them as much as he could remember. He felt oddly at home here in this house where he'd spent so much of his summer. As he looked from the duke to Marco to Garth, and even at the duchess, he realized he felt comfortable with them, as well. They were good, decent people, regardless of the differences he might have had with them at times—and he felt nothing but warmth from every one of them now. He had a feeling that this family would go back to Nabotavia and turn it into a good and decent country. In a way he envied them such a clear-cut goal.

For the first time, he met Kari's brother Damian who was now staying at the Beverly Hills estate hoping to recover from a boating accident that had left him blind. Despite that disability, he had a look very much like the others in his family and Jack knew he was going to like him as well.

Marco asked to speak to him alone and he followed him into the study, sitting down across the desk from him.

"I have something I need to go over with you," Marco said. "We've discussed finding an appropriate way to thank you for what you've done today."

"Thank me! Hah!" Jack laughed shortly. "No need to thank me. I would have done it regardless of anything at all."

"We understand that. But it's beside the point. The fact is you've done something very important, and the nation of Nabotavia must find a way to thank you for it. We've decided that the most appropriate way would be to ask you to accept a knighthood."

"A what?" For just a moment he thought it must be a joke. But as he looked at Marco, he could see that the man was completely serious.

"I am authorized to begin rewarding service to the crown. Yours will be the first knighthood of the new regime. Should you choose to accept it," he added quickly.

"Me? A knight?" Did the fairy tales never end with these people?

"Why not?" Marco smiled. "The police are a sort of paladin group, wouldn't you say? It seems only natural."

He shook his head. "I don't understand."

"There's nothing to understand," said Garth, coming in along with Damian to join them. "Just accept it. Become a knight. You'll be Sir Jack Santini."

That made Jack laugh. "You've got to be kidding."

"We don't kid about this stuff," Garth said with a grin. "Hey, come on. You'll be a knight of the Nabotavian realm. And as such, entitled to a certain status among our people."

Realization was slowly beginning to dawn in Jack's cloudy brain.

"And as someone of that status you will be eligible to be considered for the princess's hand in marriage," Garth added, just in case Jack hadn't let the facts sink in quite yet.

He shook his head, trying to clear up his thinking. Was Garth really saying what it sounded like he was saying?

"Don't worry, Jack," Garth added, laughing. "I think you know by now that when there is royalty involved, everything is carefully planned out ahead of time. Spontaneity is not our game. We've considered this carefully and we all agree."

Jack stared at him. "And exactly what is it we all agree on?"

He shrugged. "That we all love Kari very much."

Jack nodded slowly. "Yes, I'll agree to that," he said.

Damian grinned. "Take the knighthood, Jack. The rest is up to you."

Jack looked at Marco, then slowly, deliberately he rose to stand at a sort of attention before the desk. "Crown Prince Marco," he said in a clear voice, "I'd be honored to accept."

"Good." Marco rose. "I think we'll just go ahead with it, if you don't mind. We can have a public ceremony later, but I'm due in Dallas tomorrow, and Garth is going home to Arizona."

Jack shook his head. "This is your game," he told him. "I'll play by your rules."

Marco nodded. Going to a cherry wood cabinet, he took out a long, beautiful silver sword. "We'll dispense with the long version of the ceremony, if you don't mind." His smile was playful. "We'll skip the praying all night and the ritualistic assuming of the suit of armor, piece by piece. And we won't expect you to perform any tournament tricks just yet. We'll get right to the heart of the matter, shall we?"

"Let's."

Marco gestured for him to kneel, then rested the sword on one shoulder. "In the name of the people and crown of Nabotavia I dub thee Sir Jack Santini, a knight of the realm. We trust you will protect the weak, honor women and right the wrongs you find in this world. Be brave and loyal and remember that you now represent Nabotavia in all you do." He tapped each shoulder with the sword, then nodded. "Arise, Sir Jack Santini. We welcome you."

Jack rose and looked around him. This was exactly the sort of thing he should be making fun of if he were to remain consistent. Instead he found himself flooded with an emotion he hadn't expected, and his eyes grew a little misty. He was a knight of Nabotavia. Now he would have to be a good guy for the rest of his life.

Even more scary, he was gong to ask Kari to marry him. Funny how that didn't seem as crazy as it might have just days before. All the walls he'd built up over the years were melting away. Now the crazy thing would be to imagine trying to live without her. For a few short summer months she'd brought joy and light to his life. Being away from her had taught him that those were elements he could no longer live without. He needed her like he needed air in his lungs and sunlight on his face. She was a part of him.

"Now that you're a knight," Garth said, putting an arm around his shoulders, "I'd like to talk to you about a job I'm thinking of offering you. Nabotavia is going to need someone to coordinate the various armed services and the homeland security and intelligence services. With your varied background, I thought you might be the one to help us pull all that together. How would you feel about the title minister of security?"

Jack started to laugh. Marco and Garth soon joined in, and by the time Kari came down to join them, they were out of breath and wheezing and unable to explain to her what the joke was. But they all knew, and a bond had been formed among the four of them, a bond that would take a lot to break.

Kari wasn't sure where things were going. She was only sure that this had been the most amazing day of her life. Jack was now a knight of the realm. What did it all mean? She wasn't sure, but she did know that he was being treated as an equal, not an employee, even by the duchess. That was confusing, but very, very gratifying. She thought back to the young girl she'd been at the beginning of the summer and she hardly recognized her. And now she was with the man she loved, and it seemed things might work out the way she'd always wanted. So much had changed.

Some detectives showed up to question her about the kidnapping. The men involved were all in custody and one of them was providing a lot of information. As suspected they were all members of the December Radicals. They had hoped to use her as a hostage. A number of their leaders had been captured during the liberation struggle the year before and they had been planning to use her as a bargaining chip in order to free them. The detectives took her statement and made an appointment for her to come tomorrow for further questioning. She went through it all with so much more confidence, just having Jack at her side. They contacted the hospital to check on Greg and Mr. Barbera, both of whom were being treated for minor wounds and were going to be released that same evening. That was a relief.

So there was a sense of celebration at their family dinner, and afterwards she and Jack went for a walk in the rose garden. He tucked her hand into the crook of his arm and held her close to his side.

"Remember when you asked me to marry you and I turned you down?" he said, looking down at her.

"I remember it well." The joy in her eyes dimmed.

"I was wondering…what if I were to reconsider?"

Her heart leaped, but she pursed her lips. "I don't know, Jack. That proposal was made in the exuberance of the moment. I'm not sure you can hold me to it."

He gave her a questioning look. "Are you taking it back?"

She pretended to consider. "I'll have to think about it."

He sighed. "Well, maybe it's just as well," he teased.

"After all, now that I'm a knight of the realm, there's no telling how many princesses might want to marry me."

"Jack!"

"I mean, I suppose I shouldn't just fall for the first princess I see…."

"You devil!"

He laughed and wrapped her in his arms where she snuggled in as though she would never leave. "I love you, Princess. I can't fight it any longer."

"I love you, too," she said, sighing with satisfaction. "Is it really true? Are we really going to get our own 'happily ever after'?"

"Yes. It's true." He kissed her, then looked at her lovingly. "And you're finally going to get those kissing lessons you've been asking for."

"Oh, good," she said. "Can we start right now?"

"Your wish, Most Royal Highness, is my command." And he proceeded to follow through on his promise.

* * * * *

BETROTHED TO THE PRINCE

To Jean, for all the days of laughter.

Chapter 1

"Hello. What have we here?"

Princess Katianna Mirishevsky Roseanova-Krimorova, usually known as Tianna Rose, stood looking down at the man sprawled on the cushioned gazebo bench with a reluctant sense of interest. It was pretty obvious he was sleeping off the effects of a night on the town. She couldn't imagine how the staff who administered to this royal residence could let such things go on.

"Shoddy maintenance," her mother would have said. This certainly wouldn't have been tolerated at her parents' home.

But this casual attitude seemed to be common here on the Arizona estate of the Roseanova family—the home of the exiled Royal House of the Rose. She'd arrived at the address, dismissed her cab and gone to the entry gatehouse, only to find the gate standing wide open and no one in attendance. The estate where she'd grown up was much more modest and low-key than this one, and yet such lax security was unheard of there. And besides that, she'd assumed there would be a shuttle service to take her to the main house, and now it looked like she was going to have to make the uphill climb on her own.

Sighing, she started up the long driveway, only to notice the cute little gazebo overlooking a small man-made lake. She could see someone was inside so she made the detour in hopes of finding help. But it seemed she was destined to be out of luck again. The man was out like a light.

Still, he was so good-looking, even in this state, that she lingered, looking him over for a moment. He looked quite comfortable lying on a sort of window seat setup equipped with plush cushions. His dark blond hair was tousled and a little too long, but his white shirt, though partially unbuttoned, was impeccable, his leather jacket expensive-looking and his slacks still had a beautiful crease. His features were strong and even, his skin smooth and tan. The slight stubble on his chin only enhanced the effect of very appealing masculinity. All in all, he was gorgeous. They just didn't hire them like this where she came from—more the pity.

She thought about giving him a quick shake and waking him. But no. That wouldn't be much use. She might as well get back on the path and make her way to the main house. Pulling her wine-colored suede jacket a little closer in the cool fall morning air, she gave one last glance at the muscular exposure of his impressive chest and turned to go. To her horror, his hand shot out and grabbed her wrist, trapping her.

"Hey, Little Red Riding Hood," he said in a voice

low as a scratchy old cello. "Didn't anyone tell you it isn't safe to wander around alone in these woods?"

"Let me go!" she ordered once she found his grasp was like steel.

"Oh." His eyes were barely slit open. "Sorry. I thought you were part of my dream." But he still held her.

She tugged on his hold, definitely annoyed by now.

"Listen," she began, but he wasn't listening at all.

"You're sexy enough to be part of my dream," he was musing whimsically. "And you'll definitely be a part of my next dream."

"Make that your nightmare," she snapped, reaching to grab his thumb and bend it backward, hard, turning into it to make a clean breakaway.

"Hey!" he said, and swore as he dropped her wrist and began to struggle to sit up. "What the—?"

But she didn't stick around to chat. Head high, she marched toward the driveway without a backward glance, silently thanking her personal defense trainer as she went. So much for those who thought princesses were sitting ducks for any passing tormentor. It was actually rather satisfying to have run across a chance to use her training.

The entire incident was timely. She'd needed a little boost to her self-esteem to help her through the chore she'd set for herself here. She'd come to break her engagement to Garth Franz Josef Mikeavich Romano Roseanova, Prince of Nabotavia. She was going to have to be tough to make him understand that she was not going to marry him, no matter how many official proclamations of their betrothal he could pull out of the country's archives.

Not in a million years.

The inner area of the estate was set off by a long arbor covered with winding sprays of climbing red roses, and she paused at the lovely gateway to gaze in at the spires and towers and balconies decorating the huge palatial mansion ahead, giving a little cough of amusement.

"Just like an East Nabotavian prince to build himself a little Rhineland castle in the middle of Arizona," she thought to herself.

She was a West Nabotavian herself, one of a contingent of refugees who had fled the tiny Central European country twenty years before during a deadly revolution. Most had landed in the United States, living relatively good lives, working and waiting for their chance to rid their country of its oppressors. Now a miracle had happened and the rebels had been thrown off. Nabotavia wanted its monarchy back, and young people such as Tianna were preparing to return to a land they only knew in legends. But it was their home, their destiny. Anyway, it was supposed to be.

Tianna was having trouble reconciling her own plans with this new imperative. She didn't know how Prince Garth felt about it, but she had no intention of going back. And that was one reason she meant to break their engagement off right away.

A scattering of raindrops made a pattern on the walkway and she looked up at the dark clouds gathering above her in the huge Arizona sky. Somewhere not too far off, thunder crackled. Good thing she wasn't too far from the house.

A shout drew her attention. Some sort of a hullabaloo seemed to be going on in another area of the estate. She could hear some yelling, a man's voice, then a woman's higher shriek. Craning her neck, she spotted the location of the activity. Two large cows were munching contentedly in the vegetable garden while a number of people were dancing around them, yelling and waving hats and brooms and other implements of distraction. That solved the mystery of where the security guards must be.

Shrugging lightly, Tianna walked through the arbor and started toward the house, the sensible heels of her soft leather shoes making a pleasing tattoo on the flagstone pavers. But another sound stopped her in her tracks. She turned, frowning, not sure what it was. The soft noise was coming from just beyond the primrose beds that lined the driveway. It seemed to be coming from a small bundle wrapped in a blanket and was certainly something alive. A kitten? A puppy? She moved forward hesitantly and lifted the edge of the little pink blanket.

Her heart stopped. A baby. Big blue eyes stared out at her and the sweet little mouth made a tiny *o*.

"A baby!" she said to no one in particular. "Oh, you precious little thing."

She looked around quickly, sure that someone must be nearby who was in charge of this sweetheart. But there was no one in sight. Perhaps the nanny had stuck the baby here while she ran off to help with the cows. Another inept employee! What a strange place this was—and how glad she was that she wasn't going to be marrying the prince and living here, even temporarily.

But the raindrops were coming harder all the time. Without any more hesitation, she shifted her overnight case to her other hand, reached down and scooped up the baby and headed for the house. She'd been aiming at the front door, but the side entry looked closer and the door there was open, so she changed her trajectory and made a beeline for that.

"Hello!" she called, stepping in out of the drizzle and into the huge kitchen, shaking the drops from her rich copper-colored hair and setting her overnight case by the door.

A teenage girl with a snub nose and a mop of bouncing curls came forward to greet her. "Oh, did you come for the pastry job, then? I think you're a bit early."

"The job?" Tianna looked at her blankly, pressing the little live bundle to her chest. "Oh, no, actually..." She shook her head and smiled at the girl. "No, I've come to see the prince."

"The prince?" Her dark eyes widened. "Sorry. He's not here."

"Not here?" Tianna said with dismay. She'd had her family secretary call and check and they'd said he would be in all this week. *Oh!* She should have called herself, just to make sure. But she'd assumed the information would be good.

Still, she'd come here on the sly, so what did she expect? Her parents thought she was visiting an old school friend in Phoenix. Instead, she'd slipped over to Flagstaff in order to talk Prince Garth into joining her in annulling their betrothal.

They'd been engaged since they were small children, an arrangement set up in a case of influence swapping that had long since lost its importance, as far as she was concerned. And since he'd never shown the slightest interest in her—they had never even met—she had high hopes she was going to be able to pull it off and present it as a fait accompli to her father.

"Where has he gone?" she asked the maid.

The girl shrugged again. "I don't know. I think maybe Texas."

"Oh no." Tianna couldn't believe she'd come all this way for nothing. "Do you have any idea when he'll be back?"

"No, Miss. I'm sorry. He doesn't come here much lately."

The baby squirmed and made a tiny sound, more like a kitten than a child and Tianna gave it a comforting pat.

The young maid looked confused. "Is that a baby?"

"Oh, yes." Tianna held it out where it could be seen. "Someone left this baby outside in the rain. I thought I'd better bring her in."

The maid blinked. "Outside in the rain?" she echoed blankly.

"Exactly," Tianna said. "It must belong to someone here."

"No, Miss." She was shaking her head quite emphatically. "There's no baby living here. I would know if there was a baby here."

"Oh, for heaven's sake," Tianna murmured, looking down into the precious face and feeling a pang of sympathy for the poor little thing. All alone, with no one to claim her. Something tugged at her heart as she remembered another little girl lost from her own past. Wincing, she hugged the baby to her heart and murmured a comforting sound.

"Cook's not here," the little maid went on. "They're all out chasing the cows. They got out again and went straight for the vegetable garden, like they do every time." She gestured toward a chair. "Please sit and wait, Miss. Cook will be back in no time. I'll go fetch her and tell her you are here for the pastry job."

The girl bobbed her head and before Tianna could correct her again, she disappeared down a dark passageway.

"Oh!" Tianna looked down at the tiny life in her arms and her annoyance melted. "You are so beautiful," she whispered, kissing the downy head. "But what am I going to do with you?"

She looked around the room for a place to put the baby down, but though the huge kitchen managed to have a homey ambience, with copper-bottomed pans displayed over a central island and swags of herbs hanging in a window, its shining stainless steel counters and appliances didn't seem to have a niche for a baby to sleep in.

Someone was coming down the hall toward the kitchen and she turned, hoping to find an adult who could be talked to instead of the witless little maid. There was a muted groan before the newcomer appeared, a hand held to his head, his eyes barely slit open enough to make his way.

Tianna gasped. It was the reprobate who'd been lolling about in the gazebo. She stood where she was, paralyzed. A woman who prided herself on her levelheaded attitude toward life, she was not one to be bowled over by a handsome hunk, but this was, without a doubt, the most stunning man she'd ever seen, and now that he was upright, he looked even better than he had a few minutes earlier.

Her trained photographer's eye told her she was looking at a masterpiece. His physical beauty shone through despite the fact that his golden hair needed cutting and he'd changed his clothes into something more casual. Dressed in a pair of snug jeans and a cotton shirt left carelessly open to display that breathtakingly muscular chest, he was absolutely spectacular in a young-god-straddling-the-universe sort of way. She might have taken him for the prince himself if she hadn't already heard the prince was gone.

But no. The few princes she'd met over the years had mostly been effete and purposeless, dried husks of the men of power they might once have been. This man was too earthy, too vital, to be a prince. He looked more like a warrior. A warrior who'd had too much to drink recently.

"Haven't we met somewhere?" he asked, gazing at her through narrowed eyes, as though the room was too bright for him.

"You might say that," she said crisply, determined he wouldn't know how attractive she found him. "You could be having trouble remembering, since you were lying down at the time."

"Oh yes. The girl of my dreams." His crooked smile was a knock-out, but it was fleeting. In seconds he was putting his hand to his head again and wincing. "Sorry to present myself in such a state of disrepair," he added. "I'm recovering from a rather late night."

"So I see."

"Ouch. Your tone has the definite sting of disapproval." He raised a sardonic eyebrow. "I don't suppose you've ever had a hangover, have you, Red Riding Hood?"

"Never."

"No. I didn't think so. You're one of the wise ones. It's written all over you." He sighed. "I think I've finally learned that lesson myself. I know I'm never going to touch alcohol again." He looked around the kitchen as though he'd lost something. "What do you know about making Bloody Marys?" he added hopefully.

"Nothing."

She made her tone as scornful as possible, but she knew she wasn't fooling anyone. If she'd known a magic potion to make him feel better, she'd have conjured it up in a flash. As it was she just stood there, watching him, holding the baby to her chest. She'd always known pure beauty could be fascinating, but she'd never experienced it in the form of a man before.

He nodded, accepting fate for what it was, and rummaged in a cabinet, finding a remedy for himself. Tearing open a package, he poured the contents into a glass and filled it with water from the faucet in the huge stainless steel sink, then downed most of it, making a face as he set the glass back down on the counter.

"Not quite as satisfying as the hair of the dog," he murmured as he made his way painfully toward the kitchen table. "But probably more effective."

Slumping into a chair, he threw his head back and closed his eyes and wondered, and not for the first time, why he put himself through this sort of punishment. Admittedly, it had been a good long time since he'd tied one on like he had the night before. At one time it had actually seemed like fun. As the years went on, it had become rather dreary, and he'd pretty much given up the party scene. But last night...

He wasn't kidding anyone. He knew why he'd tried to drown himself in a bottle the night before. The anniversary of his parents' murder was a tough thing to get past, and last night had been the twentieth one. Hopefully by next year this time he'd be too busy in Nabotavia to go through this yearly ritual.

He opened his eyes and found himself staring right into the steady green gaze of the young woman gently pacing back and forth in front of him. Suddenly he was almost embarrassed by his condition. She was so young and bright and clean-looking. He felt shopworn and seedy in contrast. He sat up a bit straighter.

"What have you got there?" he asked, noting the bundle she carried close to her chest.

She cuddled it closer, pressing a kiss to the tiny head. "A baby," she replied, gazing at him over the top of the blanket.

Suddenly he was wide-awake. "A baby?" He sat up even straighter as the implications became clear to him. "Your baby?"

"No." She glanced at him, then away again. "Someone left her out in the yard. I just brought her in out of the rain."

"Uh-huh."

That hardly seemed likely. Now he was guarded. He tried to remember if she'd been carrying the baby when he'd first seen her in the gazebo, but he hadn't been thinking clearly enough at the time to notice much of anything. He frowned, focusing. Had he ever seen her before? No, he didn't think so. He would have remembered. And she wasn't claiming any previous relationship at this point.

"I know nothing about babies," he said, as though merely making conversation. "I've heard they have something to do with human beings, in much the same way the acorn magically transforms itself into the mighty oak, but I have a hard time believing it."

She wasn't paying any attention to his jesting declaration. Her face was bent down to the little one and she was murmuring soft sounds to it. He frowned. She did seem inordinately attached to a baby she'd only just met. He couldn't help but be suspicious.

One thing he'd been scrupulously careful about all

his adult life was to make sure there would never be a woman who could claim her baby was his. There had been a few who had tried that scam, but the claims had never held up. Still, it had happened often enough to make him very wary.

He'd learned very young that his special station in life meant there weren't many people he could trust. Everybody seemed to want something from him, whether it was influence or favors or just the extra prestige of being able to say they had been hanging out with the prince. He didn't often let his guard down. The few times he'd done that had led to pain and disaster. His carefully maintained image of vaguely good-natured cynicism was real in part, but it also served to hide an inner vulnerability he wouldn't ever risk again.

"So what's it doing here?" he asked.

She looked at him as though she was beginning to doubt his intelligence. "It's a baby," she said carefully.

"But not yours."

"No, I found it in the yard."

"So you said." His mouth turned down at the corners. "So whose is it really?"

She cocked an eyebrow at him. "I don't know, but your gate was unattended. Almost anyone could have sauntered in."

"True." He wasn't convinced, but then, it didn't really matter. He didn't have much interest in babies anyway. But he did like the look of the woman who held it. "So you think things are a little lax around here, do you?"

"That's putting it mildly," she said without bothering to soften her judgment. "This place is run like a public park."

"Oh. I suppose you think you could do a better job."

She gave a short laugh. "I know I could."

He liked her attitude. It was refreshing to meet an attractive woman who didn't seem to be bowled over by just being in his presence. "Really. If you took over management, what would you do to improve it?"

She gave him a sideways look and went back to rocking the baby in her arms. "My first item of business would probably be to fire *you*."

"Fire *me?*" He stared at her for a moment, then threw back his head and laughed.

"Absolutely." She followed up her assertion with a scathing glance that went up and down the long, muscular length of him, and was meant to convey disapproval, but ended up feeling too much like admiration for comfort and she quickly looked away. "I would never put up with an employee who acted like you do." She shifted the baby from one hip to the other. "What do you do around here, anyway?"

He grinned. She really didn't know he was the prince of this castle. That was great. "Oh, not a whole heck of a lot. Mostly they just keep me around for comic relief."

"Really?" Her look told him she halfway believed it. "Well you could make yourself useful right now. Would you like to hold the baby for a moment?" She offered the little bundle with the blanket open so that the baby could be seen.

He glanced at it and looked away, shaking his head dismissively. "I'm not much of a baby person."

She stepped toward him. "Hold her anyway, while I fix a place to put her down."

Not likely. Something about the thought of taking charge of that little piece of life gave him the willies. He threw her a baleful look. "*I'll* do it," he said, rising and looking around the kitchen, grabbing a large basket and arranging the napkins it held into a sort of bed. "Here you go."

She carefully laid the sleeping child in the impromptu bed and pushed it to a safe place on the counter, then looked down with a sweet smile. "She's so beautiful."

He'd never considered red and wrinkled to be beautiful, but he did like the look of the woman. She interested him. She kept looking at him in the oddest way. It wasn't just that she was attracted to him. Women usually were. But there was something more, something mysterious in her smoky green eyes.

She was very pretty, but it was a careless sort of beauty. The way she held herself, the way she moved, he could tell she didn't think about her looks any more than she thought about the weather. There was an innocence about her, and yet at the same time, a sophistication, as though she knew a lot, but it was mostly secondhand information, experience gained from books and not from mixing with the masses.

"Funny," he said softly, looking at the way her bronze hair lay against the smooth pale skin of her neck and wondering if she smelled as good as she looked. "You don't look like a pastry chef."

"I am not a pastry chef," she responded automatically, looking up at him. It didn't occur to her to say she was a princess. She never said things like that. If she had her way, the whole princess thing would fade from her life and no one would ever know about it again. Of course, being a princess was the very reason she was here, a fact she had practically forgotten by now.

"I saw Milla, the kitchen maid, in the hall and she said you'd come about the pastry chef position."

Tianna gave him a long suffering look. "Milla was wrong."

He frowned. Thinking wasn't as painful as it had been a few minutes earlier, but it still wasn't back with its usual zing. "What are you, then?"

"I'm a photographer."

He groaned, dropping back down into the chair and stretching. "Not another photojournalist sniffing around for a story on the royals."

"I'm not a photojournalist," she assured him quickly. "I told you, I'm a photographer. I mainly concentrate on architectural photography. And I have no interest in photographing royals."

"Good. Then we won't have to kick you out on your ear."

She bristled. "I'd like to see you try," she said sharply, one hand on her hip.

"Oh. That's right. I forgot you were the dangerous one." His blue eyes glinted at her in a way that sent a new awareness skittering along her nerve endings. "Quite the little wildcat, aren't you?" he said in a tone that made her sound downright erotic.

Her breath caught in her throat and color flooded her cheeks, but she lifted her chin and tried to ignore it. "I'm nothing of the sort. But I do know how to defend myself."

"I'll say you do. I've got the sore hand to prove it." He shook the hand, deemed it basically unscathed, but looked up at her accusingly anyway. "That was quite a nice demonstration of the old thumb trick you put on this morning. What other escape moves do you have up your sleeve?"

She looked fully at him and for just a moment, their gazes seemed to connect, fuse, and sizzle.

"I...I think I'd better keep that to myself," she said, feeling a bit muddled and looking toward the window, absently noting that the rain was coming down pretty steadily now. "The element of surprise is half the battle."

"Here," he said, coming to his feet. "I'll show you a good one."

"No thanks." She turned away, shaking her head, but he moved too quickly for her.

"If someone grabs you, like this," he said, coming up behind her and sliding his arms in, locking them just beneath her breasts, pulling her close in against him. "What would you do?"

She gasped. His face was next to hers, his breath tantalizing her cheek, his rough day's growth of beard rasping against her skin. It had all happened so fast, she had to wait a beat or two to make sure she understood just exactly what was going on here.

"You snap back your right elbow and at the same time, you make a turn to the left," he was advising, his voice silky, so very near her ear.

She could hardly breathe. He was holding her to his long, strong body and she thought she could feel every one of his muscles against her back. Her natural inclination was to do as he said and turn toward the left, but one second of clear thinking and she realized what that meant. She might be in his arms now, but if she followed his instructions she would be in his embrace and in perfect position to be kissed.

A lovely thought—if only she could believe he wasn't doing this on purpose just to mock her. Which, of course, he was! She steeled herself. She wasn't going to follow through and fall into his trap. Instead, she made another move her personal defense trainer had taught her and quickly raised her foot, coming down hard on top of his.

He yelled. She pulled out of his grip, whirling to glare at him hotly. Half-laughing, he was hobbling in pain.

"My God, woman, you're lethal. I was just trying to show you..."

She raised her hands as though to defend herself. "Stay back!" she ordered him.

And at the same time, the cook came bustling in through the outer doorway, her hair damp, her look very cross. She took in the scene at a glance, nodded at Tianna, and glared daggers at the man standing beside her.

"Young mister, you know the rules," she said sternly, shaking a finger at him. "There's to be no trifling with the help." She all but stamped her foot and pointed to show him the way out of her kitchen.

"Trifling?" He glanced at Tianna and shook his head, laughing softly. "Don't worry. This lady is definitely a no-trifling zone."

His gaze met hers and held for a moment, then he turned his full charm on the cook.

"That you, of all people, should accuse me of trifling." He had the confident smile of a man who had used charisma as his currency out of many a sticky situation in his life and was pretty sure it would work for him again, any time he chose to use it. "I was doing no such thing. I was merely keeping a visitor company while waiting for you to return and do your duty by her."

The cook was still pointing. "If you want to practice your profligate ways, you'll do so somewhere else," she insisted. "I've got work to do here."

The handsome charmer reacted with weary resignation.

"Aye aye, Cook." He gave her a somewhat disjointed salute, then leaned toward her teasingly. "My mentor, my conscience, my guide. As ever, words of wisdom fall from your lips like petals from the rose...."

The cook colored and had a hard time not showing pleasure at his affectionate mockery. "Get on with you." She swatted at him with a dish towel, but she was beaming in a way that gave full evidence to how much she cared for him. "And keep your crazy poetry to yourself."

"Hey, watch that talk," he said as he prepared to depart. "You know I have to maintain my reputation as a soldier. Don't start spreading that poetry rumor."

He stopped to drop a quick kiss on the cook's cheek, then dodged another swipe with the dish towel as he made his way toward the exit. Tianna noted with a twinge of guilty satisfaction that he was limping slightly. He paused in the doorway, looking back.

"Goodbye, lovely lady," he said to Tianna just before disappearing out the door. "I hope we meet again." A fleeting smile, and then he was gone.

Tianna thought she'd probably seen the last of him and was disappointed in herself for caring. She had to admit, it would be tempting to let herself get a healthy crush on a man like that, to start thinking about the scent of roses and kisses in the moonlight. The only love affair she'd let herself attempt had ended badly and had seemed hardly worth the effort in the end. She had the feeling things might have been different with a man like this.

"He's got a heart of gold, that one," the cook confided once he was out of the room. "But he does tease so."

Tianna smiled, her pulse still reacting to the man's presence in the room. "Is he your son?"

The cook looked shocked. "My son? Heaven's no. My dear, don't you know who that is? Why, it's Prince Garth, that's who."

Chapter 2

Tianna felt the room fade and pulse, and she barely avoided a gasp. "Prince Garth!" She put her hand over her heart. "But...but the little maid told me the prince had gone to Texas."

"Oh, aye. She thought you meant Crown Prince Marco, no doubt about it. He was here last week." She began to bustle about the kitchen. "No one thinks of Garth as 'the prince.' He's always been the younger brother, you know. The rascal. The charming one." She grinned affectionately.

Tianna sat, still dumbfounded, and growing more and more astonished as she thought over this latest wrinkle. So the man they expected her to marry really was a playboy and a carouser. Delightfully irresistible—and the last man in the world a woman would want to be married to. Hah! Just wait until she explained all this to her father. It looked like she would be able to put together a nice tight case for annulling this betrothal. And wasn't that what she'd come for?

Actually, it was getting hard to remember what she'd come for. Too much was getting in the way.

The cook had turned back and was frowning down at her. "Well, now about your business. Come about the pastry chef job, have you? We weren't expecting you quite this soon, but that's all right. We'll make do."

Tianna turned to tell her the truth, but she was rattling on.

"Now, let's see a bit of your talent. I've got some dough mixed for pies. Why don't you roll it out and we'll see what you can do with it. Try something creative."

"I'm really not here for the pastry chef job."

"No?"

"No. I'm…"

It was going to be hard to explain what she was here for at this point—and why she hadn't talked to Garth when she had a chance. Her day was careening wildly out of control. It was probably time she made herself known to everyone and tried to get some order back into things. "Actually, you see, I'm Princess Katianna of…"

Unfortunately, her words were drowned out by the sudden wail of the infant. The cook whirled and stared at the basket on the table.

"A baby!" Cook's gaze fell on the basket. "Ah yes, Milla said you'd brought your baby. We really don't have facilities for babies here. You should have asked first, you know."

Tianna considered tearing her hair out, but thought better of it. "She's not my baby," she said evenly. "I found her in the yard."

Cook rolled her eyes. "What nonsense," she said, and bent over the little thing, cooing to it.

Tianna bit her lip and silently counted to ten, then drew herself up and gazed coolly at the woman. "I assure you, I'm telling the truth."

Cook glanced up and seemed to recognize her growing irritation. "Well, that's as may be. But then where did this baby come from?"

Good question. If only someone would answer it! Stifling the urge to scream, Tianna gave her a quick explanation of how the estate had been left unguarded and open to the world when she'd arrived. The cook finally seemed to accept that, though reluctantly.

"Oh yes, we're so shorthanded right now, things are falling to wrack and ruin," she said, shaking her head. "You know, they usually leave their babies at the guard gate. We never even see them up here. And you say you found her right out in the garden?"

Tianna frowned. "Are you telling me strange babies show up here all the time?" she asked.

Cook shrugged. "Well, not all the time. But it's been known to happen. Single girls hoping we'll take the tykes in and raise them as royals. Surely you know about the legend of Baby Rose. It's an old Nabotavian story."

She didn't, but she wasn't in the mood for a story right now. "You think this one was left by a desperate young girl?" she asked, looking down at the dewy little face and wishing she didn't feel such a strong emotional pull every time she did so. The baby was starting to fuss again and she pulled it up into her arms without thinking twice, patting her little back and whispering sweet nothings against her silky head.

"No doubt about it." The cook turned and spoke to

the kitchen maid. "Milla, call the orphanage. Tell them we'll be sending another baby over."

Tianna looked up, frowning. She hated to think of letting this little angel go. "Don't you think we should call the police? And perhaps, Children's Services?"

"Children's Services? Oh my, no. We'll call the Nabotavian Orphanage, that's what we'll do. They'll take her. We Nabotavians like to take care of our own." She frowned at Tianna. "Aren't you a daughter of the Rose nation, my dear?"

"Yes, of course I am."

"Been in this country a little too long, though, haven't you? Started to think like an American. Just like my young prince. It's a good thing we'll all be going back soon." She shook her head. "We've almost lost our heritage, I do declare."

"So you're preparing for the return?"

"We're at sixes and sevens, my dear. All this moving back to Nabotavia has the entire staff in an uproar." She looked overwhelmed by it all. "The housekeeper left a week ago to manage the preparations at Red Rose Palace and she took some of our best workers with her. She left Mr. Harva, the butler, in charge, and he immediately ran off with the pastry chef. Now I'm left to try to keep things from falling apart here, and heaven knows I have my hands full."

The little maid returned at that moment, walking into the kitchen with a bouncy step. "The orphanage can't take her. They've got chicken pox. They can't take anyone new for at least four days."

"Oh my heavens! What's next?" The cook turned to Tianna, shaking her head.

Tianna looked from the cook to the baby and back again. Hesitating, she recognized that she was at a crossroads. She could hand the baby back and identify herself, and everything would change. She would be the princess and escorted to the other side of the house where she would be given a beautiful bedroom for the night and probably not see this baby again.

Or she could let them think she was a mere job seeker and stick around for a while. She looked down into the baby's face. The lower lip was trembling and the huge blue eyes were clouded. A wave of protective affection seized her. The child felt so soft and snuggly and she smelled like something fresh and new—which was exactly what she was. But she was also so helpless. Tianna hadn't been quite this young, but she had known what it was to be helpless and lost. She didn't wish that on anyone, especially not this innocent. Someone had to make sure nothing bad happened to her. And since she'd had plenty of experience helping with her sister's baby, she supposed she was the one to do it.

"I…well, I suppose I could help…."

"And what is your name, child?"

Her chin lifted. "Tianna Rose." It was the name she went by in daily life, and would do for the moment. No one would connect it to the Katianna Roseanova-Krimorova who was betrothed to the prince.

"Ah, a Rose, are you?" The cook nodded knowingly. "Related to the royal family by any chance?"

Tianna met her gaze levelly but she wasn't prepared to outright lie. "Perhaps."

"Ah, yes. Everyone likes to claim a little relationship here and there." The cook smiled sympathetically. "I'm sure you have the usual references. Well, we can put you to work, I think. Somebody is going to have to take care of this baby, and I don't dare let Milla do it. She'd probably leave it out in the yard again." She smiled hopefully. "What do you know about the nanny business, Tianna Rose?"

For Prince Garth, driving his Porsche was a major part of the joy of life. Sleek and silver, his car purred like a giant cat and was so responsive to his handling, it reminded him of a sensual woman. Maybe that was why, as he drove up the winding driveway, returning from an afternoon of boring meetings in town with lawyers and business managers, his thoughts went to the lovely woman he'd met that morning in the gazebo.

He could still feel the way her curves had fit against his body and the memory stirred his reactions in a way that made him laugh at himself. She was certainly a tempting bit of luscious femininity—which should put him on guard, as he'd recently sworn off women altogether.

Women! They never played fair. Even those who agreed to ground rules from the beginning—vowing to keep things light and playful, swearing there would be no hearts involved, ended up wanting commitments and long-range promises in the end. And if you rebuffed their come-on advances, they usually found a way to make you pay.

He was still reeling from his last scandal involving a woman he hadn't even kissed. She'd told the tabloids a wild tale of sex in public places and orgies on yachts and all because he'd stopped taking her phone calls. Sometimes you couldn't win for losing.

On the other hand, he hated to think of how many women he'd hurt over the years. But their hearts seemed to break so easily. He'd finally come to the conclusion that it was better just to stay completely out of the game.

After all, he was betrothed. He didn't need to search for a mate, so why not give up women for the time being?

Still, the lovely yet dangerous visitor intrigued him. She'd said she was a photographer, yet all evidence suggested she was here to apply for the pastry chef position. Hopefully, she was going to be preparing tempting confections for him from now on. That thought made him smile again. Leaving his car out front for Homer, the chauffeur, to deal with, he went straight into the kitchen and greeted Cook with a peck on the cheek.

"There you are," she said in a harried fashion. "Will you be having your dinner here tonight, then?"

"Yes, I think I will." He glanced around the kitchen but didn't catch sight of the woman he was searching for.

"Good." Cook gave him a baleful look. "You've been out gallivanting too much lately. It'll do you good to stay at home for a change. Any guests?"

"No." He peered around the kitchen, noting Milla shelling peas and a thin stranger cleaning off a counter. "What happened to the new pastry chef?"

Cook nodded in the direction of the slender woman. "There she is. She's hard at work."

Garth did a double take and frowned. "No, I mean the other one." He turned to the older woman in alarm. "You didn't hire her?"

"Oh, that one." She waved a hand in the air. "Tianna, you mean. Yes, she's still here. She agreed to be nanny to that baby that was found in the yard, at least until the orphanage can take her—or someone shows up to claim her. She's probably up in the nursery right now..."

But Garth was already on his way, whistling as he went. Tianna. So that was her name. A lovely and typically Nabotavian name, a lovely and typically

Nabotavian girl. Against all his better judgements, he was looking forward to seeing her again. Although he had a rather inflated reputation as a playboy, he had never actually dallied with the help. It wasn't his style. But then, the help had never been quite so beautiful before. There was always the exception that proved the rule.

He was feeling rather debonair as he knocked a quick rhythm on the nursery room door.

"Come in," her voice called.

He straightened his tie and turned the knob, a provocative smile at the ready. But when he opened the door, instead of the welcoming look of surprise he expected, he found himself gazing into a face that, though still beautiful, was set in a look that said "trouble."

"There you are!" she exclaimed.

He stopped in his tracks, but at least she didn't have her dukes up this time. "What did I do?" he asked, completely at sea.

She gave him a look that said, "If you don't know…" and rose from the rocking chair with the baby in her arms.

"I've been waiting for you to come home," she said distractedly. "I've got to talk to you."

He raised an eyebrow, surprised at her tone but happy to see she was every bit as lovely as he remembered. Her soft burnished hair set off a face that was finely boned, the lips full, the green eyes luminous and framed in thick dark lashes. He liked the look of her and he was already speculating what her touch would be like.

"I had some meetings to attend to. And very tedious they were, too. Why? Did I miss something?"

Did he miss something!

Turning, she carefully laid the sleeping baby down

in its antique crib, giving herself a moment to compose her emotions. Trailing a finger across the downy head, she felt a surge of affection for this helpless creature that was beginning to seem automatic. She looked so beautiful tucked under her lacy covers. It was official now. Tianna was her defender and protector. She would do whatever she had to do to make sure this child was safe and well taken care of.

Luckily, the nursery was fully stocked with baby supplies, as it had only been a short time since Prince Marco's two children had passed through on their way to their larger bedrooms. Milla had been sent into town to get formula and baby food, but disposable diapers and baby blankets filled the cupboards—everything a well-connected baby would need. And this sweet baby might just be a little more well-connected than everyone had first believed.

Turning, she looked at Prince Garth. She'd been sitting here for the past few hours working herself up into a lather over this situation and it wasn't going to help if she started ranting at him. At any rate, now that they were face-to-face, she knew he wasn't the monster she'd been painting in her mind. Surely he would do the right thing.

"Have you done anything yet to find the mother of this baby?" she asked carefully.

He seemed puzzled by her question but he answered readily enough. "Don't worry about that. The authorities will handle it. The orphanage finds the mothers very quickly. The mothers and babies are usually reunited within days." He shook his head. "They do this because of the Rose Baby Legend, you know."

She paused, biting her lip. This legend had been mentioned twice. It had to be peculiar to East Nabotavia, because she didn't remember ever hearing of it before. She supposed she ought to get the full background before she made her case.

"Why don't you sit down?" she suggested, gesturing toward a chair set facing the rocker. "I'd like to hear about this Rose Baby Legend."

He looked at her and almost laughed. She was talking to him as though…hell, as though she were a princess. Actually, he was used to people treating him with casual equality. After all, he'd spent quite a few years in the U.S. Army after graduating from West Point, the last few as a lieutenant colonel. But this was different. He was in his own home castle and Tianna was an employee. By now she surely knew he was a prince. It was very strange that she didn't seem to feel a need to treat him like—well, at least like the boss. A neutral observer might have come to the opposite conclusion and figured *he* must work for *her*.

"You're Nabotavian, aren't you?" he asked as he sank easily into the chair. "Surely you've heard the story."

"I may have heard it once, but if I did, it didn't stick with me." She sat down in the rocker and leaned forward. "Why don't you fill me in?"

"The Rose Baby Legend. Okay." He frowned, calling up the old story from the past. "It started about a hundred years ago in Nabotavia. It was a time of great instability in the kingdom—as usual. The queen—my great-grandmother—had given birth to three boys and then found she was unable to have any more children. She desperately wanted a girl. In fact, supposedly she'd fallen into deep depression because, as she said, the boys would all be taken from her by war and she deeply longed for a daughter who would stay beside her always. Everyone in the country knew about her sorrow. Then one day, while walking in the rose garden, she found a baby girl, wrapped in a rose-colored blanket. She adopted her, raised her as her own, even to the point of calling her a princess. She was my great aunt, Princess Elna. True to the queen's desires, she never married, staying with her adoptive mother to the end."

"Wow."

"Yes. You don't see that kind of gratitude much these days, do you?" He gave her a crooked grin. "I don't really remember her, but I've always heard a lot about her. She affected the lives of all she came in contact with. She was the first one to start a nursing charity for the poor. She founded the original Nabotavian orphanage. The whole country loved her. She was considered a sort of royal saint."

"Princess Elna." Tianna nodded. She remembered now. She'd read a biography of the woman when she was about twelve or thirteen. "Yes, of course. I've heard of her. She was a wonderful woman."

"Yes. Anyway, she became quite a legend, and eventually a myth grew up around her experience. It was thought that the royal family might take in other babies. The rose garden was open to the public in those days and women began leaving their babies there, with notes, begging for the royal family to adopt the baby. For some reason, a few years ago, the story was revived and they started trying to do that here, too. They usually don't get any farther than the guard gate, though."

"I see." She nodded thoughtfully, then glanced at the crib where the little girl slept.

Garth followed her gaze. "Now where was it you found her?" he asked, watching for her reaction.

Tianna looked at him. "Just outside, along the driveway."

"Not in the rose garden?"

"No, it was among the primroses."

She blinked and their eyes met. His eyebrow cocked.

"Too bad," he said softly. "I'm afraid we're not in the adopting mood here at the castle."

Tianna's gaze was still holding his. "What if it's not just some stranger who left her?" she asked softly. "What if it's someone you know?"

He frowned, sitting back in his chair. The wary look returned to his handsome face. "What are you driving at?"

She rose, stepping to the chest of drawers and returning with a small note card. Even from where he was sitting, he could smell the rose scent it had been dabbed with.

"Here," she said. "You'd better read this. It fell out of the baby's clothing."

He looked at it for a moment, a feeling of unease growing in his chest. This had all the earmarks of something that was going to be extremely unpleasant. Reluctantly, he reached for the card.

"My dearest Garth," the note began. He groaned softly, then went on reading.

"Why have you done this to me? You never come by and you don't write anymore. I'm at my wits' end. I don't know what to do. I can't handle this by myself. It's just too hard. I feel I've lost your love and your support. But this baby is as much yours as she is mine. I'm leaving her for you to raise. I just can't do it on my own. But I still love you and always will. Your Sunshine Girl."

"Nice try, Sunshine Girl," he said sardonically, flipping the letter down on the small table between them. He took a deep breath, then looked up into Tianna's intense green gaze. "I assume you read this."

"I…" She flushed, realizing she had intruded herself where she hadn't been invited. "I'm sorry, but I thought…"

"Of course you read it," he said, sweeping away her apologies. "That hardly matters." He fixed her with a serious look. "What does matter is that you realize it's a hoax."

"A hoax?"

"Of course." He looked at the paper as though he could start a flame if he stared hard enough. "I have no idea who this person is. And I'm not the father of her baby."

Tianna stared at him. So this was the angle he was going to take. For some reason, she'd thought he might respond with remorse at least, and hopefully promises of support. But as she looked into his clear blue eyes, she could see that he had no intention of doing any such thing.

For the first time since she'd read the note, her confidence wavered. Maybe he was right. Maybe the baby wasn't his. On one level, she would like to believe it. But how could that be? The note came across as so sincere. And women usually knew who the fathers of their babies were. It was hard for her to believe that any woman would set her baby out to be found like that without being darn sure….

"I assumed at least you would know who she is," she said, pinning him with a penetrating look.

"No. I do not know who this is."

She leaned forward, frowning. The baby seemed to be about four months old to her. "Well, if you think back…. Where were you a little over a year ago? That's when it would have happened."

"I was in Nabotavia," he said coolly. "Fighting with the underground."

"Oh." She sat back. That certainly put a different light on the subject. Still… "But maybe she was in Nabotavia, too."

A muscle twitched at his temple and his mouth seemed to harden. "And maybe she's just a local girl who heard about the Rose Baby Legend and decided to take her chances."

She held his gaze with her own intense stare. "Maybe."

They stayed that way for a long moment as the air crackled between them. Suddenly Tianna was short of breath and afraid she knew exactly why. She licked her lips, trying to mask her breathlessness, and saw his gaze darken as he followed the path of her tongue. That only made things worse. She had to focus hard to remember what they were here talking about.

"At any rate, there's no need for you to worry about it," he said at last, shrugging carelessly. "I'm sure the mother will be found eventually."

She drew in a sharp breath, back on subject and exasperated with him. "That's all you have to say about this?"

He looked very continental and above it all. "What would you like me to say?"

She shrugged, growing more and more annoyed with him. "Oh, I don't know. Maybe that you're sorry the poor little thing has been abandoned. That you'll make some effort to find out where she belongs." She threw out her arms. "How about giving some indication that just possibly you might give a damn?"

But what if I don't?

He didn't say it, but he was tempted to, more because

he knew it would drive her crazy than anything else. Of course he cared on a basic human level. But that was pretty abstract. In the grand scheme of things, he had to admit that the women who left their babies hoping the royals would raise them didn't interest him much. It had been happening for as long as he could remember. The only thing that made this instance different was that this new mother had composed a bogus note to add to the mix—and that Tianna was involved.

He had to admit, she interested him more than any woman had in a long time. Women usually swooned around him, flirted, gushed, gave every indication that they would love to be taken home and ravished. But Tianna was different. She reacted enough to let him know she wasn't immune to the attraction that had sprung up between them from the first. But she was working very hard to resist it. And that, of course, was a challenge he might not be able to ignore.

Still, he knew she wasn't going to be happy until he took some steps toward solving the problem of the baby—an annoyance he could easily take care of.

"If it will make you feel better, I'll put a real expert on the case right away." He pulled out his cell phone and quickly punched in a number. "Janus? I have an assignment for you. Please meet me in the study in…oh, say five minutes."

"My valet," he told her as he folded his phone and put it away in his pocket. "He's the most trustworthy man I know. He'll handle it."

She sat very still and drew in a slow, deep breath. Where should she go from here? It would have been nice to see more enthusiasm from him, more interest in getting to the bottom of this mystery. It disappointed her to have him brush it off, as if it hardly mattered, as if, like any rich and powerful person, he didn't have to deal with the problems of the little people. This was exactly what she hated about the monarchy—and one of the main reasons she was determined to slough it off like a poorly fitting skin.

He rose from his chair and she rose to face him. "Would you like to hold the baby before you go?" she asked hopefully.

His eyes shone with a quizzical sheen. "No thanks," he said dismissively. He hesitated, then added, "Dinner is at six in the game room."

"Oh, I can't leave the baby."

He looked pained. "Of course you can. I'll send up Bridget, the downstairs maid, to sit with the baby. She often watches Marcos's children."

"No, I really don't think…"

"Tianna."

Her head jerked up at the tone of his voice. He hadn't come right out and said, "Listen, wench, I think you're forgetting who's in charge here," but he might as well have. The implication was clear as a bell.

"I require your presence at dinner," he said, his voice low but filled with steel. "Six o'clock in the game room."

She swallowed and stared at him, suddenly tongue-tied. His face softened into a lazy, knowing smile that managed to leave her feeling caressed, though he hadn't touched her.

"We need some time to get to know each other better," he added, his voice hinting at promises of something unexpressed but easy enough to understand.

Catching her breath, she watched while he left the room, then she stared at the door after he'd closed it behind him.

"There's your problem," she whispered to herself, shaking her head in a sort of wonder. "You're letting the man hypnotize you. Cut it out!" Groaning, she turned back to check on the child.

Not many men had ever managed to penetrate her sometimes cool exterior armor. And she was thankful for that. She had the example of her younger sister, Jannika, to show her how bad things could get. Janni had not only found a way to sneak out on dates, she'd married someone her family disapproved of, had a baby and been abandoned by her young shiftless husband and was now living at home again—a fate so filled with regret and shame that Tianna would have died rather than copy it.

She'd grown up in a bookish sort of household, where trips to the library were more important than trips to the mall. On vacations, her family made reservations at museums rather than at the trendiest hot spots. She'd gone to girls' schools, and even her college had been mostly female. The few times people of the male gender had appeared on her horizon, there had always been a sense of distance, because after all, she was betrothed.

That arrangement had seemed to be the magic spell that kept her from harm for a long, long time. But once she'd begun to take her photography classes, and become quite good at it, she'd realized that the very thing that had served as her shield now acted as her jailer. As long as she was promised to the Nabotavian prince, she was tied to the monarchy, tied to certain duties and responsibilities—and would never be allowed to take off for New York to pursue her photography dream.

So she'd taken a step off the reservation. The recipe was an old one. Take one handsome and worldly instructor and one innocent but curious student, give them time alone together, and poof! One quick pulse-pounding love affair to go.

Luckily she'd pulled back from the brink in time to save herself from complete insanity—as well as from her sister's fate. But she felt she knew a lot more about men and sensual chemistry now. And she knew it could ruin your life if you let it. But she wasn't interested in affairs of the heart any more than she was interested in playing the princess part. She was a photographer.

Despite what her father might think, evidence suggested she really did have a lot of talent. She'd submitted entries to contests, won a few, and finally received a job offer in Chicago that she was determined to take. It wasn't quite New York, but it was on the way. Opening that envelope with the offer inside had been the most exciting thing she'd ever done.

Her father, of course, had scorned it. "It's of no use to you. You'll be marrying Prince Garth soon," he'd said.

She found it a little odd that he'd brought it up, actually. He hadn't said much about it over the years. As a family, they hadn't kept up ties with the Nabotavian community to any large extent. So she'd begun to think maybe it wasn't all that important any longer. And she was perfectly happy to ignore it—until it loomed as a barrier to something she really wanted to do. She had to remember that she'd come to find a way to break her engagement, and she couldn't let a momentary attraction to the very man from whom she wanted to break free deter her from her goal.

"Oh well," she told herself with forced cheer. "By

the time I make him take responsibility for this baby, he might be so sick of me, he'll be glad to see me go!"

She could only hope.

Chapter 3

Tianna entered the game room at exactly six. She came in slowly, warily, scanning the room for danger. She was so busy being careful, she didn't see Prince Garth standing just behind her and she jumped when he spoke.

"Good evening."

"Oh!" She turned quickly and tried to pretend she hadn't been startled. "Good evening," she said, nervously smoothing down the lacy collar at her neck. The dress she wore was long and clinging, buttoned high at the neck and decorated with white lace. It was like nothing she ever wore in her real life, but she hadn't brought much in her overnight case, and she'd been told she could wear anything she found in the nanny's closet. Luckily, at least one of the previous nannies had been very close to her size, if not to her taste in clothes.

The prince was dressed casually, but with understated elegance, the crease in his slacks so sharp it could have cut wood, the fabric of his white shirt so soft, it clung to the hard lines of his muscular torso. The virility of the man made her heart jump and she couldn't avoid backing up a step as he came toward her, just because his appeal was so darn scary.

"Won't you sit down?" he said smoothly, gesturing toward two chairs set up at the other end of the room. "I thought you might like to have a drink before dinner."

"Where are the others?" she asked, looking about the room suspiciously.

"There are no others," he told her, giving her a significant half smile. "We're it."

She hesitated, looking at him sideways, perfectly willing to let him understand that she didn't trust him. "I don't know about this," she said archly.

"Sure you do," he replied, taking her hand and bringing it to his lips. "I've invited you down here to seduce you," he said, his eyes ravishing her in a mocking way. "It's perfectly obvious. I do this with all the nannies. Sort of an initiation ceremony, if you like."

She gave him a long-suffering look. He was teasing her again and she wasn't going to fall for it. Still, she did reclaim her hand and turned to look at the room again. Paneled in dark wood and lined with tall bookcases, it sported card and gaming tables, along with a large green felt billiard table and a huge fireplace at one end. The two wing chairs with a small coffee table between them faced the fireplace.

"About that drink," he began.

"I thought you'd given up alcohol," she said, eyebrows raised.

"I have." He gestured toward the coffee table set between the chairs where she could see a ceramic pot and two delicate cups waiting. "I'm having green tea. Good for the digestion. You can join me, or I'll have Janus bring you something else."

She looked at him, not totally convinced of his reformation. He was still laughing at her. She didn't know if that irked her or made her want to laugh, too.

"Green tea would be lovely," she said.

He offered her a seat with a flourish and she gracefully lowered herself into it, then leaned forward and began to serve the tea. He stared at her for a moment, startled. The nanny didn't usually take it upon herself to go ahead and serve the tea without being asked to do so. She was acting as though *she* were the hostess, completely comfortable in the role—as though this was what she normally did. He frowned. Nothing about this woman fell into patterns for him. She was unusual, to say the least. Unusual, and somewhat annoying.

As he sank into the opposite chair, he wondered why she seemed to be able to get under his skin in a way no other woman ever had. He knew very well that he was not the father of that baby she was now so fiercely guarding, and yet he'd spent the entire afternoon racking his brain, trying to remember every contact he'd had, every woman he'd dated, every night he might have had too much to drink to remember what he was doing.

But the last didn't happen very often these days. And even when it had in the past, he never really lost control. Which was the main reason he was pretty confident nothing could happen, no big surprise could fall out of the sky, no young woman who called herself his Sunshine Girl could appear and provide proof that he was the guilty party. Because there was no such girl.

And still, Tianna's reproachful looks made him think twice every time. At any rate, she had played havoc with his emotional equilibrium since the first moment he'd woken to find her standing beside where he slept in the gazebo, like a vision, a manifestation of his dreams. He grimaced. This wasn't like him. It had to stop.

But never mind. He was used to dealing with women. Surely he could handle even this.

He accepted the cup of tea she offered, then raised it in a mock salute. "To love and beauty," he toasted.

Her eyes flashed and she raised her own cup. "To integrity," she countered, making him sputter on his first sip.

"Tianna," he began warningly. "You're much too beautiful to waste your time being a nag."

A nag! Setting down her cup, she sat back and crossed her arms, gazing at him levelly. "I think we had better get something straight. You seem to have quite a reputation as a playboy. But I'm not a plaything. And I'm not here to play around."

She thought she sounded wonderfully confident and that was good. If only she felt as sure as she sounded. But whenever she looked at him, she sensed she was walking on quicksand. Humor simmered in his gaze, but something else was lurking there as well. She wasn't sure what it was, but she knew it was making her very nervous.

"Never say never, Tianna," he advised in his most world-weary tone. "In the long run, everything's negotiable."

"No." Slowly, she shook her head, her eyes clear and bright. "You're wrong. Some things are just too important for that."

He shrugged. She would learn with time and experience.

They chatted about inconsequential things for a

few minutes and then Janus came in carrying the soup course. She smiled a greeting his way. A tall, handsome man in his late forties, Janus had come by the nursery that afternoon once Garth had filled him in on the particulars. He was a gentle-looking man with something of a twinkle in his eyes. He had gone right to the baby when she'd let him in, lifted her up and spoke soothingly to her.

"I can see you've had babies of your own," she'd said, smiling. Her own skills came from helping her sister. She had never realized how much she would come to rely on what she'd learned there.

"Oh no, I've never married," he said. "But I have plenty of nieces and nephews. I know my way around a nursery."

She was reassured to know that he shared her concern for the little one. She could see that he loved children and she'd felt a lot better about putting the investigation in his hands.

"Dinner is served," he said now, bowing graciously.

Prince Garth offered Tianna his arm and they went to the table which had been set up in the middle of the room. The service was informal but still stunning, the sterling silver heavy, the bone china fragile as eggshells, the crystal glittering in the lamplight. Janus ladled out shrimp bisque and went back to the kitchen to prepare the second course.

"I'm impressed with your valet," she said as he left the room.

Garth nodded. "Janus is a multifaceted man. Not only does he keep me from falling off the edge of the earth on occasion, he's also quite the amateur artist. Oils, mostly. He spends most of his free time down at the artists' colony in Sedona." He smiled at her. "If you play your cards right, he'll do your portrait."

"That would be lovely." She thought of the official portrait that hung in her family's library. She was dressed as Diana, goddess of the hunt, for some strange reason. The artist who had done the work liked to see life in terms of Olympian gods. She'd loved it when she was eighteen. Now, it was just plain embarrassing.

And then Garth said something, rather softly, that stopped her in her tracks.

"Janus is the one who rescued me during the revolt and brought me to America," he said, adding simply, "I owe my life to him."

They were both silent for a moment. Tianna was remembering that his parents had been murdered in the revolution. He must have been a young boy when that happened. Suddenly, she felt a wave of sympathy for him. The history of her country was full of tragedies and his was just another one. But something in his eyes told her the tragedy lived in him still.

"Tell me a little about yourself," he said as though to fill the quiet space. "Where have you been living?"

"I was raised in the Seattle area," she said after a brief hesitation. Giving the location might set off a chain of recognition in him. After all, not many Nabotavians lived in the Pacific Northwest.

In fact, she sometimes thought her parents had taken the entire sojourn in America as a welcome respite from the responsibilities and duties of leading a regional state. She and her sister and brother had been brought up in a very nice well-to-do neighborhood in suburban Seattle. But their house had been no grander than anyone else's on the block. No one except very close friends had even known they had royal connections. She'd had a pretty normal childhood. There had been an estate manager and some minimal security, just in case, but for the most part, they hadn't had any more servants than any of their wealthy neighbors.

So admitting to living in the north might sound odd to him, might even make him wonder. But she wasn't going to lie. So if it did, it did.

But he gave no sign of surprise. "So you went to school there?"

"Yes. To a small college just outside the city."

He nodded, buttering a roll. "You have something of the Seattle look."

"Tweedy and damp?" she asked, laughing.

"Not at all. It's that vigorous youth thing, well-educated and interested in the world around you."

She colored slightly. It seemed to be a sincere comment and she appreciated it. "I'd return the compliment and say you have an Arizona look, but I'm not really sure what that would be."

"Sunburnt and wind-whipped," he said, dismissing it. "You said you were a photographer, didn't you? Tell me about that. What got you started?"

She hesitated, but once she got going, there seemed to be a lot she had to say on the subject. He sat back, nodding at Janus as he took the soup plates and set out the salmon, listening to her with only part of his attention, while the rest was engaged in a study of this puzzling female.

He was becoming more and more entranced by her careless, yet luminous beauty. He liked the way her eyes lit up while she was talking about the profession she was learning to love, the way she used her hands to emphasize a point. He liked the way the white collar gave her a virginal look that was undercut by the generous proportions she displayed beneath the dark dress that hugged her curves. And the way the silver clasp that was holding back her hair was falling out, letting strands slide free to curl around her face.

For just a moment he wondered what it would be like if he weren't royal. Would he be dating women like this? There was something very appealing about that thought.

Soon he would be heading back to Nabotavia to take his place among the leadership of his native country. He'd been there during the fight to throw off the rebels the year before, but he'd been incognito, fighting with the underground, helping the effort that was ultimately sweet in its complete success. He'd thought that defeating the thugs who'd killed his parents and stolen his birthright would change everything. But it really hadn't. The hole in his heart was still there. Maybe it just wasn't meant to heal.

"I think we should talk about the baby for a moment," she said suddenly.

He frowned, jolted back from his reverie. "If we must," he murmured.

She nodded resolutely. "Putting Janus in charge of the investigation was a great move."

"So you're happy now?"

She gave him a look very close to outrage. "Certainly not."

He sighed. "And why is that?"

She leaned toward him. "Janus is wonderful. But can't you see that you should be doing the searching yourself? In some way or other, you seem to be responsible for this baby's existence."

His mouth tightened and his fingers began playing with the silverware. "So you want me to do what exactly?"

Taking a deep breath, she said, "I think you should be a little more hands-on in looking for the mother. After all, you probably know her."

"I don't know her."

Her voice rose with the intensity of her passion for this subject. "How do you know that when we don't know who she is?"

His eyes flashed. "You know what? You're the most insubordinate employee this castle has ever had."

"Good. It's about time someone told you the truth, isn't it?"

They glared at one another for a moment, and then Prince Garth's anger faded. "Tianna," he said quietly, "calm down. There's no need to get excited about this. We're not adversaries. I'm not trying to put one over on you in any way." He smiled at her. "I'm not even really trying to seduce you."

"Hah!" she said, her own smile wobbling. "You had me believing you there until that last bit."

He laughed, but she laughed along with him. And she realized he was right. Why was she so on the defensive with him? He was just a man, after all.

Taking a deep breath, she tried to center her emotions. She'd come here to make an ally out of him, not an enemy. She still hoped that he would join her in nullifying this silly betrothal. For now, she'd gotten shanghaied into taking care of the baby, but that was okay. The baby came first. Once she was certain the little sweetheart's future was assured, there would be time to deal with her own life. She would get much further if she took it all on an even keel. After all, he was just a man.

Then she took another look at him and fell back into the reality zone. Who was she kidding? Of course she had to be on guard with him. He was so darn gorgeous, so charming, so desirable. She was like a girl who'd been denied ice cream staring at a large bowl of French vanilla. With hot fudge dripping over it. Steeling herself to resist temptation, she turned back to him.

"You're right," she said. "Truce?"

He held out his hand and she hesitantly put her hand in his. "Truce," he said in a low husky voice that made her want to whimper.

Luckily, Janus arrived with dessert, two small cups of crÈme brûlée, and the tone lightened quickly. By the time they had finished the delicious custard, Garth had launched into an explanation of the preparations for the return to Nabotavia. To her surprise, he seemed quite enthusiastic about it.

"But don't you think the monarchy has had its day?" she said to him at last. "They've become nothing but fodder for the tabloids."

"That may be the way it is in some countries, but Nabotavia is going to be different." He said it with such authority, she had to think he really believed it. "My brother Marco and I have been preparing for this all our lives. We're going to be running that country and we're going to run it right."

She shook her head. "Well, I'm glad *you're* so optimistic about going back and ruling. But as for me…"

"You?"

She bit her tongue. She'd forgotten he didn't know she was just as royal as he was.

He leaned forward, looking at her. "Are you planning to join the return?"

She quickly shook her head. "Not me. I told you, I'm a photographer. I have a job lined up in Chicago."

"Really?" He gazed at her speculatively. "Then why were you here applying for a job as a pastry chef?"

She opened her mouth and then closed it again. Oops. The way things had turned out, it would be best to pretend she had been after the pastry chef job after all. "Uh... I just needed a job to tide me over for a bit, before my position in Chicago starts," she improvised quickly, her heart sinking as she spoke. "So taking care of the baby for a few days will be perfect," she added lamely.

He stared at her, hard. He distinctly remembered her saying she hadn't come for the pastry chef job, but she had never really explained what she *had* come for.

"Who are you, Tianna?" he asked softly, searching her eyes. "Where did you come from?"

"I told you. Seattle."

"What is your last name?" the prince asked, still looking at her curiously.

"Rose," she said, stealing herself again.

"Rose!" He frowned at her in alarm. "Is that short for Roseanova?"

"Roseanova is not my last name." And that wasn't a fib. It was the next to her last name, but not the last one.

"Good. I was suddenly afraid you might have been one of my crazy cousins." He sighed. "A flock of them is descending upon us tomorrow, as a matter of fact. That's why everyone is racing around trying to get ready. We've got about half our normal staff, and Marco isn't even here."

That gave her pause. Any cousins of his might just be cousins of hers. They shared a great-great-grandfather from almost one hundred and fifty years back, and all the royals were tied together in one way or another. It might get a little sticky keeping up this masquerade if someone she knew showed up. But she would worry about that tomorrow.

"Where is your brother?" she asked him.

"He's in Dallas, I believe, looking over some princess he might be marrying."

"Oh." She knew about Marco, knew about the tragic loss of his young wife. "His story is so sad," she said quietly.

"True." Garth nodded. "Marco deserves happiness. I just hope he finds it in Dallas."

He didn't sound convinced that such a thing was possible. It was quite apparent to her that he was a cynic. He probably didn't believe in love. The question was, did she?

"And you have a younger sister, don't you?"

She had met Princess Karina at a luncheon celebrating the younger woman's graduation from college a few months before. Kari was a lovely young woman and she'd enjoyed talking to her. When she'd asked her about Garth, Kari had laughed once she'd mentioned the betrothal.

"Oh you poor thing," she'd said.

"It wasn't my idea," Tianna reminded her. "In fact, if I could think of a way to get out of it, I would."

Kari had laughed again. "You'll probably find a willing accomplice in my brother. I'm sure he will want to put off tying the knot as long as possible."

And that was when the plan was first born. If there was a chance that he wasn't any more eager for an arranged marriage than she was, she knew she had to follow up on it. So she'd come.

She'd met Garth. She'd found him just as appealing as everyone said he was. She was pretty sure he didn't care much about the betrothal on anything other than a convenience level. But would he be willing to give it up? At some point, she was going to have to confront him with that. Something told her that he wasn't going to be easy to deal with, no matter how smooth and charming he might seem right now. He was, after all, the second son of the king. And that certainly meant something in Nabotavian society. It all hinged on just what sort of man Prince Garth really was. But that was exactly what she'd come here to find out, wasn't it?

It was time to get back to the baby. She rose, making her excuses, and started for the door. Prince Garth followed her, reluctant to see her leave so soon. She was a beautiful woman and he was beginning to realize that he wanted her, wanted her badly, with a deep burning pulse such as he hadn't felt in years.

Maybe that's not it at all, he told himself a bit caustically. *Maybe I just need a drink.*

But he knew the truth. He wanted to kiss her. He wanted to undress her slowly and see her beautiful body in the lamplight and stroke and touch her until she cried out with need for him. That was what he wanted. All he had to do was figure out how to get it.

He was playing an old game. It was a great game. He'd played it often in past years. And he usually won. But something was different this time. Somehow the usual game didn't feel right with this one. Maybe he was going to have to step it up, take things to a higher level. Whatever that meant.

"Tianna," he said softly.

She turned in the doorway, looking up at him with her beautiful green eyes rimmed with dark lashes. He touched her cheek and looked at her mouth. Desire was frothing inside him like champagne. One kiss ought to do the trick. Staring at her lips, he began to lower toward them.

"Oh," she said suddenly. "I forgot to tell you. I think I know what the baby's name is."

He drew back, annoyed. "What?" he said, not asking for the name, but asking why she would interrupt this wonderful moment with such mundane information.

She went on, earnestly. "I was looking at the little baby clothes she came in and there seems to be a name embroidered into the edging. Marika. Isn't that cute?" She smiled at him as though she expected him to be as delighted with it as she was. "Marika. An old-fashioned Nabotavian name, isn't it? I love it."

Garth choked. He felt the blood drain from his face.

"Good night," Tianna said cheerfully. Turning, she walked briskly down the corridor toward the nursery and he did nothing to stop her.

Marika. That was his mother's name, a nickname that was only used in the family. Marika. How could a stranger have known?

He turned back into the game room, shaken. Coincidence? It had to be. And yet...

A sense of impending doom slipped over him for a moment, but he shook it off. No. Facts were facts. That baby couldn't possibly be his.

Chapter 4

Tianna had a lot of time to think over her situation during the night. Baby Marika didn't seem to be real clear on the difference between the time to be awake and the time to be asleep. It wasn't that she was fussy. In fact, she didn't appear to have an ill-natured bone in her tiny little body. She was wide-awake, however, gurgling happy baby sounds and playing with her thumb.

Tianna's experience in putting a baby to sleep was limited but her attempts ran the gamut—walking, talking, rocking. She even tried a soft song or two, and was rewarded with big smiles, but no signs of sleep. Finally she gave up with a sigh and just stayed in the creaky old rocker, holding her, waiting for her eyelids to droop. And thinking over this strange day. As the hour grew later and the house grew quieter, the shadows seemed deeper and her thoughts grew more haunted.

Rocking the baby, she looked about the room. It was

lovely with gingham curtains and an antique baby crib, along with the usual chests and baby-changing table. There was a handy sink, a tub for baby baths, and an attached bathroom. A simple adult bed sat along the wall, and that was where she would sleep—once she was allowed to! All in all, it was a comfortable situation.

But what in the world was she doing here? She'd come to discuss breaking her betrothal to Prince Garth, and ended up taking care of what was probably his illegitimate baby. What an unbelievable twist to her plans.

And yet, she knew she didn't have to stay. She didn't have to do this at all. All she had to do was announce who she was and they wouldn't allow her to act the nanny any longer. Which was exactly why she was staying quiet. There was something about this baby that tore at her heart. One look and she'd been hooked on the child.

She knew it was partly because Marika was a beautiful and good-natured baby. But surely there was more to it than that. Misty, faded memories of her own childhood had something to do with it. Seeing this baby left abandoned to the unknown called up barely remembered recollections of dark days, of loss and loneliness and reaching out for comfort, only to find a stranger holding her hand. Shuddering, she pushed the thoughts away and looked down into Marika's sweet face. Resolution steeled within her heart. This baby would not be frightened the way she had been if she had anything to do with it.

"And that, my *petit chou,* was how I became a nanny to the most beautiful baby in the world," she whispered softly as Marika cooed. Her long silky lashes were fluttering. Tianna held her breath. Yes! The eyes were closing. Finally, they were going to get some sleep.

The first rays of the sun appeared all too soon, and Marika met them with a loud crowing sound that signaled a new day was beginning. Tianna groaned as she tried to work up the same enthusiasm. Still groggy from lack of sleep, she rose and washed her face before cleaning and changing the tyke. Looking in the "nanny closet," she chose a tan rollneck cotton sweater and brown linen slacks. They fit just a bit larger than she would have liked, but all in all, she was lucky she had such a supply. Changing done, she wrapped Marika in a fresh blanket and carried her along on a trip to the kitchen.

She'd explored the floor where the nursery was the night before. The castle was beautiful, full of hardwood floors with Persian carpeting, velvet drapes and high-ceilinged rooms. Somehow the builders had managed to make it look as though it had been there for centuries.

Delicious smells wafted around her before she opened the double doors to find the large kitchen buzzing with activity, even though it was barely dawn. Cook looked up and saw her right away, gesturing for her to come on in.

"Let's see her, then," she cried, holding out her flour-dusted arms. "How is the little angel this morning?"

Tianna handed her over and smiled as the other kitchen workers gathered around, oohing and aahing.

"She doesn't sleep much," she said as she turned to find the bottles and formula she knew Milla had stockpiled for her. "In fact, she was quite the night owl last night."

"Oh, she'll settle down once she's used to us," Cook said comfortably, then frowned and drew away when Milla offered to hold the baby. "You all get back to work now. We've got visitors coming this afternoon and we're way behind. I'll just hold on to this little darling while Tianna gets her breakfast ready. Shoo now, get on with you."

Her scolding didn't have much effect. Milla and the new pastry chef lingered along with Bridget, who'd stopped by for her morning coffee. They laughed softly over the baby, touching her little fingers, kissing the top of her downy head. It warmed Tianna to see them react that way to her. *Almost as though she were really my own,* she thought, then winced. That was the first time she'd let herself give form to a thought like that and she knew she would have to nip it in the bud. Marika was not hers and never would be. She had to guard against letting the child become too important to her.

"Do you know her name?" Cook asked, laughing as the baby grabbed for her finger.

"I believe it's Marika."

"Marika. That's a real old-fashioned Nabotavian name, isn't it? You don't hear it much these days." She smiled down at her armful. "Oh, I wish we could keep this one. She's a peach."

Tianna finished filling the bottle with warmed formula and took the baby from the cook, sitting down in a chair at the table to feed her. The servants bustled around her and she sat enjoying the smells and the small talk. But most of all, she enjoyed the whole experience of holding and feeding the baby. There was something about it that filled her with a delightful sense of happiness, and she really wasn't sure why.

As she finished up, she noticed that Janus had entered

the kitchen and was preparing a tray. "Good morning," she said to him with a smile. "I certainly hope you have some luck today."

"Luck?" He looked at her blankly for a moment. "Oh, you mean in finding the child's mother? Oh, yes. Well, I plan to do a thorough investigation as soon as I can get away."

He stopped by, smiling down at Marika and touching her sweet cheek.

"Yes indeed," he said rather absently. "Yes indeed."

Tianna liked the way he interacted with the baby. Something about the man gave her a feeling of security. He would find the mother, and probably very soon. He turned to go and she looked at Cook. Her stomach was definitely complaining it was being ignored.

"In what room is breakfast served?" she asked, looking forward to a proper meal.

Cook looked at her strangely. "Well, the nanny usually eats her breakfast here, with the staff, if she doesn't have it in the nursery," she said.

"Oh." Mentally, she kicked herself. She'd forgotten. She wasn't a princess here. She licked her lower lip, wondering how to repair the damage from her mistake.

But Janus saved her. He was just leaving himself, but he turned back and said, "I meant to tell you, Miss, His Highness is breakfasting in the morning room right now. He asked me to request that you join him as soon as you are free."

"Ah." She rose, trying to avoid meeting Cook's gaze. "I'll go to him right away," she said, then glanced at the woman and saw the disapproval she had known would be there. Cook seemed on the verge of stepping forward and giving her a piece of advice, but Tianna turned away. Advice was something she didn't need right now.

"Would you like me to hold the baby while you have your breakfast?" Milla offered.

"Oh no," Tianna said breezily as she started for the door. "I can have the prince hold her for me."

She had the impression of mouths gaping all around, but she didn't stay to see it. Janus led her to the morning room. He, at least, was smiling his approval.

Garth looked up and rose as she entered, and she favored him with a radiant smile in return. The room was lovely, shaped like an octagon and glassed in from floor to ceiling on four of those sides. The morning light flooded in, turning everything golden, including the prince's hair.

"Good morning," she said brightly.

He nodded, almost bowing. "Good morning to you," he said softly, and when she looked into his eyes, she saw a look that made her shiver. It seemed he liked what he saw. At least, until his gaze fell on the baby in her arms.

"Why don't you send her up to the nursery with Bridget?" he suggested. "You can't eat your breakfast with a baby on your shoulder."

"You're right," she said, noting that he had finished eating himself, and was relaxing with a cup of coffee. "But I have a better idea. I think you should hold her."

"Me?"

"You."

With no further ado, she plopped the baby in his arms and turned toward the sideboard to begin filling a plate with food. She watched him out of the corner of her eye. He stood thunderstruck for a moment, then appealed to his valet.

"Janus," he said. "You'd better take this thing quickly...."

"Sorry, sir," Janus said with a sly smile. "I'm just on my way to catch Homer before he takes the car in for repairs. You said you wanted to make sure he remembered to have that whistling sound checked."

"Oh. Of course." Garth stood where he was as Janus, his last hope, left the room. He held the baby as though it had something contagious. "Tianna, this is ridiculous," he said.

After looking things over and deciding he wasn't going to drop Marika, Tianna ignored him, humming a cheerful tune as she collected strips of bacon, mounds of scrambled egg, and pieces of buttered toast and arranged them neatly on her plate. Turning back to the table, she gave him a look of pure exasperation. "Oh, do sit down. She won't break."

He shot her a look that was meant to inflict pain, but he did as she suggested, sitting gingerly on the edge of his chair, trying to hold the baby without having her touch any part of him except his arms. Marika cooed and laughed into his face.

Tianna sat down and picked up her fork, watching him with growing amusement as he glowered down at the child. "What can you possibly have against a sweet little innocent baby?" she asked.

He glared at her, too. "Oh, I don't know. Let me count the ways. They cry, they smell, they make demands, they want to be carried around..."

"They smile, they laugh, they look so adorable..."

"They spit up milk."

"Well, sometimes, but..."

"No, I mean right now. Take her!" His voice held a note of horror.

"Oh!" Tianna jumped up, but instead of taking Marika herself, she threw a cloth diaper onto Garth's shoulder and propped the baby up against it in burping position. "There you go. Burp her."

"Burp her?" He said the word as though it were in a foreign tongue.

"Pat her back softly. Here. Like this."

She guided his hand. For just a moment, their gazes met, and suddenly it seemed that what they were doing together was awfully intimate. Tianna drew away and sat down. Looking rebellious, Garth went on patting Marika, awkwardly at first, but then more and more gracefully. Slowly, imperceptibly, he began to get his bearings.

Tianna ate her scrambled eggs, but her mind wasn't on food. She watched as Garth tried hard to do what the baby needed. He wasn't complaining any longer. He looked to be getting into it, though he was still frowning fiercely and making sure she knew this wasn't his idea of a good time. Marika's head was bobbing up and she was making enough noise to announce the fact that she didn't feel very comfortable. Another moment, and she might actually get fussy.

And then something magic happened. For just a moment, Prince Garth forgot himself, and he murmured a soft endearment against little Marika's downy head.

Tianna held her breath, staring down at her plate. What was that he'd said? Had she heard him whisper, "That's okay, sweetie?" She very carefully didn't look at him and kept the smile that threatened to shine from her face at bay. There! She heard it again. Putting her napkin to her lips, she allowed the smile to break through.

"What's so funny?" he asked, growling.

"Who's laughing?" she asked innocently.

He glared at her, but a huge burp burst from the tiny baby mouth, the sound echoing around the room, and suddenly they were all three laughing.

Bridget appeared in the doorway. "Cook told me to ask if you needed any help with the baby," she said, her eyes big as saucers at the sight of Garth holding the baby against his shoulder.

"Thank you, Bridget," Tianna said, taking charge as though it were the most natural thing in the world. "I think His Highness has done enough bonding with Marika for one morning. I would appreciate it if you would take her up to the nursery and sit with her until I come up. I have a few things to talk over with His Highness. I won't be long."

"Yes, Miss." Bridget did as she'd been told and Garth relaxed for the first time since Tianna had thrust the child in his arms.

That had been quite an adventure. No one had ever dumped a baby in his arms before. Actually, it hadn't turned out to be as monstrous as he'd thought it would. The sense of a small life in his hands had been strange, but rather appealing. Even so, he hoped he wouldn't have to repeat the experience and he was very glad Bridget had come to save the day.

"Now, back to business," Tianna was saying, clearing her plate to the side and leaning forward on her elbows, her green eyes bright with anticipation. "About finding Marika's mother."

Looking at her, he wondered how she could be so enchanting and so annoying at the same time. "Janus is handling that," he reminded her.

"I know. But I thought maybe we could go into town

and ask around at some of the places where Nabotavians hang out...."

"Tianna." He took her warm, slender hand in his and
held it. He could see how important this was to her. It
shone from her face, resonated in her voice. He could
almost feel it in the pulse at her wrist. "Why do you
care so much about this baby?" he asked, searching her
eyes for the answer.

She blinked, took in a ragged breath and pulled her
hand from his, reaching for her glass of orange juice
to mask the move. "The question really is, why do you
care so little?" she countered, taking a sip.

That was an easy one.

"Because that baby isn't mine."

He'd been thrown for a few minutes the night before
when he'd heard the baby's name. It still seemed an odd
coincidence. But Marika had once been a common and
endearing name in Nabotavia. It wasn't all that unusual.
Just an accident. That was all.

"How can you be so sure?" she asked him.

"Because I know. What more can I say?"

She shook her head. His gaze followed the movement
of her silky hair, the way it brushed against her slim
neck, the way one deep wave curled around her chin
line, and he felt a deep response that made him wince.
He couldn't believe he was reacting to something so
ordinary. But then, it wasn't really the hair, was it? It
was the totality of the woman. He wanted her. Frowning hard, he suppressed the thought. This was no time
to get bogged down in plain old garden-variety lust. He
could see that she was making an effort to get through
to him, that she was about to ask something she knew
wasn't going to be well received. So he waited, giving
her a chance.

She twisted her hands together and stared down at her entwined fingers. "Are you trying to tell me it would be impossible?" she asked hesitantly.

He knew what she was getting at, but he didn't make it any easier for her. "I would say so, yes."

Her lashes fluttered. "Are you…unable to have children?"

She made herself look him in the eye as she asked it, and he almost laughed at how brave she was being. There was no need for her uneasiness. He wasn't offended by the query. Still, he couldn't help but tease her a little.

"Tianna, I'm surprised at you. That's a rather personal question."

The flush that flooded her cheeks only made her more beautiful. "The entire topic is personal," she said stoutly, nonetheless. "Very personal. And I only ask because…"

"I know, I know. Your whole concern is for the good of the child."

She took a deep breath and looked relieved. "Yes. And you didn't answer the question."

He looked at her and laughed. "Come on," he said, rising and putting out his hand to take hers. "Let's go out on the terrace. I want to have a cigarette."

"You shouldn't smoke," she said automatically, but she rose and let him take her hand, leading her out through the French doors onto the wide terrace that overlooked the rolling lawns which swept out from the castle. Down below was a series of ponds connected with small waterfalls. They stood together at the railing, looking down at the grounds. The beauty of the stark horizon peaks, so different from the lush forest-covered mountains of her Washington State home, was beginning to grow on her. The sky seemed so big. And the rain the day before had left everything feeling so clean. For a few minutes, she took it all in, breathing the fresh air, letting her gaze travel over the landscape— and wishing she had brought along a camera or two. And Garth stood silently beside her, a presence she couldn't ignore. The more she avoided looking at him, the more he seemed to loom in her awareness, touching all her senses. Maybe it would be better to face him. She turned with dogged determination.

"You still haven't answered my question," she said.

He chuckled. "Don't worry about my ability to carry on the name, Tianna," he said. "As far as I know, there are no problems along those lines." He turned, leaning on the railing, looking at her in a way that made her think of candlelight and the scent of gardenias. "There is no way I can prove it to you, but I know I didn't father that baby."

She started to say something, then cut it back and bit her lip. He could see that she was searching for some way to reach him. How was he going to convince her that it was no use?

She avoided his gaze again, looking out toward the mountains. "Maybe you just don't remember," she suggested. "Maybe you were drinking and…"

"I'm not that much of a drinker, Tianna." He said it smoothly, but she could detect the underlying annoyance that was growing. "In fact, the other night was the first time in a long time…." He hesitated, hating the way it sounded like making excuses. "Believe what you want to believe," he said shortly. "She's not my baby. And I don't plan to have a child outside of wedlock. It doesn't do anybody any good, from what I've seen."

"And you've never been married," she said, stating the obvious as though she had to get it nailed down.

"You know I've never been married." He shoved his hands into his pockets and gazed at her speculatively. "Of course, I *am* betrothed."

"Betrothed?" She turned slowly to face him, her eyes wary, her cheeks blushing more than ever.

He frowned, not sure why he'd brought it up. It wasn't something he thought about much. Somehow it had popped into his head and he'd expressed it out loud.

"A technicality, really," he added quickly. "A hangover from the old days. I shouldn't have mentioned it."

She was looking determined again. He'd never known a woman who was so bad at hiding her feelings. And for some strange reason, he found that absolutely charming, even though her feelings so often seemed to run against him.

"No, I'm glad you did," she said, looking at him obliquely. "I find this quite interesting." She turned so that she could see directly into his eyes. "Who's the lucky girl?"

"A minor princess." He shrugged it off as though it were hardly worth mentioning. "From West Nabotavia. I doubt you've heard of her."

"A minor princess." Tianna had to turn away so that he wouldn't see the fire in her eyes. *Minor, eh?* "Fascinating. Do you have a wedding planned?"

"Uh…no, not really." He wished he'd never brought it up. "It's sort of just looming in my future somewhere. I think she's too young or something." He reached into his pocket for his cigarettes. He didn't know why an uneasy feeling was beginning to nag at him. There was something about this subject that felt strangely awkward at the moment.

"So you're in no hurry to marry." She turned, her back and elbows on the railing, and looked at him almost challengingly.

"Are you kidding?" His laugh was utterly genuine. "Do I look like marriage material to you?"

She put her head to the side and pretended to look him over. "Oh, I don't know. A good wife might be able to make a man out of you."

One dark eyebrow rose. This had to be the first time in many years anyone had implied he lacked manhood.

She waited a beat before amplifying, enjoying his surprised response. "A *mature* man," she said at last. "A man who is ready to take on life instead of hiding from it."

"Hiding from it?" he said, and now he was finally offended. "Listen Tianna Rose, I've seen more of life than you'll ever dream of."

"Really?" She sniffed. "Too bad you don't seem to have learned much from all your experience." Her eyes flashed. "For instance, don't you know that those things will kill you?" She nodded at the pack of cigarettes he held in his hand.

He looked at them, then back at her with a cynical smile. "No, they won't. I'm quitting. This is my last pack."

"Hmm." She'd heard that one before. Her father had smoked for years. The whole family had celebrated once he'd quit for good.

"*I'm* from West Nabotavia, you know," she said, not sure why she was pushing it. She really didn't want him to realize who she was. Not yet. But at the same time, the fact that he thought so lightly of her...or of the "minor" princess he was betrothed to...drove her crazy.

"Ah, a Westie," he said, using the vaguely patronizing word regular Nabotavians often used for her sort.

"No, not a Westie," she said icily. "A White Rose Nabotavian."

"Yes." His smile was so darn dazzling. "If they all look like you, maybe she won't be so bad."

She choked and looked away. Talk about a double-edged compliment. It was too bad she couldn't show him just how angry this talk was making her. "I guess you aren't expecting much?"

"No, from what I hear, she's a real homebody. They say she's quiet, though forthright with her opinions, but would rather read than go to parties." He gave her a comical look as he tore open the package in his hand. "Now does that sound like any sort of match for me?"

Oh, the conceit of the man! She itched to wring his neck. "So you've asked around about her, then?" she said carefully, seething inside.

Setting the pack of cigarettes on the polished wood railing, he began to search his pockets for a light. "Actually, Marco was trying to get me to go visit her. He told me she is supposed to be 'very pretty.' Now, when Marco says 'very pretty' in that tone of voice, it's time to head for the hills. I have no doubt she's plain as toast. And just as dull."

Oh! She wanted to throw something at him. The urge was impossibly strong. She looked around for something, anything, to get her hands on, and her gaze fell on the pack of cigarettes sitting on the railing while he searched his pockets for his lighter. Slowly, deliberately, she reached out and flicked the pack with her forefinger. It shot through the air and went sailing down into the pond below. She leaned over the railing, staring after it, feeling triumphant.

"Tianna," he said, looking at her strangely.

"Oops," she responded, still watching the pack float among the lily pads. "It was an accident. I'm so sorry."

"No, you're not." He stared at her, fascinated. "You did that on purpose."

Looking up, she met his eyes. She lifted her chin and gazed at him defiantly. "I did not."

"Yes, you did," he said with a half laugh. "You very carefully knocked my cigarettes down into the water. You little devil!"

She began to back away, her eyes very large. "I said I was sorry."

"But you're not sorry at all." For every step she took backward, he took one toward her, his eyes filled with amusement and resolve. "And I'm going to have to exact some kind of retribution. Just for my own self-respect, you understand."

Beginning to worry about just what he might have in mind, she shot him a blazing look and turned on her heel. "I'm going in," she said breezily. "I'll see you later."

But she hardly got two steps before he'd cornered her against the wall.

"You're not going anywhere until we settle this," he told her, his eyes sparkling with the fun of the chase. "Now I've got you right where I want you." With both hands flat on the stone wall, he had her effectively trapped and he leaned closer. "What should I do to get my revenge?" he asked musingly.

"Your Highness, let me go this instant," she ordered, with somewhat more spirit than an employee would normally use toward her employer.

"Oh no. I can't do that."

"Yes, you can. I'm...I'm sorry about the cigarettes. I'll buy you another pack."

"There are some things," he said in a very low and provocative voice, "more addictive than smoking."

"Are there?" she said breathlessly, then shook herself. "I mean, let me go!"

He leaned closer, so close that she could smell his crisp, clean scent, so close that she thought she could feel the heat rising from the open neck of his cotton shirt. "Say 'uncle,'" he said softly, his gaze caressing her face in a way that was almost tactile.

"Uncle?"

He shrugged lightly, his breath tickling the tender skin below her ear. "It's traditional. You've got to say it to be set free."

Well, then... "Uncle! Uncle!"

"Hmm." Leaning even closer, he didn't show any signs of relenting. He dropped a small kiss on the cord of her neck, giving her a delicious shiver, then drew back enough to see her face. "No, try 'strawberries.'"

"What for?"

He smiled. "To put your lips in a kissable position."

"What?" she cried, outraged.

"That'll do."

She put her hands up to stop him and found her fingers curling against his muscular chest. She raised her chin to show defiance, but quickly realized it seemed more like acquiescence. And then his warm mouth was meeting hers and her brain went into a snow pattern.

She hadn't meant to let this happen, but once it did, she found herself powerless to stop it. And then she didn't want to stop it. She'd been kissed before, and she'd definitely liked it. But this was something else again. Instead of awkward groping and noses getting in the way, this felt as though the two of them had been specially made to go together. Their bodies seemed to fit, their arms were in exactly the right place, and their lips touched, and then clung together, fused together, causing their mouths to melt together, all smooth, liquid heat and sweet, intoxicating taste, with just a touch of exotic spice to add excitement.

She loved this. She wanted more, and she reached hungrily for all she could get, yearning toward him. His arms tightened around her, held her so close, she could barely breathe. But she didn't care. She was living in the moment, and all she needed in her lungs, in her life, in her heart, was this wonderful strong man.

Garth wasn't quite as blind to all sensible intelligence as she was, but it was darn close. It had been a long time since he'd lost his head over a woman. In fact, he would have had a hard time thinking of an instance where it might have happened before. In all his romantic adventures, there always seemed to be a part of him that stood aloof, watching it all with a cynical air, waiting for the pretending to be over, waiting for the masks to come off and the real human beneath the veneer to emerge and ruin everything. He'd never really been in love. He didn't think much of the concept. In his mind, love was an excuse people made for doing something foolish. Love meant losing control. And he always had to keep control.

Still, something about this warm and wonderful woman was making his head spin. She tasted so good, and her body seemed to be made for his. This simple kiss was giving him more gratification and satisfaction than many a full half hour of sexual interaction ever had in the past. For just a moment, he lost himself in the magic of her copper-colored hair, the smell of her buttery skin, the feel of her full breasts against him, the provocative way her hips seemed to invite him to linger, the taste of her hot, willing mouth. It wasn't until a phrase drifted into his mind that he regained control of his senses.

Do you realize you are kissing the nanny?

He reacted almost as though someone had spoken it out loud, his head jerking back, his body pushing away from hers. And he stared at her.

She stared right back. "Wow," she said raggedly, her heart beating wildly, her breath coming in shaky gulps. "We'd better not do that again."

He stared at her a moment longer, and then he began to laugh. She ducked around him and made her escape. When she reached the French doors, she looked back. He was still laughing. She turned and made her way back to the nursery, her heart pounding.

She didn't know if she was insulted or pleased. Her hands were still shaking. That kiss had really thrown her for a loop. What exactly was going on here? Stopping outside the door to the nursery, she took a deep breath and steadied herself. She had to keep her focus. Baby Marika was what mattered. Kisses on the terrace could only cloud the picture. If she didn't watch out, she might find herself falling for the very man she'd come here to get rid of!

Chapter 5

"Don't you think it would be a good idea to get the police involved? At least they might be able to canvas the neighborhood and ask for any suspicious sightings."

Tianna watched as Janus picked up Marika and held her above his head, murmuring nonsense noises at her. The baby gurgled and wiggled with happiness. It was wonderful to see this man with this baby. But it did give her a pang to think the man holding her should probably have been Garth.

"No police," Janus said in a tone that brooked no argument as he swung the baby down again and held her in his arms. He'd just come back from a trip into Flagstaff but had not been lucky in finding out anything much. He had collected a few contacts he planned to call, though, organizations and individuals who he thought might be able to help. Tianna wasn't exactly thrilled with how slowly this seemed to be going.

"What do you have against the police?" she asked, frowning.

"No police," he repeated, putting Marika back down in her bed. "We don't deal with the police here. Leave it at that."

She wanted to argue with him, but held her tongue for now.

"Another thing," she said. "I'd like to set her up with a doctor's appointment. She seems to be fine, but I do think a basic checkup is in order."

He nodded. "I will call the pediatrician Marco uses for his children. I'll take care of that right away."

She sighed. Another item marked off her list. But she still had a feeling she was leaving something out. She wished she had more experience.

"I'm going to give her the first full-fledged bath she's had since she came," she told him, nodding at the little baby tub she'd set up on the counter. "And I'm a little nervous about it."

He smiled. "You'll do fine. Just don't leave her alone for even one second."

"Oh no, of course not."

He seemed to know so much about babies. It made her smile. He was reassuring. And she supposed he was doing everything he could to locate Marika's mother. She wanted to jump in and help, but he probably knew best. She would leave it to him for the time being.

Still, time was running out. She couldn't stay here forever, pretending to be a nanny. She'd called her sister, Janni, who knew all about her trip, and told her things had changed and that she wouldn't be back home for a few more days than she'd planned.

"You'll cover for me with the parentals, won't you?"

"Of course. You covered for me often enough in the old days."

"True." Tianna answered ruefully, knowing it might not have been the best thing she ever did for her sister.

"But have you broken the engagement yet?" Janni had asked her.

"No, not yet. I have to get this baby taken care of first." She'd sighed. "Once Prince Garth knows why I'm really here, he'll want to get rid of me as quickly as possible. And I won't be able to do a thing for the baby."

"So tell me, what's he like?"

Tianna opened her mouth but she couldn't seem to get out a statement. "Uh…"

"I heard he's very handsome. True or not?"

"Oh, uh…yes, that's certainly true."

There was a pause, then Janni gave a little cry.

"Ohmigod. You're falling for him, aren't you?"

"No!"

"You are! Oh, this is too rich!"

"I am not. I'm getting out of this betrothal if it kills me."

"Sure, but just not quite yet," Janni noted with a sisterly laugh.

Tianna wasn't sure why sisters who could be so helpful and loving could also be so darn irritating, but it really was true. She told her sister goodbye rather icily and went back to watching Marika. About an hour later, Janus had arrived to give her his disappointing progress report. And here they were.

"Janus, what will happen if we can't find the mother?"

Janus looked almost as worried about that prospect as she did herself. "It will have to be the Nabotavian orphanage I suppose," he said. "I don't know of any alternative."

No, she thought, looking down at the antique crib. A chill skittered down her spine. *No. Anything but that.*

"Janus, tell me the truth. Do you think she's the prince's child?"

He looked shocked and she realized he might not know all the details that would make her say such a thing. But there was no time to linger over protocol.

"I know you think that an impertinent question," she said quickly. "But I am really very attached to this baby and I'm trying to do what's best for her. There has been an allegation that Prince Garth is her father, and I'm only asking if you think that might be possible."

Janus looked uncomfortable. He cleared his throat and stood back, folding his arms across his chest.

"I don't know, Miss," he said at last. "But I do want to say this. Prince Garth plays the part of the libertine, but it is mostly just that—an act. There was a time, a few years ago, when he got into the wild life, the international jet set scene, a little too heavily. But these days, you'll rarely find him drinking anything more than a simple glass of wine with dinner. And as for the women…" He shrugged in a very continental manner. "Those have been few and far between as well, for the last three years at least." He looked at her earnestly. "I've known him all his life and this I can say without hesitation. He's a very decent man. I know that doesn't answer your question, but it is the best I can do."

Tianna bit her lip and sighed. "Thank you, Janus. You've answered my question quite nicely."

And he had, really. If Prince Garth insisted he wasn't the father, maybe it was time to stop accusing him. Because her instincts were telling her Janus was right.

The prince was a good man, despite all that others might think. If he thought he was responsible for this child's existence, she was beginning to believe he would assume the burden as a matter of course, regardless of how he felt about the issue.

She frowned, wondering if these thoughts she was having were tainted by his having kissed her. Was she giving him all this credit because he deserved it— or because she was, as Janni had screeched at her, "falling for him." Who knew?

Prince Garth rapped on the nursery door. He didn't know why he was here. He had better places to be, more important things to do. He'd spent the past few hours completely unable to concentrate on his work and he had a lot of correspondence that needed answering, phone calls to return. In other words, he had work to do. And yet, here he was.

The door opened and he was surprised to find his valet visiting. He glanced from one face to the other. Looking into Tianna's emerald eyes, he caught a flash of wordless communication. They both were remembering what had happened on the terrace. Something had changed between them and they both knew it. Still, she was looking at him expectantly, wondering why he was here.

And why not? He was wondering, too. Why the hell *was* he here? He ran a hand distractedly through his hair and frowned.

"I...uh...thought I'd come see how the baby is," he said, knowing that sounded transparently feeble. But it elicited such a look of shining happiness from Tianna, he immediately felt better about it. In fact, Janus looked pretty pleased, too.

But at the same time, the valet was beating a hasty retreat.

"If you have no need of me, Your Highness, I am anxious to make a few phone calls before it gets too late." He gestured toward where Marika lay. "They have to do with the parentage of the child."

"Of course. Do what you must."

Janus hesitated. "Miss Rose, you might see if the prince will help you with the baby's bath, if you are still feeling nervous about it."

"Good idea," she murmured.

Janus gave his employer a significant look and left the room.

The prince nodded to him, but his attention was filled with his sense of Tianna's presence. Meeting her gaze again, he caught a flash of apprehension. Yes, they were going to be alone together once more. He felt the same quiver of excitement that he could see in her. This was dangerous stuff and he wasn't sure why he was tempting fate.

She turned to the baby, bending over the crib, in an obvious move to avoid looking at him. "Look, Marika," she said softly. "Look who's come to see you."

He bent over the crib, too, as it seemed to be expected. "Hi," he said. The baby turned her sleepy blue eyes toward him and stared. "Hi, Marika."

Marika. That name. Suddenly he was transported back over twenty years, and his mother was the Marika he was seeing, not this baby.

"Marika," his father was saying, reaching for his beautiful wife. "Darling one, I promise we will all be safe. Trust me."

His mother's arms wrapped around him and held him close, even as his father pulled them both closer into his protective embrace. He could smell the rose scent his mother wore, feel her kiss on his cheek. They would all be safe. His father had promised.

But his father couldn't keep that promise. Within days, both his parents were dead. The old, familiar sense of loss choked him, but anger rose quickly to take its place, burning in his chest. Reflexively, his hands clenched into fists.

"What's the matter?" Tianna asked.

He looked at her, startled back to the here and now. "Nothing," he said, shaking his head.

"There was something," she insisted, putting her hand on his arm. "Are you in pain? Is something wrong?"

Surprised, he looked deep into the misty depths of her eyes. He saw real concern there. This wasn't merely a social nicety. She cared. That touched a chord in his soul, resonating inside him and for just a moment, he had a lump in his throat.

And then he wanted to kiss her again. It was getting so that he couldn't look at her without wanting to touch her. He made a move toward her, and almost imperceptibly, she shook her head, her eyes huge.

He stopped. She was right, of course. It would be skating a bit close to the edge to risk holding her in his arms with a bed so close by. He really ought to get out of here and back to his work.

She watched his face, wondering what he was thinking. Marika babbled something babylike and he turned to look down at her. Almost against his will, she saw a smile begin to curl his wide mouth, and he put his hand into range, forefinger extended. Marika gurgled and reached for it, her tiny fingers trying to grab his finger, her little perfect mouth open with her effort.

He laughed and Tianna came up next to him, looking down as well, watching the prince play with the baby. Just the day before he'd refused to even think of holding her, so some progress was being made. That gave her the nerve to ask him the same question she'd asked Janus.

"Prince Garth, tell me this. If we can't find the mother and the final determination is that you had nothing to do with this baby, what will become of her?"

"She'll go to the Nabotavian orphanage, of course," he said without hesitation. "That's what it's there for."

She sighed. They'd both said the same thing. That made it just about the final word, and it worried her. For just a moment, she had wild thoughts of trying to adopt Marika herself. But she knew that wouldn't work. She was going to Chicago to start a career in photography. She couldn't take a baby along. It wouldn't be fair to the baby.

Maybe her sister…? But no. Janni had her hands full with her own baby as it was, and raising her child at home with their parents was no picnic. Her mother and father were wonderful and loving in many ways, but they did disapprove of things Janni had done and they weren't afraid to let it show on occasion.

"After her bath, I'm going to put her in a play suit and take her outside for a ride around in the stroller," she told him. "Would you like to come with us?"

"I'm sorely tempted," he admitted. "But my cousins should be arriving very soon. I've got some work I must get done before they get here."

"Oh. Of course." She'd forgotten about the cousins, though she'd heard the upstairs maids rushing about freshening rooms all day. She was going to have to be careful once they got here. "How many are coming?"

He shrugged. "They can't seem to go anywhere without bringing all their friends along, so it's liable to be a large group. They are only staying the night. They're off in the morning to Gallup, New Mexico to see the Native American dances and buy some turquoise."

"Good," she said. "I guess I'd better get our little outdoor excursion underway so that we can get back inside and out of sight before they arrive."

He started to ask her why she felt she had to be out of sight, but Marika, feeling neglected, let out a piercing squeal that had them both laughing at her, and he let it go. Tianna began filling the baby tub for Marika's bath, while the prince found himself playing peekaboo—and only feeling slightly ridiculous.

"One thing's for sure," he said to Tianna. "Whoever wandered in and left Marika in the yard must have been heartbroken to do it. This is one adorable baby."

Tianna nodded, pleased he could finally admit it. "Speaking of wandering in," she said. "Have you done anything about the security on this property?"

He turned to look at her. "Pushy, aren't you?" he noted. "Don't worry about it. We've got it under control."

She bit her tongue and held back the sharp retort she had ready for that statement. "Have you ever had any sort of real problem with people breaking in?" she asked instead.

"Nothing serious. Not here at any rate." He helped her move the tub full of warm water onto the counter where she would be using it.

"My sister Kari, who lives with our aunt and uncle in Beverly Hills, has to be protected at all times. There have been a few attempts to kidnap her. But no one has tried to kidnap me or my brother as yet. They wouldn't dare. They know they would never get away with it."

Tianna stopped and looked at him, suddenly chilled. After all, the history of his family was rife with tragedy. "Kidnapping might not be the only way to get to you. What if they only want to…to kill you?"

"True. That's a possibility. But no such attempt has been made, so…" He shrugged.

"That doesn't mean it might not happen."

She thought about what her father had told her about the background of the rebellion in Nabotavia. Her own branch of the family was never under threat. They didn't have much real power. So they had been able to move into a nice neighborhood in the Seattle area and live like anyone else, keeping a low profile and quietly going on about their lives. But the Roseanovas were different. They were the ones who'd had all the power, and therefore all the danger. Suddenly she was alarmed that Garth wasn't taking better precautions.

"I don't care about you, personally," she said quickly to make sure he didn't get the wrong idea. "I care about Nabotavia, especially in this critical time."

And that was true, she realized suddenly, and it surprised her. How strange. She hadn't ever thought so much about being Nabotavian as she had since she'd arrived in this place. Knowing the prince was giving her a whole new perspective on her background.

"Of course," he said, but amusement was shining in his eyes.

She couldn't help but smile back at him. "Hand me the washrags, please," she said to change the subject.

He turned toward where she'd pointed and located the items she'd asked for, but something caught his eye before he'd completed the move toward them. Reaching around the changing table, he pulled a crumpled piece of cloth out of a pile of laundry and frowned at it.

"Tianna," he said carefully. "Where did this come from?"

"What? Oh, that cloth? It was with the baby. It was inside the baby's blanket, sort of as a liner. Why?"

He spread it out, flattening it with his hands. "Look," he said, drawing her attention to the pattern woven into the damask cloth. "It's the family crest. The Red Rose crest." He looked at her strangely. "We used to have this sort of thing when I was a child. No one was allowed to use this except the royal family in those days."

She met his gaze. "How strange," she murmured, not sure what he was thinking.

He nodded. "Too strange." His voice was almost angry now. "Dammit. I wish Marika's mother would show up. I'm getting tired of all the mystery surrounding this baby."

Tianna found it rather reassuring that he was beginning to let the situation touch him a little more deeply. She wanted to talk to him about his reactions, but his cell phone rang.

"Can you handle the bath by yourself?" he asked, grimacing. "I've got a long distance call from Nabotavia. I'm going to have to go down to the study to take it."

"Go ahead," she told him. "We'll be fine."

He looked at her and for one fleeting moment, she thought he might lean forward and drop a kiss on her lips before he left. But the moment passed and he only gave her a smile before he went out the door.

She sighed. Finding the cloth seemed to bother him a lot and Tianna wasn't sure why. Had it shaken his faith in his own position?

But she didn't have a lot of time to think about that. The bath loomed, a little scary, but soon underway, and going well. Marika splashed in the water, enjoying it just as she seemed to enjoy everything in life. And once Tianna had pulled all her clothes off, she discovered something she hadn't noticed before. Just over her heart, on her chubby little baby chest, there was a wine-red birthmark about an inch and a half long. And for the life of her, Tianna couldn't shake the opinion that it looked very much like a rosebud just beginning to open.

"How very appropriate," she told the wet and wiggly baby. "You see, Marika? You were made for this family."

The cousins arrived sooner than expected and caught Tianna as she was coming in from her walk with Marika. She had just unstrapped the little girl from the huge stroller and taken her up in her arms when two long black limousines drove up to the front door. There was no time to run. Before she fully realized what was happening, the drivers were out and opening the car doors. Two footmen from the castle came out to carry in the luggage, and suddenly women of all ages and all shapes and sizes were leaving the cars and descending on the castle—"Like flies on a week-old pizza," Tianna muttered to herself, using one of her brother's favorite phrases.

Oh well, maybe they would all be strangers. It was quite likely, after all. The members of her family weren't exactly a bunch of social butterflies. She would have to hold her ground and hope for the best.

As she stood between the cars and the castle entryway, the entire entourage was coming straight for her when she suddenly realized she knew one of the

women. She clutched the baby tightly to her chest and
gulped, her heart beating a bit faster. The jig was up,
she supposed. Her charade would be exposed. The third
woman coming her way was the Duchess of Tabliva,
an old friend of her mother's. She'd been taken to visit
her once years before, at her beautiful bay-view apartment in San Francisco. She remembered it well, mostly
because of that stunning view. Tea had been served
on the terrace and they had watched fog roll in across
the water while the sun retreated into the mist. She'd
thought at the time that was one appealing thing about
being royalty—you did tend to get good housing.

She had an urge to turn and dash out of the way and
hope for the best, but it was too late. They were marching right past her. She pasted a smile on her face and
lifted her chin, determined to take her medicine bravely.
The first woman brushed on by without a glance. The
second woman seemed to see right through her. And the
duchess, the woman her mother counted as one of her
dear friends, let her glance touch briefly on the baby,
then made a face, as though children didn't please her,
and walked on past without a sign of any recognition
at all.

Tianna stood where she was, stunned. They were
passing her as though she were a potted plant. Anxiety
gave way to annoyance, and she began to glare at the
remaining women as they hurried past her. No one noticed. Not one of them met her gaze. Even two beautiful young ones who brought up the rear.

She couldn't believe it. Most of these women were
royals or close to it. How could they be so unutterably
rude? She certainly wasn't used to being ignored this
way. How dared they?

And then it came to her.

They treated you like the servant you're pretending to be. What on earth do you expect?

She stayed where she was for a few more minutes, digesting what had just happened, rummaging through her memories, trying to recall if she'd treated servants as she'd just been treated. And she couldn't remember. Was that because she hadn't done it? Or because doing it came so naturally, she didn't retain the incidents? She wasn't sure. But she *was* sure she would be more aware in the future. Being ignored didn't feel good. She hated it.

Two footmen who'd travelled with the group were coming up to the stairs now, and she looked at them. They weren't ignoring her at any rate. The older ducked his head and reined in a smile, but the younger one, a short but cocky-looking fellow with a snub nose and a wide grin gave her a wink.

"Hey, honey, meet ya' later in the kitchen?" he suggested hopefully as he walked past her.

She drew herself up, astounded, even though she now realized he thought she was a nanny and was just treating her accordingly. Her outrage dimmed and she gave him a toss of her head rather than the tongue-lashing that first came to mind.

Obviously, she was going to have to deal with the way she was treated, and the way she was treated was molded very much by the image she projected to the world.

"Come on, sweetheart," she told Marika, leaving the stroller behind as she started for the castle herself. "Let's go in and work on our attitudes."

Chapter 6

The visitors seemed to have turned the castle upside down. There was constant commotion, people rushing down hallways, doors banging, voices calling out. An entirely different atmosphere settled over the house.

Tianna sat restlessly in the nursery, feeling like a caged animal.

"A bunny in a box," she told Marika reassuringly. "Nothing too scary for little girls."

Marika pursed her lips and seemed to be considering what her nanny had said, making Tianna laugh.

She wanted to go out and see what was going on but she knew that would be too risky. So she sat, playing with Marika while she was awake, pacing the floor when the baby was asleep, wishing she had a good book with her. Late in the afternoon, things seemed to settle down and she assumed they had all gathered in the garden for tea—earlier she had seen the footmen setting up tables. Taking her chance, she picked up Marika and headed for the kitchen to restock the baby's food supply.

As usual, the kitchen staff was delighted to see Marika, even though they were busy serving little sandwiches and tarts on silver plates.

"I went into town and got you that baby food you wanted," Milla told Tianna after she'd given the baby a hug. She produced tiny jars of swirled peas and banana cereal.

"Oh good. I really do want to try some of the cereal with her. I'd say she's old enough."

Milla put her head to the side. "How old would you say she is?" she ventured.

"About four months." She shifted the baby so she could take hold of the bag full of baby food. "Does anyone know where Janus is?" she asked. She was anxiously waiting to hear his latest report on how the search was going. But no one seemed to have an answer.

"If you see him, please tell him I'd like to talk to him," she told them all. "I guess I'll get out of your way for now."

She started back toward the nursery but the laughter of the garden party drew her to a bank of tall windows on a landing where she could look down on the group. There were four or five decorated tables set up beneath the arbor. It looked like everyone was having a good time. She wondered who they all were, and where Prince Garth was. Craning her neck, she began looking for him among the throng.

"Want to join the party?"

She whirled, and found the prince leaning against a doorjamb, smiling at her. He looked tall and elegant in a casual suit, the shirt open at the neck. Her breath caught in her throat for just a moment.

"You look like a child who wasn't invited to the birthday party," he continued. "Why don't you come on down and join in?"

She shook her head, marveling at the charge of excitement that seemed to sweep through her system at the sight of him. This wasn't good. "No thanks," she said quickly. "I've got…things to do."

"Ah, the ubiquitous 'things to do.' They're always first on my list."

"Yes." She avoided his mocking gaze and glanced back out the window, though she was turning to go.

"Tell you what," he said, straightening. "I'll have someone set up a little table for you here at the window. You can watch the group and have some afternoon tea of your own right here."

Suddenly that sounded like a lot of fun. She knew how good those little finger sandwiches had looked in the kitchen. She could symbolically join in and yet not risk identification from the duchess.

"What a good idea," she told him radiantly.

Pulling out his cell phone, he made a quick call to the butler's pantry to make arrangements. She waited for him to put the phone away, then put Marika in his arms, startling him.

"Here, hold her for a moment, and I'll run these things back to the room and get her sling chair. I'll only be a second."

Not waiting to see if he was really willing to babysit, she turned and hurried toward the room, humming as she went.

The prince looked down at Marika. She smiled up at him. He had to laugh. He was dead sure she couldn't be his, despite the name business and that royal cloth she'd come in, but once he had a baby, he would be darn lucky if she turned out half as cute and personable as this one.

Tianna was back in a flash, just as she'd promised, and by then, he was holding the baby as though he were an old hand at it.

Which, in fact, turned out to be a lot closer to the truth than either of them had imagined. Cook arrived with a tray of goodies just as a footman showed up with the table. The good woman took one look at Prince Garth and began to laugh.

"I declare, that does take me back some. You always were so good with babies."

Prince Garth looked at her as though she'd gone demented. "What are you talking about?"

"Don't you remember? When you were a young 'un. You used to carry your little sister Kari around like a rag doll. You wouldn't let anyone else near her." She set down her tray and began to serve tea. "He was quite the protective brother, you know. I think all that horror of fleeing the country and our beloved king and queen... well, you know the story. It made our little prince want to protect what he had left. At least that was the way we saw it at the time." She shook her head, her eyes seeing a past twenty years back. "They were so young for so much heartbreak," she murmured. "Well, you enjoy the eats, now. I think you'll like what I've brought you."

Cook smiled at the picture the prince made holding Marika, but Tianna noticed she had to wipe her eyes as she turned to go. It was interesting how much more immediate the ties to Nabotavia were in this household than they had been in the atmosphere she had grown up in. It was as though the past were only yesterday, and everyone made reference to it all the time. In her family, the past was the past, and they all tried to push it into the background as they looked forward to a future without all the heartache and pain. Her own trauma from those days was never mentioned—as though it could somehow be erased by ignoring it.

"Thank you so much," she said to the prince as she took the baby into her own arms and put her in the sling seat. She noticed there were two chairs at the little table, but it still surprised her when the prince sat down with her.

"Shouldn't you be entertaining your guests?" she asked him, taking a bite from a watercress sandwich and rolling her eyes with the deliciousness of it all.

"They entertain themselves quite nicely." He watched her, seeming to enjoy what he was looking at, making her feel a bit self-conscious.

"But they came to visit you," she reminded him.

He leaned back sideways in his char, throwing one arm over the back of it. "In a manner of speaking. Actually, they came to take charge of my life. And since I'm not about to let that happen, they will be much happier talking about it among themselves." His eyes shone with suppressed amusement. "Once I get into the conversation, I'm afraid there will be much rending of garments and gnashing of teeth. Tears will be shed. Oaths will be spoken."

She was laughing and trying not to. But something about the way he gave his narrative struck her as funny and she couldn't help it. "And what are they trying to get you to do that you are so determined to resist?" she asked him.

"Take a look for yourself." Looking down at the assembled guests, he nodded toward the dark-haired of the two pretty young ladies Tianna had noticed when the group had arrived. "There she is," he said. "What do you think of her?"

Tianna sighed, popping a salmon tidbit into her mouth. "She looks so young."

"She *is* young." His brows furled as he pretended to consider that concept. "But young can be good. You can train them when you get them young. Older women are already so opinionated." He cocked an eyebrow, teasingly. "Like you."

"Older women?" she protested, looking askance. "I didn't know I'd already crossed the line."

But he was calling her attention down onto the grass again. The two young ladies were talking, leaning close and whispering to each other. They looked as lovely as spring flowers, and careless as children.

"Ah, and there is the other one," he told her. "One is blond and one is dark-haired, you see. A variety to choose from."

She laughed again, though she wasn't sure why. This was beginning to sound a little odd. "What are you talking about?"

He put his head to the side and his gaze trailed down the line of her neck. She could almost feel it, and she couldn't stop her natural reaction to reach up and ward it off with her hand. The ghost of a smile shadowed his eyes.

"I don't much like being managed," he said quietly.

She nodded, tingling from the way he was looking at her. She knew she ought to resist it, that she ought to feel annoyed, maybe get up and speak sharply to him, turn and leave him sitting here on the landing. She ought to. But she wouldn't. "I've noticed," she said.

"Good."

"So I take it, some of the visitors are trying to 'manage' you?"

"Most definitely. It is my Aunt Cordelia's mission in life to take hold of me and mold me into the sort of man she thinks I should be."

Cordelia. Yes, she knew who that was. A very important woman in Nabotavian society. She thought she could pick out which one she was just by the way the others were deferring to her down below.

"Your Highness," she said, looking straight at him, "just what is it your aunt wants you to do?"

"She wants me to marry one of those pretty girls, of course."

Tianna's mouth dropped with outrage. "But you're betrothed."

He nodded and sighed. "You know, that betrothal business has held me in good stead for years. But lately people are starting to disrespect it. They seem to think I should have fulfilled my obligations by now, and since I haven't, I ought to dump the whole thing."

"Why…that's outrageous!" The irony of it all was clear to her, but she brushed it aside. It was one thing for her to want to break the promise made so long ago. It was quite another for outsiders to decide these things for her. And for him.

"You think so?" He looked thoughtful. "I don't know. It does seem that the days of betrothals have pretty much faded from the scene, don't you think?"

"Not at all," she argued stoutly. "These arrangements are made for very specific reasons. And studies show that arranged marriages have a better record of lasting than love relationships do." She could hardly believe this was coming from her own mouth. These were the very arguments her own mother had used when she'd chafed under the rules herself.

They hadn't done much to change her own opinion. Why on earth did she think they would work on Garth? And why did she want them to all of a sudden? Looking at him, she realized knowing him was changing her.

"Well, I've loved being betrothed," he went on. "It's kept me safe through many a relationship when I was younger. Whenever some lovely young thing began to speak of commitment, I gently reminded her of the betrothal, and that was that."

No outrage. Not this time. She was getting wise to him. Instead of swallowing his tale whole, she gave him a gimlet eye. "Why are you trying so hard to make me believe you're really a cad?" she asked him.

"What?" He pretended shock at her lack of faith in him. "You don't believe it?"

She favored him with a mysterious smile and turned away.

"Wait. What do I have to do to convince you?"

"I'm not falling for it anymore," she announced. "I think I know you too well." She flashed him a look. "Try as you might, you can't keep me from liking you."

"Liking me?" He sounded surprised, but more than that, he sounded as though her saying that had touched him in some way. "Really?"

Suddenly it seemed too big a confession and she wished she hadn't made it. Confused, she turned to look at Marika, hoping to use fussing with her to hide her consternation, but Marika was sound asleep in her little chair, her arms limp, her breathing soft and even. Tianna's emotions calmed at the sight of her and a smile tilted her lips. Who could resist such a beautiful baby?

She looked up at the prince to see if he was enjoying

Marika's charm as well, but found him looking at her, not the baby, with an intensity that startled her.

"Don't."

"Don't what?"

"Look at me like that."

"Can I kiss you instead?"

She swallowed and tried to look unperturbed. "Why me? Why don't you go kiss one of them?" She nodded toward the two young lovelies.

"They are beautiful, aren't they?" He said the words, but his gaze was still on her and it was clear his interest was, too. He even moved his chair closer to where she sat.

"Yes," she said breathlessly. "Beautiful girls. Pick one and kiss *her.*"

Slowly, he shook his head. Leaning closer, he touched her cheek with his finger. "I don't want to kiss one of them. I want to kiss you."

Try as she might, her foggy brain couldn't dredge up one good argument against it. "Why?" she asked a bit agitatedly, but as he leaned even closer, she didn't back away.

He shrugged as his arm came around her, pulling her into the warmth of his body. "You got me," he murmured, burying his face in her silky hair.

"I...I thought we agreed that it would be better not to do things like...like kissing," she said, shivering deliciously.

"I don't remember agreeing to any such thing," he whispered, and then his lips were on hers, making soft love bites, teasing her, enticing her.

She sighed and began to kiss him back. She'd never felt anything as warm and exciting as his touch and she wanted more of it. His kisses were intoxicating, drugging her senses, and she was about to float away on pure sensation.

But his cell phone rang. For a moment, they both ignored it. The second ring came, and he sighed, drawing back. Reaching for it, he flipped it open and said, "Yes?" but his gaze never left her.

She closed her eyes, still drifting in the aftermath of his embrace, feeling foolish but happy anyway.

He listened for a moment. "Alright," he said, just a bit impatiently. "I'll be right down. Tell Cordelia I'm sorry to be so late about it, but I've been delayed by something much more important." One side of his mouth lifted in a semigrin. "Yes, use those exact words. I'll be there in a moment."

Closing the phone he gave her a look of regret and began to pull away from the table.

"We'll be eating at seven in the main dining room. Will you join us?"

Her head came up. Her lips still tingled from touching his. She wanted to join him in anything, everything—breathing, even. But she had to touch down to earth again, and reluctantly, she did so.

"Absolutely not," she said, and managed to sound firm about it. "I'll be eating in the nursery." She felt she had to remind him. "That's where the nanny belongs, you know."

He gave her a slow grin. "And when did you start acting like a proper nanny?"

"Do you have any complaints?"

"Not a one. But I have noticed that you tend to act more like the lady of the manor than you do an employee." He gazed at her quizzically. "Have you noticed that yourself?"

She gave him a look and didn't answer.

"Why don't you come with us?" he coaxed. "It would be a lot more fun if you were there. You can sit at my right hand and keep me company."

She laughed just thinking about the looks on the faces of those women when they realized the nanny was going to eat with them—sitting in the place of honor no less! But she really didn't want to risk having the duchess suddenly jump up, jab a finger in her direction and yell out, "Your Highness, that woman is an imposter!" That wouldn't go down well and she still had a job to get done here.

She shook her head. "I'd better stay with Marika," she said, and he nodded, giving her one last long look before departing.

She watched him go, the blood still racing through her veins in a way she found exhilarating—and very scary. Was Janni right? Had she really fallen for him? And if that was the case, what on earth was she prepared to do about it?

The dinner hour had come and gone and the party had retired to the sitting room. Tianna had finally succeeded in getting Marika to fall asleep and she wanted to do the same as soon as possible. She had only had a couple of hours sleep the night before and she was feeling it. Still, she wanted to get something to read, as she thought chances were good she would be up with Marika again at some point during the night. She was pretty sure she could slip past the sitting room without being seen.

Making her way to the library, all went well. She could hear the laughter and the high female voices, set against the low tone that had to be Garth, and it made her smile. He was quite the king of the hill, alone with all those women.

Then she remembered the pretty young pair and her smile faded. He could make fun all he wanted to, those were very pretty girls. She couldn't deny that she felt a pang of something close to jealousy to think of them spending time with him.

Jealousy! Where had that word come from? She wasn't jealous. She didn't need to be jealous. After all, she was the one who was as good as engaged to the man! Oh, the irony of it all.

"What a tangled web we weave," she muttered as she sped along.

The library was empty, just as she'd thought it would be, and she went immediately to the shelves and began browsing the history section. There was a great selection of volumes on Nabotavian history, and though that hadn't been what she'd thought she would choose when planning her reading, something about the subject drew her attention and she decided it had been too long since she'd read anything on her country of birth. Reaching out, she took three books down and carried them to a large, overstuffed couch where she curled up to leaf through them and make a choice between them.

The first thing she did was to look up the history of the Great Nabotavian Rift of 1860. The rift had cut the country in two, leaving the Roseanovas to rule, but giving her own family a long, thin slice of the country to manage themselves. She had only a sketchy picture of what exactly had happened to force the change, but she quickly found a description.

It seemed her great-great-grandfather—and Garth's—King Marcovo I, was frustrated by the activities of his first son and heir, Marcovo II, who spent his days fox hunting with his dissolute friends, and his nights getting local ladies "with child." One famous minister of the crown was quoted as saying, "At the rate he's going, half the children in the kingdom will soon be claiming the Crown Prince as their daddy."

"Oh my," Tianna said, stifling a giggle. "Garth, you come from the wild side, don't you?"

On the other hand, her own great-grandfather Peter, Marcovo the First's second son—and his favorite—was a serious young man who did his duty and studied voraciously and started the national institute of sciences. Angry that the country had to be handed to his good-for-nothing son, the king decreed that the country be cut along the banks of the Tannabee River, giving Peter a kingdom of his own. The entire area consisted of less than a quarter of the land of Nabotavia, and it was arguably too mountainous and desolate to amount to much. Still, the rest of the government refused to let it leave the actual authority of the Nabotavian kingdom. So Peter was given a sort of paper kingdom, one that was still really a part of Nabotavia, but could pretend to be independent. And, as she well knew, it would exist as a thorn in the side of the Nabotavian royalty from then on. Her marriage to Garth was supposed to heal the rift. But did anyone really care anymore?

She'd just put down one book and picked up the next when she heard voices, and then her place of refuge was invaded by two of the visitors. The couch faced away from the entry side of the room and she sank down into it, out of sight, as she realized one of the women was her mother's friend. Her heart began to skip and she felt downright silly to be hiding. But what could she do? Nothing but wait and hope they left quickly.

"Well, I think it's just senseless the way he's clinging

to this betrothal," one of the women was saying. "I know you think a lot of the West Nabotavian royal family and I'm sure they are very nice people, but the point is, they are unimportant people."

Tianna stifled the outrage that rose in her throat. They were talking about her family! Who did this woman think she was? Suddenly she realized she could see both of the newcomers in the large mirror at the end of the room—and that they could see her if they turned in that direction. Her pulse raced, but she was torn between wanting to remain hidden and wanting to rise up and confront this witch.

"Who needs West Nabotavia, after all?" the woman was going on. "It's all mountains. No industry, no society or community to speak of. And these two young things I've brought to meet Garth are the daughters of very rich captains of industry who have a lot of money to throw around. And money is what we're going to need to bring Nabotavia back to glory, believe me."

"Of course, Cordelia," the duchess agreed. "But I don't really understand why you put such stock in Prince Garth. After all, he's not the crown prince."

Cordelia sighed. "I've always had a special warmth for Garth. I often took care of the boys when they were young, you know, and he and I just seemed to have a special rapport." She sighed again. "Besides, he is the only one of the three who bears the mark, you know."

"The mark?"

"The mark of the rose."

"I had no idea."

"Oh yes. And in the traditional position, too. Right over his heart."

Tianna's head lifted and she listened more intently. She'd never heard of this mark of the rose before.

"I'd heard of it years ago, of course, but I thought it was a sort of historical myth. What is it, a birthmark sort of thing?"

"Yes. It looks like a rose just beginning to unfurl its petals. My brother, the late king, God rest his soul…he had it. Our father had it, too. But of the children, only Garth has it. And I can't help but think that the one who has it is specially marked for greatness."

Tianna frowned, trying to remember just what the birthmark she'd seen on Marika had looked like—and where it was placed. It seemed to her it was very much like what Cordelia was describing. How strange. How very, very strange.

"Oh, I see," the duchess was saying agreeably.

"Yes. And that is why I think it is very important who Prince Garth marries. It's a new age. We need fresh blood in the line. These girls both come from dynamic families. Their fathers have done great things. Either one of them would be a wonderful match for Garth. If only I can convince him to void this betrothal."

As though summoned, the prince himself appeared in the doorway. His gaze connected with Tianna's in the mirror. Noting the way she was scrunched down in the couch, he took in the situation at a glance. Quickly, he turned his full smile on the two older women.

"Ladies, dessert is being served," he announced.

"Oh!"

"Please hurry back to the sitting room." He made a sweeping gesture as though ushering them to the door.

"And you?" his aunt asked. "Aren't you going to join us?"

"Of course. I just need a moment, if you don't mind. I have a few things I want to think over."

"Oh, of course." The two ladies started for the door,

but Cordelia stopped and turned back. "But tell me, my dear, what do you think of the girls?"

"The girls?" He looked at her blankly for a moment. "Oh, the two young ladies?" He made a move as though to get them started out the door again. "Yes, quite beautiful. And charming."

"Yes," Cordelia said, still resisting the push he was making to get them out of the room. "I'd like you to have a little more time with them before we leave in the morning. You should get to know them better."

"I'll certainly do my best." He put his hand in the middle of her back and literally guided her to the door. "See you in a few minutes," he promised, then closed the door and turned to face Tianna.

"What the hell is going on here?" he demanded.

She rose to face him, her cheeks flushed. "That is what I'd like to know," she retorted. "So you're going to break your betrothal in order to marry one of those Bobbsey twins? How crass can you get?"

His frown was almost angry. "Who said I was doing any such thing?"

"Cordelia."

He groaned. "My darling Aunt Cordelia has been working her chubby little fingers to the bone trying to get me to do just that," he admitted. "But I told you I didn't like being managed. I have no intention of marrying one of those two empty-headed little flirts."

"Oh." Taking a deep breath, she began to calm down. "That's good."

She started to turn away but he pulled her back, holding her upper arm in his strong hand.

"But why would you care about something like that?" he asked her softly.

She gave him a superior look. "I just wouldn't want to

see you throw your integrity away on those… those…"
She stopped. What was she doing? The girls were perfectly fine young women for all she knew. If she went on like this, she would sound like a jealous lover. "Oh, never mind," she said, avoiding his gaze and suddenly wishing he would kiss her. "You'd probably better go join your party."

He let go of her arm and she could tell he was drawing away.

"Wait," she said, and this time she was the one who grabbed *his* arm—though she pulled her hand back right away. "Do you know where Janus is?" she asked him. "I haven't seen him all evening."

The prince shrugged. "He must be around somewhere. He laid these clothes out for me to wear."

She looked them over. Sleek and trendy, the suit fit him like a glove, emphasizing his muscular body in a way that would make strong women swoon. "And very handsome they are, too," she admitted.

"Thank you."

He smiled into her eyes and she wanted that kiss again. Could he tell? But if he could, why wasn't he kissing her?

Then she remembered there was something else nagging at her—the mark of the rose that Cordelia had been talking about. She'd better find out anything she could about it while she still had him here.

"Your Highness," she said quickly. "Your aunt said you have the mark of the rose. What did she mean? Is it a tattoo?"

"Actually, it's a sort of birthmark that runs in the family. If you have a really vivid imagination, it looks like a rose. It doesn't pop up on everyone, but I've got it. Marco and my baby sister Kari don't."

"Is it considered special?"

He nodded. "Sort of. It's strongly identified with the House of the Rose. Why?"

The implications were finally coming clear to her. This could be big.

She grabbed his arm more tightly. "I have to show you something. Come with me, quickly."

He put his hand over hers. "What's the matter?"

She shook her head. "Please. Just come with me."

He searched her eyes, frowning, then turned toward where the sounds of silver against china emanated from the sitting room.

"I don't think that would be such a good idea, Tianna. I've promised the others...."

She took a deep breath. Of course, he was right. "Then meet me in the nursery as soon as you can."

"All right." He looked at her curiously. "I'll be there within the hour."

He was as good as his word. Tianna had been pacing the floors waiting for him and when he arrived, she felt relief mixed with apprehension.

Marika was still asleep. Tianna peeled back her little shirt and let him see the mark on her chubby little baby chest, just above her heart. The reddish-brown discoloration was still there, and it most definitely could have been called a rose.

He stared down at it and it seemed to her that for just a moment, he turned to stone. Not saying a word, he very carefully shrugged out of his suit coat, slung it across the back of the chair, then began to unbutton his shirt. She waited, her heart beating in her throat. He slipped out of the shirt and stood silently, his beautiful, muscular body displayed before her. The birthmark, just above his heart, looked very much like the smaller version on Marika's chest.

Tianna was expecting exactly what she saw, but even so, she gasped when she saw it. It was so perfect. *He* was so perfect. Hesitantly, she reached out and touched the mark with her fingertips, then looked up into his eyes.

Taking her by the shoulders, he pulled her up against him and kissed her, hard on the mouth. The heat from his naked skin burned her, but the kiss only lasted for seconds, and then he put her back where she'd been, slipped back into his shirt, grabbed his jacket, and left the room. The entire time, neither of them had said a word.

Chapter 7

A baby was crying. Garth tossed and turned in his bed, not sure if he was dreaming or if there really was a baby in distress. Finally he was wide-awake enough to tell the difference. It was for real.

He lay listening. It wasn't so much what he heard as what he felt. Marika was crying. Did that mean *his daughter* was crying? Was she his?

No. She couldn't be. And yet…and yet…

Rolling over, he looked at the clock. It was two in the morning. He lay still for another moment, then began to get up, shaking the sleep from his head, reaching for a sweatshirt and jeans. A few minutes later he was outside the nursery, listening for any evidence of what was going on within.

There it was. Marika's fussy voice, Tianna hushing her. He knocked softly on the door, then let himself in.

"Oh." Tianna looked dead tired as she gazed at him

from the middle of the room. She was holding Marika, whose face was red and blotchy and wet with tears. She'd obviously been pacing the floor with the baby for a very long time. "Did we wake you up? I'm sorry."

"No problem," he said. "Here. Let me take her."

He reached for her and Marika's little arms shot out, ready to be taken. She babbled something unintelligible and actually seemed to be smiling through her tears. Tianna released her and Garth took the weight of her in his arms. Life, warm and sweet and magic. He seemed to know just how to hold her now. She fit in his arms as though she'd been born to be there. Marika. Was she...?

He looked up at Tianna. Her eyes were shadowed by dark smudges, but she was still as beautiful as ever in the dim lamplight, standing there in her lacy night-gown, covered by a soft blue robe.

"Get in bed," he told her. "You're dying for some sleep. I'll take care of Marika."

She stared at him. "What?" she said, as though she didn't understand.

"I can do it," he reassured her. "I can walk around patting her back as well as you can. And if she falls asleep, I'll put her down in her crib and go back to my room."

"But...but what if...?"

"I'll wake you up." He gestured toward the bed with a nod. "Go on. Get in there."

A slow smile began to grow, first in her eyes, then to include her wide mouth. "When did you become the nurturing one?" she asked, but she started toward the bed, slipping out of her robe and sliding beneath the covers. She sighed, but she still looked tense. "I don't know if this will do any good," she told him. "I'm so wound up, I can't relax."

He'd started to pace the room with the baby to his shoulder. The space was long enough to allow ten steps before he had to turn and go back. Marika gave a shuddering sigh and put her head down, but he could feel that she was far from sleep. Just as Tianna was.

"Why don't you talk for a while?" he suggested. "That might help you let go."

She considered, nestling into the pillow. "What shall I talk about?"

"I don't know." He dropped a kiss on Marika's head and glanced at where Tianna lay, her beautiful hair spread out around her head. "Talk about your favorite movie. Or the latest good book you read. Or—how about this—why did you form such a deep attachment to this baby so quickly? I have a feeling there must be a background to it."

"Oh." She snuggled into the fluffy pillow. "All right." Drawing in a deep breath, she began. "I was five years old during the escape. In the confusion, I was separated from my family. My old nursemaid took me across Europe, racing to the sea where I was supposed to meet up with my family. But something happened and I was placed aboard the wrong boat, and from then on, strangers took care of me. They were kind enough, but I remember being so alone and so cold and so very frightened. I wanted my mother and they couldn't tell me where she was. I think these people didn't really know for sure who I was. I was shuttled from one Nabotavian immigrant community to another. It was almost six months before my parents managed to make it to the States and another few months of looking before they found me." Her voice grew softer. "By then, they said I wouldn't talk. And even after I was reunited with my family, it was months before I would say anything."

"Poor Tianna." He thought of her as a child and smiled. "I'm sorry you had to go through that."

She sighed. "That, or something like it, happened to all of us, didn't it? A lot had it worse than I did. You…well, you lost your parents for good. And that is so much worse. Still, my experience stayed with me in ways I am still only starting to understand. And when I saw that helpless little baby lying there, all alone, her mother gone…" Her voice broke and she paused for a moment, regaining her composure. "Well, I just had to make sure she wasn't hurt in any way, if I could help it."

The baby against his shoulder was still moving, but he risked sitting in the rocking chair and she seemed to respond favorably while he gently rocked her. He understood only too well what Tianna had been telling him. His experience in the escape was still with him as well. He imagined it would probably color the rest of his life.

"How about you?" she said sleepily. "You said Janus got you out. What happened when you got to the States?"

"We were shuttled about, just like you were, at first. Though we were staying with people we knew, so it wasn't quite as bad. Marco was the oldest, and the crown prince, so he was expected to be almost an adult. They were always including him in meetings and things that were way above his years and experience. And Kari was just a baby." Funny how Cook bringing up the memory of him carrying Kari around had opened up a whole chapter of his life he'd pretty much forgotten about. "So I took care of her. We used to hide together, so they wouldn't make us eat oatmeal." He smiled as more memories flooded him. "Finally our father's half brother and his wife, the duke and duchess of Gavini, took Kari to live in Beverly Hills, and our uncle Kenneth brought Marco and me here to Arizona to live in his castle."

"That's right," she said, yawning. "I'd forgotten about him. Where is he now?"

"He went to Nabotavia last year with me when we were working with the underground, and he stayed on."

She didn't say anything in response and he looked over at the bed. Her breathing was even. She was finally asleep. He stayed where he was, watching her sleep, watching her breathe. What was it about this woman that set her apart from all the rest? In a short time she'd become very important to him—indispensable. He didn't like to feel that anyone was that vital to his own well-being. He was always the one in control, the one who could let go and not look back. But things were changing.

Maybe it had something to do with the return to Nabotavia. Maybe it had something to do with his time in the life cycle. He didn't know for sure, but he knew he didn't want to lose her. What, exactly, was he willing to do to make sure that didn't happen? That was the question. And for that, he didn't have an answer yet.

Marika fell asleep against him, but he didn't rise and put her in her crib. He didn't want to risk waking her. Instead, he sank down into the chair with the adorable baby in his arms and fell asleep as well.

Tianna woke in the first light and saw Garth in the chair with Marika. Laughing softly, she slipped out of bed, dropped a soft kiss on the prince's cheek before she took the baby from his arms and carried her to bed.

When she turned, she found that he'd already come to his feet and looked ready to leave.

"Everything okay?" he asked, wincing in the light.

She nodded, looking at him with love in her eyes. He smiled and touched her chin with his forefinger.

"What do you think?" he asked her softly. "Do you think she's mine?"

Her eyes clouded and she shook her head. "That's up to you," she told him.

He nodded. "I still can't see how it could be possible. But there are so many signs pointing that way."

Tianna took a deep breath and said something she knew she probably shouldn't. "Could...could she be Marco's?"

His eyes widened and he choked. "Don't make me laugh. Marco is as straight-arrow as they come. He's not like me."

"There's nothing wrong with you," she said defensively.

He looked at her oddly, wondering why she felt that way. "In a strange way I always felt I had to protect Marco," he admitted slowly. "I always tried to keep the real world away from him. He was always so good."

"You're good, too."

"No. Not like Marco." He looked into her eyes for a long moment, feeling a sweeping wave of affection for her, along with the usual sensual interest. She was the one who was good. And goodness like that was a rare trait. Knowing her almost made him believe that a world without lies and treachery was possible. Almost. But not quite.

His mouth touched hers. Her lips parted and his tongue played with hers. She felt so good against him. He could close his eyes and still see her, every detail.

He'd memorized her, her smell, the feel of her skin, her voice. And soon, he would know her body as well.

But he was the one who was dead tired now. He felt like death. Drawing back, he told her, "I'm going to go get some sleep. Wake me if anything momentous happens."

"I will."

Watching him go, an apprehensive excitement crept over her. There was no use denying it any longer. She was falling for him all right. Falling pretty hard.

But you've only known him for two days!

True. And untrue. In some ways, she'd known him all her life.

"And after all," she whispered to herself. "We're engaged."

For some time that morning, she could hear the sounds of the cousins packing up and marching down to the limousines. Finally it was quiet and she assumed they had gone. A few hours later, after breakfast and playtime for Marika, a knock came on the nursery door.

"Miss," Bridget called. "Come quickly. Prince Marco wants to see you."

"What?" Tianna opened the door and stared at Bridget in surprise. "He's here?"

"Yes, Miss. He's in the study and he said, please come right away, and bring the baby."

"Of course."

She said the words automatically, but she swallowed hard and had to steady herself before getting together the wits to do as she'd been asked. The crown prince was, after all, the putative king of Nabotavia, and as such, he was the top authority figure in her culture. Prince Garth must have told him about the baby and the unusual bits of evidence that she might be connected in some way to the royal family. And of course, he would want that confirmed or proven false right away.

"Come on, Marika," she said at last. "We're going to see the king."

He was sitting behind the wide desk in the study, but rose when she entered the room, and came toward her, nodding politely but obviously interested in Marika most of all.

"So this is the mysterious baby," he said. "What a beautiful child."

Tianna found herself tongue-tied, which was rare for her. The man had the presence one would expect of royalty, and was just as handsome as his brother, though in a very different way. He had a lean, wiry-looking body, strong without being ostentatiously muscular, reserved rather than friendly. Handsome in a rugged sense, his face had a rather gaunt look, as though he'd been through too much too early in his relatively short existence. She thought she could see evidence of his haunting agony from losing his young wife reflected in his dark eyes. All in all, she was impressed.

"May I see the mark on her chest?"

"Oh. Of course." She pulled back the shirt to show him.

He nodded and she put it back again. Suddenly she found him looking straight into her eyes, as though he were ordering her to reveal the truth, and she gulped, ready to bare her soul if need be.

"There's been some talk that since you arrived at the same time the baby did, and you have been such a staunch advocate for her, there must be some connection which precedes your arrival."

"No, Your Royal Highness," she managed to stutter

out. "I'm afraid that is not correct. I can understand how that misapprehension could come about, but it has no approximation to reality."

He stared at her for a long moment, then smiled coolly. "I'll accept your word on that. Still, it is strange, isn't it? The name, the cloth, the birthmark, all implying a direct connection to the royal family."

"Yes."

"Well, there is obviously only one thing to be done."

"What is that?"

"A DNA test, of course. I've brought a professional with me. He'll do a swab from inside the baby's cheek and compare it to the family DNA. It should take a few days to get the results, and then we will know for sure."

"Oh. Of course."

He bowed and turned back toward the desk, and she realized she'd been dismissed. Holding Marika to her chest, she started back to the nursery, then thought better of it and made a detour. She found Bridget in the library and asked her to take the baby up to the nursery and wait. That done, she took a deep breath and started for the second floor. She knew which room was Garth's and she went to his door, knocking softly.

He opened the door as though he'd been expecting her, and the next thing she knew, she was wrapped in his arms and being kissed like there was no tomorrow—delightfully kissed, hungrily kissed, deliciously kissed. But still, she pulled away, laughing.

"Hey," she said, gazing at him lovingly. "I didn't come here for this. We've got to talk."

He put his head to the side, considering her. "Okay," he allowed. "We'll talk. Then we'll kiss. And then…"

She laughed softly, pressing her palm to his cheek

and enjoying the light in his eyes. "Now be good," she told him. "I've just met your brother."

"Marco?" He turned his face and put a kiss right in the center of her palm. "Good old Marco. I told him all about Marika. I suppose he's ordered DNA testing, hasn't he?"

"Yes." She turned away and looked at his room. Larger than the average living room in a normal house, it was lined with bookcases, most of which were taken up with a beautiful stereo system. A huge bed filled one side of the room, and French doors opened onto a terrace balcony.

Turning, she browsed along the bookcases and came upon a very expensive camera.

"Nice piece of equipment," she said, picking it up and getting a feel for it, admiring the optical zoom lens.

"I haven't used it much. Go ahead and try it out if you like. Why don't you take some portraits of Marika?"

She set the camera down and turned back toward him. "I don't really have any experience with baby pictures."

He shrugged. "What's special about baby pictures?"

"Nothing. It's just that my field is architecture. You know, skyscrapers against the sky, interesting entryways, angles and crannies. That sort of thing."

"You're going to be like a kid in a candy store if you go back to Nabotavia."

Her eyebrows rose. "How so?"

"The revolution was over in hours and this recent fight to throw off the usurpers only lasted a few days. Not many buildings were damaged. You'll be amazed. It looks like a little piece of nineteenth-century Europe in Kalavia, the capital. And since Nabotavia has been cut off from the rest of the world for the last twenty years, the beauty of our cities is relatively unknown."

"Really? That is interesting." And it was. The idea of being one of the first to document the architectural scenes in the newly liberated country intrigued her for a moment. She was beginning to realize how little she really knew about the old country.

But she did know one thing—she was in love with its prince. Looking at him, a wave of pure affection surged in her chest, making her gasp with its intensity. And the beautiful thing was, he seemed to feel something for her, if evidence was to be believed. Still, one thing stood between finding out how real this feeling was. She was living a lie. How was she going to tell him who she really was? And when?

He came toward her and she knew he was getting impatient. Coming close, he took her face in his hands and looked down into her eyes.

"I've been trying to figure out what I like about you," he said softly as he studied her face.

"Difficult to pin down, isn't it?" she teased. "There's just so much to choose from."

"Exactly." He smiled. "You're beautiful, of course. You're good. You're loving. You care about people." He dropped a kiss on her soft lips and sighed happily. "But I think the thing that gives you that special edge is your basic bedrock honesty."

Her heart jumped, but this time with dismay. "No," she said softly, shaking her head with warning. "No, it's not that."

"Why not?"

"Don't you know? I'm lying to you all the time."

He laughed, not taking her seriously. "And that's another thing," he said. "You do have a sense of humor." He kissed her again. "You couldn't lie if you tried."

"Oh Garth," she wailed, but he didn't let her get any more words out.

His mouth covered hers, hot and urgent, and she tried at first to push him away, to catch her breath so she could make some attempt at telling him the truth. It was time. It was way past time. She should have told him before…should never have let him think she was not who she really was…should have known her play-acting would get her in trouble.

But all those fears faded as his kisses did the work of changing the subject for her. Very quickly, she forgot what she'd been worrying about, forgot that there was ever anything to worry about. Life seemed too good for worrying. In the arms of this strong, wonderful man, she felt safe and adored in a way she never had before. Sinking into the sensual fog he created around them, she needed his touch, craved the taste of his mouth, de-lighted in the scent of his skin, loved the sound of his husky voice uttering sweet nonsense in her ear. Every kiss made her hungry for more, and the sense of need began to build in her very quickly.

When his hand slid under her sweater and cupped her breast, she sighed with pleasure, and suddenly she wanted to feel his muscular chest under her hands, wanted to press herself to him with nothing in between them, wanted to feel her breasts rub against his naked skin. The shock of recognition flashed through her. She wanted to make love.

"Oh!" She drew back, staring at him, her eyes very wide. "Wait a minute," she said breathlessly. "Hold it. What the heck is going on here?"

He laughed down at her, keeping her in the circle of

his arms. "I don't know, Tianna. What do you think is going on?"

"We're going to end up in bed," she warned, her eyes flashing. "I feel like I was just on the edge of a cliff and about to leap over. One more minute of that and..." Her voice trailed off and she shook her head in wonder.

Chuckling, he kissed her lips, then nuzzled her ear. "You're damn right we're going to end up in bed," he told her softly, his breath hot on her neck. "Not today. But soon."

"You think so?" she asked him, melting against his body again.

"I know it, Tianna." He held her face in his hands and his eyes lost all trace of amusement. "It's meant to be," he said, very seriously.

She searched his eyes, then nodded, slowly. "It's meant to be," she repeated.

But what would happen once he found out how true that was?

Chapter 8

Tianna knew it was time to tell Garth the truth about her identity. She wasn't sure how he was going to react once he found out. He would be annoyed, of course. Anyone would be. But maybe he would be as amused as she was with the fact that a match that had been set up when they were children was turning out to be more or less made in heaven after all.

Would they end up getting married? She had no idea. But she knew it was past time to let him in on the facts, so he could consider that, too.

She finally worked up the courage to spill the beans and she started toward the library where she thought he might be, to get it done. But the library was empty and when she turned toward the kitchen, she found him hurrying toward her along the hallway.

His face was set and his eyes were stormy. Taking hold of her arms, he held her before him. "Marco and

I are going to Los Angeles right away. There's a heli-copter landing on the grounds to get us to the airport more quickly."

As he spoke, she thought she could hear the sound of the rotor blades. "Garth, what's happened?"

He took a deep breath. "My sister Kari has been kidnapped. I don't have time to give you all the details. We're going right now. But Tianna—" he pulled her in closer, his gaze holding hers "—promise me you and Marika will be here when I get back."

She looked up at him, surprised that he would even have any fears along those lines. "Of course we'll be here. I promise."

His gaze darkened and he kissed her firmly on the mouth. "You're such a mystery to me, Tianna. You came out of nowhere and changed everything. I suddenly had this crazy feeling that you might disappear just as mys-teriously."

For no reason she could put her finger on, tears filled her eyes. "I'll be here," she whispered to him. "I'll wait for you."

He kissed her again and turned to go without another backward glance. She ran to the windows on the land-ing, watching as he and Marco hurried to the helicop-ter. And then she gasped, because Janus was coming quickly behind them. Janus, who had been avoiding her like the plague—he was going too.

"Janus!" she said aloud, knowing he couldn't hear her. "What's the deal? I want to know what you've found out!"

Of course, there was no answer. He certainly wasn't going to do much searching in Los Angeles. She fumed, but there wasn't anything she could do about it now. She stayed where she was, watching the helicopter lift off, hover for a moment, then whisk away in the direction of the airport. She hoped they would get to Los Angeles in time, prayed that Kari would be unhurt. But she couldn't stop wondering about Janus and his strange behavior.

An hour later, with Marika asleep, she had made her decision. If Janus wasn't working on finding Marika's mother, she was going to have to do it herself. The problem was, where to start?

Had Janus checked the doctors in town? Had he contacted the hospitals and investigated births from the period when Marika would have been born? She just didn't know. So what should she do?

"Why not start at the beginning?" she muttered to herself. Hadn't Cook said that when foundlings were sent to the orphanage, they conducted their own investigations? Why not call there and get some recommendations on what to do? Maybe they could give her the name of a professional investigator who specialized in these matters.

Looking the number up, she dialed it and asked to speak to the head of the orphanage. Unfortunately the woman was out and not due back until late that evening, and the receptionist who took the call didn't sound competent to give out the time of day, much less investigating advice, so Tianna would have to wait.

There wasn't much to do other than take care of Marika and worry about Princess Kari. She called her sister to let her know about what was going on, and Janni was suitably anxious about Princess Karina's fate. But she also had some rather disturbing news of her own.

"Father wants to talk to you," she told Tianna. "I told

him you were out sightseeing and couldn't be contacted, but he's not going to be satisfied with that for long."

"Why does he want to talk to me?"

"That's just it. I don't know. He's had a couple of long phone calls and he and Mother have been conferring in whispered meetings all over the house. Of course, I'm not invited to share in the discussions, seeing as how I'm the black sheep of the family. Or would that be 'sheepess'? 'Sheepette'? 'Black ewe'?"

"Janni!"

"Sorry. At any rate, I'm out of the loop. But after all this conferring, he told me he had to talk to you. I think you'd better call him."

Tianna sighed. She really wasn't up to it just now. "Tomorrow," she promised, and rang off.

Then she went back down to be with the others and worry. Cook and Milla and all the rest of the staff spent most of the day wringing their hands and asking if anyone had heard anything. The princess was very popular with them all.

"Oh, if this gets into the papers," Cook fretted. "You know we do hate that."

Tianna nodded. She understood the feeling. "It's been my impression that the Nabotavian royal family has been rather good at staying out of the tabloids," she noted.

"Exactly. The house of Roseanova is determined to avoid ending up as fodder for the scandal rags like most of the European families. It's all so demeaning."

"Well, a kidnapping is pretty hard to keep away from the press," Tianna said. "We'll just have to wait and see."

Finally the call came. "She's been rescued!" cried Cook, who answered the phone. "She's just fine."

Cheers erupted all through the house and out in the yard where the chauffeurs and gardeners were gathered as well.

"Prince Garth would like to speak to you," Cook said, handing the receiver to Tianna. "Now the rest of you get back to work."

Tianna felt her cheeks flush as everyone in the kitchen turned to look at her.

"Hello?" she said.

"Hello." Prince Garth's rich voice sent a thrill cartwheeling through her soul. "I just wanted you to know Kari is fine."

Quickly, he outlined what had happened, how Kari had been kidnapped by a group allied with the defeated rebels in Nabotavia, how a security guard named Jack Santini had stormed up the ramp of the airplane the kidnappers were using for their getaway and grabbed the princess right out of their clutches.

"And now, believe it or not, it looks like the two of them will be getting married."

"The princess and the security guard?"

"That's Sir Security Guard to you," Garth told her, chuckling. "Marco has knighted him. At any rate, we'll be coming home in the morning. I'll tell you all the rest when we get there."

"Good."

"I miss you."

She glanced around the kitchen. Everyone was finally hard at work and didn't seem to be paying any attention any longer. "I miss you, too," she whispered into the receiver. "And so does Marika."

It was only after she hung up that she realized she hadn't thought to ask about Janus. Well, there would be time to deal with that the next day, once they were

all back and she could confront Janus on her own—
something she was itching to do. It made her crazy to
think he might have actively hindered their search for
the mother. Had he? She had no proof. But she was beginning to wonder.

And by the middle of the next day, she would
wonder even more. She got up early and changed and
fed Marika, then gave her to Bridget for safekeeping
while she went to call the orphanage.

"My name is Tianna Rose," she said once she had
the manager on the phone. "I'm staying at the castle. I
understand you have an outbreak of chicken pox there
at the orphanage and…"

"What?"

"Chicken pox." Tianna blinked. She hadn't meant to
get bogged down at this point. She was only launching
here. "I had heard you couldn't accept any new orphans
until you had handled your chicken pox situation."

"I don't know where you got that information. We
have no chicken pox problem. Haven't had one in years."

Tianna paused. This was certainly odd. "Are you
telling me you could accept new babies right now?"

"Of course. We've had no restrictions at all this year."

"I see," she said slowly. "Well…thank you very
much."

She didn't pursue her original intentions. This little
bombshell needed to be fully explored first. Sitting very
still, she tried to remember just what had happened that
first day. Cook had sent Milla to call the orphanage, and
Milla had come back saying they had chicken pox and
couldn't accept any new babies for the time being. She
remembered that distinctly. What exactly was going
on here?

Rising, she marched very deliberately down to the kitchen and strode through the double doors.

"Milla," she said, trying to remain calm. "May I have a word with you?"

"Of course, Miss." The young maid came bouncing over to where Tianna stood waiting for her. "What can I do for you?"

Tianna did not answer her smile. "You can tell me why you told us that the orphanage had chicken pox."

Milla looked startled. "Oh."

"The orphanage claims there has been no such thing. So why did you say so?"

"Oh, but that is what Mr. Janus told me. I didn't call them. I went to call them, but Mr. Janus, he said he would do it, and he came back very quickly and told me about the chicken pox."

Tianna felt thunderstruck. "Janus told you that?"

"Yes, Miss." She nodded her head energetically. "I have to take Mr. Janus's lead, you know. If he says, 'I'll do it,' I have to let him."

"Of course you do." Tianna's shoulders sagged but her mind was racing. Janus, once again. What was his angle? She had to think this over. They wouldn't be back until late in the afternoon. That gave her a lot of time. Probably too much time.

The day dragged. She thought about calling her father, but she didn't want to. If she talked to him, she would have to lie. And despite all this craziness she'd been living here at the castle, she hated lying.

Of course, she told herself quickly, she hadn't really lied as yet. She'd just let people believe things that weren't quite the truth. *Which is as good as a lie, Tianna,* she heard her mother's voice saying. And she knew the voice was right.

Yes, it was way past time to begin telling the truth. She had to tell the prince who she really was, and she had to do it right away. Suddenly, she was impatient to tell him. She couldn't imagine how she could have left it so long. She had to clear the slate.

Finally she heard the car coming up the drive. She was tempted to run down to greet them, but she knew that wouldn't be wise. Better to be patient. Dressing Marika in a pretty pink outfit she found in the closet, she waited, and when she couldn't stand it any longer, she went to the kitchen.

"Have you heard?" Bridget cried as she passed her in the kitchen doorway. "There's going to be a wedding!"

"A wedding?"

She turned, looking after her. *Whose?*

"As if we didn't have enough on our plate," Cook was fussing. "And now a wedding. And in seven days. How am I supposed to prepare for a wedding in seven days? Can't be done!"

"What's this wedding?" Tianna asked.

"Why, Princess Karina and her fiancé, haven't you heard? They are coming here in just a few days and we're supposed to put on a wedding. It's impossible."

Things were already in a frenzy, so Tianna turned and left the kitchen. And practically ran into Prince Garth in the hallway.

"Ah, there you are," he said. He reached for Marika, but his gaze was taking in everything he could get of Tianna.

"Hello," she said, glowing. She wanted a kiss very badly, but she knew it would be too risky here in the hallway. "I hear there's a wedding in the works."

"Yes. A very small wedding. Just the immediate family, really." He grimaced. "We want to get it done before the tabloids get wind of it. They were already crawling all over the house in Beverly Hills, wanting stories about the kidnapping." Giving Marika a big kiss on her round cheek, he handed her back. "You're looking very beautiful this afternoon," he told Tianna softly.

She grinned at him happily. "You don't look so bad yourself," she told him. Then she remembered some more sobering issues. "Where is Janus? I need to talk to him."

"Janus stayed behind to help Kari pack up and move her things here to Arizona."

"Oh no." Quickly she explained why she was afraid that Janus had been hindering rather than helping in the search for Marika's mother.

The prince was worried, but skeptical as he thought over what she told him. "Tianna, that doesn't make any sense. Why would he want the baby kept here rather than at the orphanage? Why would he care?"

"That's just it. Why does he care? Why did he do the things he seems to have done?"

The prince frowned, shaking his head. Finally, he looked into her eyes and said earnestly, "Listen. Janus was like a substitute father to me when I was growing up. He's still one of the closest human beings in my life. You're going to have to give me more evidence than this before I will start suspecting him of doing anything underhanded."

She knew this was hard for him to take. It was hard for her as well and she didn't have the same emotional attachment to the man. "I don't want to condemn him any more than you do," she protested. "I just want some answers."

He nodded thoughtfully. "We'll talk to him when

he gets back." He had the restless look of a man with things to do and he started to turn away.

"One more thing," she said, stopping him with a hand on his arm. "I need some time to talk to you tonight."

"Talk?" He brushed her face fleetingly with the palm of his hand, his eyes darkening as he looked into hers. "Let's make out instead."

"I'm serious. I have to tell you something."

"About Marika?"

"No. About me."

He looked puzzled. "Oh. Why can't you tell me now?"

She took a deep breath. "I need a little time. And privacy."

"All right. But it's going to have to be rather late. We have a visitor coming soon. I'll be tied up with him until dinnertime, at least. So after dinner?"

She nodded.

"Okay."

"I'm glad you're back," she whispered as he turned to go.

He looked back and smiled. "Me, too."

An hour later, she knew the mysterious visitor had arrived and she wondered idly who it might be. She'd asked, but everyone was being a little cagey, which only piqued her interest. As the afternoon stretched toward evening, she grew restless. Marika was asleep and she had nothing much to do, so she decided to take a stroll past the study to see if she could figure out what was going on.

To her surprise, voices were being raised behind the study door. She paused, listening. There seemed to be a pretty strenuous argument in progress. And something about one of the voices sounded very familiar, but for the moment, she couldn't place it. Then she thought she heard her own name spoken. This had gone beyond curiosity. If she was being discussed, she was darn well going to find out why.

Throwing open the door, she marched into the study. And then wished she could march right out again. There in the room were Crown Prince Marco, Prince Garth, a man who looked very much like a lawyer, and last but not least, her very own father. Oops.

He bolted from his chair, staring at her. "Katianna!" he cried, his usually handsome face red, though probably from some previous shouting. "What are you doing here?"

"Uh...visiting?" She tried to smile. "Hello, Father."

Garth rose, too, staring at first Tianna, then her parent. "What does this mean?" he said, bewildered.

But Trandem Roseanova-Krimorova, king of West Nabotavia, wasn't paying attention to him. He was too busy being furious with his daughter.

"So you are conspiring behind my back!" he roared at her. "Katianna, what have you done to make this man no longer want to honor his betrothal to you?"

"What?" She turned to look at Garth. "You're breaking our betrothal?"

The prince shook his head. "Who the hell *are* you?" he demanded, his eyes burning.

She winced at his tone. "I'm Katianna, princess of West Nabotavia. The one you are betrothed to. That's what I was going to tell you later on tonight."

He shook his head, looking as though he could hardly believe it, or his eyes. "You tricked me."

"No!"

A shadow of some strange form of agony filled his eyes. "What the hell…?"

But their own conversation was getting drowned out by her father's rant.

"Father, wait," she said, shaking her head at him. "Stop shouting and tell me why you're here."

"Why am I here? To try to stop our family from being swindled, that's why I'm here. I received a communication from this shyster of a lawyer telling me the prince wanted to break off the betrothal so I rushed down here to have a face-to-face meeting with him. And now I find that you are somehow involved in this travesty. Aren't you?"

"Well, sort of…"

"I have told you before. The betrothal stands. I will not rescind it. This was a bargain made years ago between me and King Marcovo, to heal the wounds of four generations of Nabotavian royalty. Our country needs this to bind it together. The selfish concerns of you two are of no interest to me. You will do this for the good of your country." Seemingly satisfied that he'd made his point with her, he turned back to the others. "The arrogant Roseanova family once again thinks it can lord it over the rest of us and dictate what we can and cannot do. Well, I won't stand for it." He frowned fiercely. "I haven't been the best, most attentive king in the world, but at least I will have the reunited nation of Nabotavia as my legacy." He pointed his finger at Prince Garth. "You are going to marry my daughter. It's time we discussed a date."

Complete silence met his demand. No one seemed to know what to say. Her father went back to grumbling, but Tianna could tell the brunt of his anger was spent and she hardly listened. Her attention was all on Garth.

She still needed to explain to him, but what she saw in his face didn't give her a lot of hope that he would understand.

It was an hour later before things calmed down and they had a chance to talk. They met in the library. She walked in hesitantly and noticed right away that his eyes didn't have their usual warmth. If only she could think of some way to make him understand how it had all come about almost without her knowing it.

"Well, I feel like a proper fool," he said, looking down at her, his face hard and unreadable.

She shook her head helplessly. There was really no reason for him to feel that way, but she didn't know how to make him stop. "I'm so sorry."

"What was the point of lying to me?"

"Well, I didn't...technically I didn't really lie, I just..."

His gaze was cold. "You thought you would come play a joke on us?"

"Oh, no!"

"You came to check us out, see if you thought you could stomach the prospect of marrying me?"

"Garth, that wasn't it at all..."

"Then what? Why did you come here?"

She took a deep breath and then looked beseechingly into his eyes, willing him to understand. "I came to talk you into breaking the betrothal."

He stared at her for a moment, then gave a mirthless laugh. "I've got a headache."

"No, listen. I told you I wanted to take a job in Chicago. I came to see if you were as disenchanted with the idea of marriage as I was, and if so, maybe we could work on doing something about it."

"If that was your object, you took a long enough time getting around to it." He shook his head. "Sorry, Princess. I don't buy it. I don't know why you did this, but I really wish you hadn't. It's going to take me some time to digest it all." He walked toward the door, then looked back. "You were the one person I thought I could count on," he said softly, his eyes haunted. And then he was gone.

She stayed behind, feeling numb. She'd known he would be upset, but she hadn't expected this. For the first time, she faced the possibility that he might not get over it. That whatever had been sparked between them might be dead, forever. And that was a fate she dreaded.

Chapter 9

The story of Tianna's true identity spread through the castle faster than a summer cold and Tianna had to endure her share of stares and whispers. Cook tried to get her to move into a more elegant bedroom, but she refused. She also refused a direct order from her father to accompany him back to Seattle. She was Marika's nanny for the duration. Once the baby's fate was settled, she would leave. Until then, she was staying. Her first and most important objective had been protecting the child, and she would see her task through to completion.

The next couple of days passed quickly, which was lucky, because she was in misery most of the time. The staff obviously felt awkward around her, not sure how to treat her now. Prince Marco seemed cool and removed. And Prince Garth seemed to see right through her most of the time. He was hurt and angry and she didn't blame him. But she thought he should let her give her side to it all. And so far, he hadn't wanted to talk.

Meanwhile, she used every spare moment to look for Marika's mother. The orphanage referred her to a good investigator, but he was out of town for the week, so she was on her own. She called every hospital, every woman's shelter, every doctor's office in the area, but no one could remember a single mother giving birth to a little girl in the time frame she gave them. And no one mentioned that anyone else had recently called, asking the same question. So much for Janus and his search.

But soon she was caught up in the preparations for the wedding, too, making place cards for the banquet, designing flower arrangements for the tables and the chapel, calling around for the best prices on supplies.

"A small wedding," Garth had said. His idea of small wasn't hers. Over two hundred people were coming. No wonder Cook was nearly hysterical.

"This will be the end of me," she moaned over and over as she hurried from one task to the next.

The saying made Tianna wince. Somehow it seemed a bad omen, spelling doom all around. She didn't want to think that way, not now, while everyone was so excited about the wedding. But she just couldn't shake the feeling that everything was going wrong.

Princess Karina arrived on the fourth day. She recognized Tianna right away, and they hugged and she exclaimed over the baby. She didn't seem to find it strange that Tianna was there, or that she was acting as nanny. Perhaps it was because her mind was fixated on Jack Santini and his many virtues, and that was all she seemed to want to talk about.

Unfortunately, Janus wasn't with her.

"He's wrapping up some details in Los Angeles and will be coming soon," Princess Kari told her airily.

That was disappointing. But Tianna and Kari hit it off right from the first, and soon Tianna found herself deeply enmeshed in the princess's personal preparations for the ceremony, including helping with the dress, picking out a veil, choosing a cake style.

"Think of this as a dress rehearsal for your own wedding," she told Tianna breezily. "I hope I'll get to help you out when you and Garth get married."

Tianna murmured something polite, but she wasn't sure there would ever be a wedding. And did she even want one? What had happened to wanting the job in Chicago? Why had she let go of that dream so easily?

"Because you've fallen in love," came the answer. So maybe she should change the question.

She had a talk or two with Garth, but they were brief and always ended in hostility. She tried to explain to him why finding the baby had thrown everything off balance and ended up leaving her pretending to be something she wasn't. She reminded him of her own background.

"I remember that fear I felt as a child, and when I look at Marika, I can't stand to think of her going through anything like that and growing up with that fear always in her heart. I had good parents. They helped me get over it. But what will she have? I want her to grow up feeling loved and secure, and always welcome in this world, the way every child should. And that is why I didn't announce who I am. I thought I could protect her interests better..."

"You still could have told me the truth," he said stubbornly. "I believed in you."

That was what hurt the most—having disappointed

him. Every time he looked at her with that hollowness in his eyes, it cut like a knife.

"Why were you trying to break our betrothal?" she asked him at one point.

He looked at her coldly. "Because I was pretty sure I was falling in love with you," he said. "Or with Tianna Rose, loyal nanny, at any rate. So I wanted to be free."

She heard his words and thrilled to them, but then hopes were dashed. He was describing how things had been, not how they were. She shook her head. "That's real irony, isn't it? You were casting me off in order to keep me."

He didn't seem to find it amusing at all.

"Tell me this," she said, steeling herself for the answer. "Are you still determined to break free of the betrothal?"

His dark eyes clouded. "Are you?" he asked in return.

She stared back at him, and neither of them said another word.

Princess Karina had an epiphany.

"Be my maid of honor!" she cried impulsively. "My friend Donna will be here to be a bridesmaid, but I'd like you to stand beside me."

"I'd love to," Tianna told her, so it was settled. And now there was another dress to think about.

Kari was completely wrapped up in preparations for her wedding and floating on a cloud of pure joy, but even from that vantage point, she could see that something was wrong between her brother and their visitor. She asked Tianna about it and her new close friend filled her in on all the details—hesitantly at first, and then in an emotional rush that gave full evidence to how much she cared for Prince Garth.

And Kari went right to her brother, sure she could fix this in no time at all.

"What is your problem?" she demanded once she'd set up her subject. "Forgive her for that small masquerade and get on with life."

The prince looked at his beautiful little sister moodily. They were both in the rose garden, and the day was gorgeous, all blue sky and golden sunshine. "Don't worry about me, Kari. I'm doing fine."

"If this is 'fine,' I'd hate to see 'poorly.' She shook her head. "And even if you can stand it, you're hurting Tianna. She loves you, you know."

His smile was bittersweet. "And you, in your innocence, think that love is all that matters."

Her eyes flashed. "I'm not a ninny. I know other things figure in. Some of them very strongly." She put a hand on his arm. "But love is like water. It is necessary to sustain life. And once you find it, you'd better drink deeply, oh brother of mine. Because you might not find a reservoir like this again."

He loved her for her concern. And he loved Tianna. There was no getting around that. But he couldn't trust Tianna. Could he build a life with her this way? When every time he looked at her, he remembered her deception, and with that memory came others, of the days of the Escape, when lies told to him had caused the deaths of his beloved mother and father?

He was overreacting and he knew it. But emotions were hard to control. Maybe, with time, these thoughts would fade. But did they have that much time?

Even though Garth didn't seem to want to be alone with Tianna, he did take Marika for a little while each day. She assumed that meant he was beginning to accept that Marika was his child and she loved watching the two of them interact. It gave her hope that Marika's future was assured.

So she was shocked when she realized that the rose-shaped birthmark over Marika's heart seemed to be fading. At first she thought it must be her imagination, but the next day, after the baby's bath, it seemed even lighter. Her heart beating in her throat, she took a wash cloth and a dab of liquid cleanser and rubbed lightly on Marika's chest. Marika giggled as though she were being tickled, but Tianna wasn't in the mood for laughter. Because the "birthmark" was almost completely gone by the time she finished rubbing. All that was left was a splotch of brown, perhaps a birthmark in itself, but hardly shaped like a rose in any way.

Someone had drawn a rose shape on Marika's chest with permanent ink. And it had certainly fooled them all for long enough to help plant the seed that this baby was Garth's.

The prince knocked on the door of the nursery half an hour later for his daily visit. She let him in and immediately showed him what she'd found. He stared at the spot, then turned and looked into her eyes.

"Who would have done something like this?" he asked, and she knew right away that he was wondering about her.

Her heart dropped. Was he always going to suspect her now? If so, it was over. Because she couldn't live that way. And he shouldn't have to, either.

"I didn't do it," she told him evenly. "Whoever did do it obviously wanted you to think she was yours. And the only person doing suspicious things in that regard that I know of has been Janus."

"Janus." He grimaced, rejecting it out of hand. "That's crazy."

"Didn't you tell me he was an amateur artist? Who probably has permanent ink pens and the ability to draw a believable-looking rose?"

"But no motive." He shook his head, reaching to pull Marika's little shirt down and wrap her in her blanket so that he could lift her and take her with him. "The DNA results are due tomorrow. That ought to answer a lot of questions. Let's wait until then before we start blaming people."

That infuriated—and worried her. What was going to happen to Marika if it turned out she had no genetic ties to the Roseanovas? Everyone had been pretty clear. She would be going to the orphanage.

Tianna couldn't let that happen. But how could she stop it?

"Find Marika's mother," she muttered to herself, and suddenly she had another idea. Talking about Janus's artistic talent had reminded her that Garth had said he spent a lot of time at the artists' colony in Sedona. Since the man seemed to have a strange connection to this case, perhaps she should try calling some of the medical facilities there.

By the next morning, after some interesting phone calls, she did something even better—borrowed a car and headed down through the red rock canyons to Sedona herself. And in one doctor's office, she hit pay dirt.

"I know exactly who you're talking about," the office clerk told her, looking concerned. "Danielle Palavo. Yes, she was a patient of ours and I remember when she had that baby. Just a second, let me pull her file. I think we probably have a copy of the baby's birth certificate."

Tianna waited anxiously, and when the clerk came back and thrust the photocopy of the birth certificate across the counter at her, she did a double take. Baby Marika had been born in the local hospital to Danielle Palavo. And the father was listed as Garth Roseanova. Tianna caught her breath, feeling a little stunned.

"Did you ever see the baby's father?" she asked.

"I don't think so," the clerk said, wrinkling her nose. "There was an older man, tall and distinguished-looking, who sometimes came in with her. He always seemed so courtly and so concerned about her. But they never seemed like a couple to me. He was more like a father or an uncle or something like that. At least, that was the way it seemed to me."

"Janus," Tianna murmured, guessing but pretty sure she had it right. "Do you have Danielle's address?"

The clerk hesitated. "Well, we would have her old address, but I don't know if I should hand it out, you know. And…" She bit her lip and winced. "She died a little over a week ago. I guess you didn't know that?"

Tianna gripped the edge of the counter. "Died! Oh no."

The clerk nodded sadly. "Yes, she had a very weak heart and childbirth just about did the poor thing in, I'm afraid. And such a cute baby." She shook her head. "Doctor took it pretty hard. He'd known her since she was young, I guess."

Tianna steadied herself. "Can I talk to the doctor?"

"Sorry, he's out of town right now. But if you leave your name and number…"

Tianna drove back to Flagstaff in a daze. What would this do to Marika's future? Nothing good, she was afraid. But there still was the mystery of Janus's part in all this. And why the baby had ended up in the castle yard. Not to mention Garth's name being on the birth certificate.

Bridget had been watching Marika and she jumped up when Tianna came in.

"Oh, Miss…I mean, Your Highness, they're all waiting for you in the library."

The DNA results.

Thanking Bridget, she took a deep breath, kissed Marika and started out again.

The meeting didn't take long. The results were indisputable. Baby Marika's DNA showed no connection whatsoever to the Roseanova family. The full scientific report was read and they all sat quietly for a moment, mulling over the implications.

Tianna was numb. So much had been explained today, but there was still an awkward question. What was Marika's poor mother thinking, putting Garth on the birth certificate? It was all so incredibly sad.

One by one, the others rose and left, first Marco, then Princess Karina, then the doctor who had brought in the report. Prince Garth and Tianna were the only ones left, and they sat silently for a few moments.

"I guess I owe you an apology," she said at last.

He cocked an eyebrow and waited for her to explain.

"For thinking you were Marika's father, I mean," she said quickly. "For being such a pest about it."

His wide mouth quirked at the corners as he regarded her. "It was a perfectly natural mistake to make," he said.

Her gaze met his. Was he almost smiling? She was dying for a real smile from him, one that crinkled the corners of his eyes and lit his face with tenderness.

"You might be interested in this," she said. "I found Marika's mother."

Garth rose and came to the couch where she was sitting, sinking down beside her. "Really."

Quickly, she related what she'd found out in Sedona. He watched her steadily as she talked. He didn't seem very surprised, and when she finally paused for breath, he shook his head and said, "Poor baby. What a way to start her life out."

His first thought was for Marika and that warmed her. But when she said, "I think the tall man the clerk mentioned might be Janus," he nodded.

"It was."

She stared at him. "How do you know?"

"I had a long talk with Janus while you were gone."

"He's back?"

"Yes. And I caught him going into the nursery with his pens, obviously planning to touch up that phony birthmark."

"No!" She covered her mouth with her hands, her eyes huge. "So that was him, too!"

"Yes." He looked uncomfortable, his eyes haunted. "He crumpled before my eyes when I caught him. Emotionally. I'd never seen him like that before." He shook his head. "How can you be that close to someone for that long and yet not really know him?"

She reached out and took his hand. It felt so good to touch him again, but her purpose was purely comfort.

"But he told me about Danielle," the prince went on. "She used to work here, you know."

"No, I didn't know."

"Yes. She was an upstairs maid for a couple of years. I vaguely remember her. But according to Janus, she was a sweet and very vulnerable person and he sort of fell in love with her. He says she didn't ever think of him as anything but a friend," he added quickly. "And he is not the father of the baby. But she had no family and he took her under his wing and saw her often down in Sedona. He says she had a crush on me from the beginning and eventually wove a whole web of fantasy around a relationship she imagined between the two of us. When she got pregnant, she insisted I was the father, even though Janus knew that wasn't possible."

"Was she mentally ill?"

"I would say the evidence suggests she was, to some degree. At any rate, Janus loves Marika, but he knew he couldn't care for her himself. So he decided to see if he could manipulate us into adopting her into the family."

She shook her head. "Why didn't he just ask?"

"I wish I had a good answer for that, Princess Katianna."

At the sound of Janus's voice, she jumped and turned to see the tall man coming into the room. He looked gaunt, broken, and her heart went out to him despite everything.

"I can only plead a sort of temporary insanity of my own," he continued, standing before them abjectly. "My judgement has been sorely impaired for the last few weeks. And I have come to say goodbye."

Tianna looked at Garth. He looked tense, a muscle working at his jaw, but he didn't say a word. She turned back to Janus.

"Tell me about the letter, the one naming the prince as her lover that fell out of Marika's clothes that first day," she said. "Did she really write it?"

He nodded. "That was only one of many letters that she wrote. She lived in a dream world much of the time toward the end."

"Poor thing."

"Yes. It was agony watching her slowly fade away.

And I promised her I would make sure Garth took Marika and raised her in the family. Of course, that was a foolish thing to promise." He smiled gently at Tianna. "Still, there were times I had some hope. When you arrived and took such a shine to the baby, I couldn't believe the luck of it. It couldn't have worked out better if I'd planned it. It all fell together, like some kind of destiny was at work."

He looked at her sadly. "I was a little bit crazy when I left the baby in the yard the way I did, not really sure what would happen, living in a kind of a fog. I was still mourning the death of Danielle, you know. It hit me particularly hard, I must admit. And then you came and picked the baby up. I saw you. I was watching from the window, keeping an eye on her. You picked her up and I knew right away that fate had stepped in. And once I realized who you were—well, it was all so perfect."

"You knew who I was?" Tianna asked in surprise.

"Of course. I keep up on these things."

"Why didn't you say something?" Prince Garth demanded.

Janus drew himself up in something very close to his usual fashion. "I would not presume to interfere, Your Highness."

"Oh," Garth said sarcastically. "Of course not. What was I thinking?"

Tianna grabbed his hand to quiet him. "Tell us more, Janus," she said. "I want to know all of it."

He explained how he had the idea to create the rose birthmark on top of the natural little mark Marika already had. And how he found the cloth from the old country to wrap her in. How he intervened to pretend the orphanage had chicken pox.

"I apologize," he said quite humbly. "Of course, I

can never make up for what I've done. And it is impossible for me to stay in your employ. I'm leaving you my address in Sedona, in case you feel the need to get in touch with me or pursue some sort of legal action."

"Don't be ridiculous, Janus," the prince said shortly. "I don't want you to go."

Janus didn't bend. "I think it best, Your Highness. If upon reflection you decide you would still prefer me by your side, I will return with alacrity. But I think you should have some respite to think over all the ramifications of such an act. And in order to facilitate this I bid you adieu."

Bowing, he left the room. Garth looked at Tianna. She looked at him. And despite everything, they both had to struggle to keep from laughing. The man was over-the-top with formality.

"Hush, he'll hear us," she said.

"He deserves to hear us. He deserves to be laughed at. The old bugger."

"Oh, no, Garth. You have to have some compassion for him. He was only doing what he thought was best for Marika."

"Compassion is dangerous," he told her gruffly. "It makes you let things go you should take care of."

Is that why you can't forgive me?

She didn't say the words out loud, but her eyes conveyed them. Instead of answering, he pulled her close and kissed her hard, trying to blot out that question. She melted in his arms, opening to him with a warm abandon that told him she would be his, if he would take her. Her arms slid around his neck and she arched beneath his hands. And he felt his system react, wanting her, needing her, aching to take possession of her body so that he could be sure he'd won her heart, touched her soul. He could love this woman, take her into his life forever. If only his demons would let him.

He pulled her close against his chest, cradling her in his arms, pressing her to his heart. Tears filled her eyes. She knew he was fighting a battle inside. He wanted her, and yet there was something in him that wanted him not to want her. She wished she knew which would win out.

"What about Marika?" she asked him, drawing back so that she could look into his handsome, beloved face. "Will she be going to the orphanage now?"

A storm came up quickly in his eyes, his face, and he rose from the couch without answering. She watched as he left the room and a hard fist of despair formed in her chest. If only she'd known the consequences of pretending to be someone she wasn't from the first.... If only.

Chapter 10

"There are times when castles really seem like castles, and when a wedding is being held it's one of those times."

Tianna smiled when she overheard a middle-aged woman say this as she passed her group in the hallway. She pretty much agreed.

The castle was filled with people, most of whom she'd never seen before, although she had come across a cousin or two here and there and the reunion squeals had been deafening. The excitement was contagious. There was definitely something in the air.

Looking around the place, she could hardly believe they had been able to make such a transformation in such a short period of time. Huge bouquets of white carnations spilled out from every corner. White streamers were draped from the rafters. Bunches of white balloons made attractive backgrounds to sprays of greenery studded with white lilies. And here and there against the lacy magic of all the whiteness, long-stemmed red roses, a symbol of love, of the Roseanovas, of the royal house itself.

The ceremony was to be performed outside, under an arched arbor decked with climbing red roses. Tables were set up all through the rose garden, each set with bone china and tall crystal champagne flutes. The centerpieces consisted of cages with white doves inside. The members of an orchestra were arriving and setting up in the area allotted for them, each dressed in white formal wear.

It was going to be a beautiful wedding, and Tianna was looking forward to it. But in some ways, she was dreading what would come after the ceremony was over and the last toast had been made. Her own personal deadline would come then. What was she going to do?

Her future hinged on what the prince decided to do about Marika. He'd once told her that the baby would go to the orphanage if she wasn't biologically his. Was that still his plan? He hadn't said anything different. She had to know. After agonizing for hours, she'd made her decision. She would adopt Marika herself, if she could find a way to do it. She had no legal standing. That was a problem. But she would do anything she could to keep that adorable baby from being dumped in the orphanage.

Whatever happened, she would be leaving soon after the wedding. It was high time she got back to Seattle and tried to pick up the pieces of her life and get on with it. Leaving Garth behind would be a wrenching experience, but staying here would be heartache as well. Besides, no one had asked her to stay.

She gave one last lingering glance to the garden and

started back inside. It was time to begin getting ready. The ceremony was only a few hours away.

Tianna wished her mother could see her in the dress she was wearing as Princess Karina's Maid of Honor. It was very much the type of thing her mother liked, sort of prom dress meets wedding gown with a little Las Vegas thrown in. The bride was all in white lace and at first she'd wanted Tianna in white, too. Luckily, Tianna and Donna, Kari's friend who'd arrived to be a bridesmaid, were able to talk her out of it and the dress Tianna wore was a very pale sea-green instead. Donna was wearing a lighter shade in the same style.

The wedding itself was about half an hour away and Tianna was wandering in a side yard, waiting for her call, trying to avoid running into any more cousins. She especially hoped to avoid Cordelia, who, she'd heard, was searching for her in hopes they could have a nice long talk.

"No thanks, Cordelia," she muttered, turning the corner on a hedge and almost running into Crown Prince Marco.

"Oh!" she said, moving aside.

But he smiled, more friendly than he'd been lately. "You look very beautiful, Princess Katianna."

"Thank you Your Royal Highness." The truth was, she felt beautiful. The hairdresser had done wonders with her hair, with a little consulting help from Kari's friend, Donna, and it settled around her face in a frame of subtle ringlets that made her feel like something out of a medieval fairy tale. The dress fit perfectly, its long skirt swishing around her legs as she walked, its tight bodice showing off her form to advantage. "That is very kind."

"Call me Marco."

"Then you must call me Tianna."

"I will. Especially as I believe we are destined to be brother and sister very soon."

"You think so?" She looked doubtful and he took her arm, leading her to a wrought iron bench along the side and inviting her to sit beside him while they talked. From where they sat, they could hear the cooing of the doves and the various sounds of the orchestra musicians tuning up.

"Why do you doubt it?" he asked her.

She shrugged. "He resents me now. I don't think I can be married to someone who feels the way he does."

Marco looked into the distance, silent for a long moment. Then he turned back to her.

"I know Garth is a tough nut to crack," he said. "He won't be easy to live with, either. But I think you will find the effort to be worthwhile." He smiled at her. "You have to understand that in some ways, Garth was scarred more than any of us by what happened during the Escape, when our parents were killed."

She shook her head. "I'm afraid I really don't understand…." Her voice trailed off.

"Of course you don't. So I'll try to explain it to you." He settled back and narrowed his eyes as though picturing the past. "Garth was about eight or nine when it happened. He was an active child and he'd been befriended by our martial arts instructor. Hendrick cultivated Garth, took him hunting, taught him special moves, made him feel very important. So on the night of the Escape, when our section of the city was burning and we were hiding, preparing to be smuggled out of the country, he used that friendship to get Garth to let him into the storage area that was our hiding place."

He shrugged. "Garth had no way of knowing Hendrick was with the rebels. And that is how our parents were killed."

"Oh, no." She put a hand to her mouth. In her mind's eye, she could see a young Garth, see his eyes as he realized how he'd been betrayed, how his mistake had led to the betrayal of his parents. No child should have to bear such a burden. She wanted to jump up and run to Garth, to comfort him, to tell him it wasn't his fault. At this point, though, she wasn't sure he would accept any such sympathy from her. "How terrible," she whispered.

"I just wanted you to know that story so you might understand some of the background for why it's hard to get Garth's full trust." Taking her hand in his, he raised it to his lips and brushed a kiss on her fingers. "But once you do, I think you'll find you have a staunch defender in Garth, a partner whose allegiance will last a lifetime."

Rising, he bowed and strode quickly away. Tianna stayed where she was and thought over what he'd told her. It did throw some light on why Garth acted the way he did. But she wasn't sure understanding his motives would do anything about changing his actions. Or his feelings.

The ceremony was beautiful. The music lifted it onto an ethereal plane. Princess Karina was stunningly lovely and Jack Santini, with his dark, Italian looks, was as handsome as the Roseanovas themselves.

Tianna was standing beside a radiant Kari and Garth was only a few feet away with Marco and Jack. Dressed in the Nabotavian military uniform, all in white with gold braid and epaulets, with a glittering array of medals on his chest, he looked breathtakingly handsome.

The minister was repeating the familiar words about love and commitment and forgiveness and Tianna's gaze met Garth's. She didn't shy away and neither did he. They might have been alone under the arbor. For a few minutes, they stared into each other's eyes and time stood still. Tianna could hardly breathe. It was as though a connection had been made between them, a mind meld, a bond that was too strong for either one of them to break, no matter how much he might wish to. All the longing she felt for him was there, all the sadness. All the love.

And then the spell was broken. She blinked and suddenly it was as though it had never happened. The ceremony was over, Jack was kissing Kari, and people were standing up to applaud. She took a deep breath. If only…

The next half hour was mostly confusion as people shouted greetings and reached across others to shake hands or grab her for a kiss. She laughed and kissed back and answered questions, but her mind was on Garth. Out of the corner of her eye, she always knew exactly where he was.

Bridget came out from the house carrying Marika, and Tianna turned to watch her in surprise. She made her way directly to Prince Garth, who reached out and took her as though he'd expected her. Curious, Tianna moved closer to the crowd around him, trying to hear what was being said.

"Her name is Marika," he was saying, smiling at Cordelia who was staring at him in shock. "After my mother."

The murmuring was subdued but only out of uncertainty.

"Prince Garth," a stout lady said firmly. "Are you telling us that this is your child?"

Tianna held her breath. Suddenly he looked out and met her gaze again.

"Yes," he said deliberately. "Marika is mine."

Tianna turned away. She was trembling and she wasn't sure if it was because she was so glad he'd done this, or because she was disappointed that her dream of adopting the baby herself was up in smoke. Someone spoke to her but she couldn't stop. Quickly she made her way out of the area. A moment later, she found herself striding down the driveway and she realized she was heading for the little gazebo where she'd first seen Garth. Could that really have only been a little over a week ago? It wasn't until she stepped into the little building that she felt she'd found a place she could be. She turned slowly, remembering the different person she'd been when she'd stopped here before.

Dropping to sit on the window seat, her skirt billowing out around her, she leaned against the backdrop and closed her eyes. She would be leaving soon. But at least Marika was taken care of. That was only right, and she was deeply relieved.

She opened her eyes again when she heard someone approaching. She wasn't really surprised that it was Garth. Her heart began to race like a locomotive. There was no help for it. Wherever he was her heart would be.

He stepped into the gazebo looking tall and handsome. "We've got to stop meeting here," he said softly, his eyes unreadable.

She smiled at him. "I don't think that will be a problem," she said lightly. "I'll be leaving in a few hours."

His face didn't change and she went on, quickly. "I want to tell you how glad I am that you've accepted Marika as yours. I was prepared to ask if I might adopt her myself if you didn't do it."

"Really?" He gazed down at her steadily. "What happened to your career in photography?"

"I wouldn't have given that up, not entirely," she said.

"Good," he said firmly, his head to the side. "Because I'm hoping you will consider taking charge of documenting the return to Nabotavia. We're going to need an official photographer, you know. We don't have one as yet."

Her heart jumped at the thought. What an exciting job that would be! And she would get to be with the royal family, and with Marika…. But she shook her head. "I don't really see how I could do that," she admitted sadly.

"It wouldn't take up all your time," he told her, as though that was her main concern. "It would be a package deal, you know."

She frowned, wondering why she had the feeling there was a spark of amusement brewing in those eyes. "What are you talking about?"

"Well…" He shrugged casually. "Marika's going to need a mother."

Her heart skipped. "I suppose that would be best."

"I thought maybe you and I could go ahead and get married…."

Her breath caught in her throat, but she wasn't going to let him see her excitement. She pretended to frown at him. "Does this mean you're sort of hiring me on as a permanent nanny?"

The corners of his mouth twitched. "Actually, I was thinking of a more well-rounded role for you."

"Really?"

"Really." Reaching out, he took her hands and pulled her to her feet, then drew her in against him, his arms around her, his face against her hair. "I'm crazy about you, Tianna. You do realize that?"

She shook her head. Tears were filling her eyes. "No, you can't be."

"But I am." He tilted her face up and dropped a kiss on her lips. "I can't help it. It's just there. So don't forget to throw that in with your other equations."

She was almost afraid to hope, but he sounded so convinced—and convincing. "Garth, are you sure?" she asked, searching for the truth in his eyes.

"Watching you today during the ceremony, seeing the pure goodness and honesty that shines in your eyes, I realized what a fool I've been. It's taken me a few days to come to my senses." He kissed her lightly. "Can you forgive me?"

"I don't know," she said, laughing up at him. Her heart was so full. "Compassion can be dangerous. Or so you've advised me."

"I'm not asking for 'compassion,' he said huskily as he nuzzled into her neck. "Plain old 'passion' will do quite nicely."

"That, sweet prince," she said as her body began to celebrate his touch, "you don't have to worry about."

He tasted her mouth and she clung to him, floating on happiness, but the sounds of yelling and crashes that had been growing in the background finally caught their attention and they both looked back up toward the castle, straining to see what was causing all the commotion.

"Oh no!" Tianna cried. "Look! The cows are out again. They're heading right for the reception!"

"Is that a fact?"

She looked up at Garth, surprised by his reaction. "Is Marika...?"

"Bridget took her back in."

"Oh, good." She sighed, then looked back up the hill. Tables were overturning. Doves were fluttering free. People were yelling. But the three black and white cows marched relentlessly on, not seeming to notice the pandemonium they were creating.

Garth pursed his lips, but his eyes couldn't mask his amusement. "This always seems to happen when you let people set up events in the area between the livestock pens and the vegetable garden," he noted dryly.

Tianna shook her head. "We can't just stay here and let this go on."

"Can't we?" He pulled her close again. "I say, let the chaos commence. We have other things to concern ourselves with."

She looked up at him uncertainly. "But..."

"Hush," he said, pulling her down onto the window seat with him. "We have a lot of missed kissing time to make up for."

"Well, when you put it that way." She sighed happily as he curled his arms around her and began dropping tiny nibbles along her jaw line. "I think you've just given me an offer I can't refuse."

* * * * *

*If you enjoyed this story from Lynne Graham,
here is an exclusive excerpt from her upcoming book
BRIDE FOR REAL.*

Available September 2011 from Harlequin Presents®.

"SANDER..." Shattered by that admission of continuing desire from the husband she was in the midst of divorcing, Tally stared at him, her emotions in turmoil.

"In fact, wanting you is driving me absolutely crazy, *yineka mou*," Sander admitted darkly.

And for the first time in longer than Tally could remember, her body leaped with actual physical hunger. She was astonished as she had felt nothing for so long that she had believed that that side of her nature might be gone forever. Was it the dark chocolate luxury of his deep voice that provoked the sudden rise of those long-buried needs? Or the sinfully sexual charge of his dark golden eyes? Tally had no idea but she felt a sudden clenching tight sensation low in her pelvis and her mouth ran dry.

She gazed back at Sander, feeling as vulnerable as if he had stripped her naked and marched her out into a busy street. *Yineka mou*, my wife, he'd called her. And she *was* still his wife, she reminded herself helplessly.

"Any idea what I can do about it?" Sander husked that question, strolling closer with the silent elegant grace that was as much a part of him as his physical strength.

"No, no idea at all."

"You push me much too close to the edge, *yineka mou*," Sander murmured, tilting down his darkly handsome head and running the angular side of his jaw back and forth over the smooth, soft line of her cheek like a jungle cat nuzzling for attention. The familiar sandalwood and jasmine scent of his expensive aftershave lotion made her nostrils flare while the faint rasp of his rougher skin scored her nerve endings into life.

Suddenly, Tally felt like someone pinned to a cliff edge, in danger and swaying far too close to a treacherous drop. She didn't want to be there; she didn't want to fall, either, but any concept of choice was wrested from her when Sander found her mouth and kissed her, strong hands firm on her slim shoulders to hold her still....

Make sure to pick up Lynne Graham's title
BRIDE FOR REAL
to find out what happens between Tally and Sander!

Available September 2011.

Exclusively from Harlequin Presents®.

REQUEST YOUR FREE BOOKS!

2 FREE NOVELS PLUS 2 FREE GIFTS!

ALWAYS POWERFUL, PASSIONATE AND PROVOCATIVE

Harlequin® *Romance*

Discover small-town warmth and community spirit
in a brand-new trilogy from

PATRICIA THAYER

*Where dreams
are stitched...patch
by patch!*

Coming August 9, 2011.

Little Cowgirl Needs a Mom

Warm-spirited quilt shop owner Jenny Collins promises to
help little Gracie finish the quilt her late mother started,
even if it means butting heads with Gracie's father,
grumpy but gorgeous rancher Evan Rafferty....

The Lonesome Rancher
(September 13, 2011)

Tall, Dark, Texas Ranger
(October 11, 2011)

HRI7745

Love Inspired

Everything Montana Brown *thought* she knew about love and marriage goes awry when her parents split up. Shaken, she heads to Mule Hollow, Texas, to take a chance on an old dream—being a cowgirl…while trying to resist the charms of a too-handsome cowboy. A wife isn't on rancher Luke Holden's wish list. But the Mule Hollow matchmakers are fixin' to lasso Luke and Montana together—with a little faith and love.

Her Rodeo Cowboy
by Debra Clopton

MULE HOLLOW
HOMECOMING

Available September wherever books are sold.

LI87691

Harlequin SHOWCASE

2 GREAT NOVELS
1 GREAT PRICE

Reader favorites
from the most talented voices in romance.

COMING NEXT MONTH
Available August 30, 2011

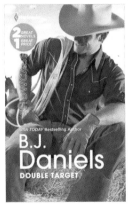

USA TODAY Bestselling Author
B.J. Daniels
DOUBLE TARGET

Carla Cassidy
SHATTERED TRUST

You can find more information
on upcoming Harlequin® titles,
free excerpts and more at
www.HarlequinInsideRomance.com.

ISBN-13:978-0-373-68832-6

HARLEQUIN SHOWCASE
Reader favorites from the most talented voices in romance

Secrets and passion abound in these two royal family
romances from popular author Raye Morgan

Jack and the Princess

Cracking the security system at the Roseanova estate
seemed like a surefire way for Jack Santini to prove to the
royal family that he was the man for the chief-of-security
position. But he hadn't counted on waking up a beautiful,
golden-haired princess! Karina Roseanova thought the
brooding bodyguard who scaled her balcony was the perfect
person to free her from the confines of her ivory tower
and show her the ways of the world. Before long, Karina's
irresistible girlish wonder gave way to a love beyond her
wildest dreams. All she had to do was convince her family
that this gruff commoner was her one and only prince!

Betrothed to the Prince

Princess Tianna had no intention of honoring her lifelong
betrothal to Prince Garth Roseanova. But when she arrived to
disengage herself from the playboy prince she'd never met,
she ended up going undercover as a nanny—to protect the
abandoned baby girl who might be the man's illegitimate
heir! Dashing Prince Garth was nervous around the child, but
her sweet cooing soon won him over, just like her beautiful
nanny. Before long, he and Tianna were drawn together,
propelled by forces beyond their control. But could their
fairy-tale romance survive the shocking truth?

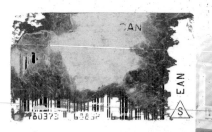